DANCE OF GOVINDA

Ashok K. Banker is the author of the internationally acclaimed Ramayana Series® and other books. He lives in Mumbai with his family. Visit him online at www.ashokbanker.com.

BOOKS BY ASHOK K. BANKER

FROM HARPERCOLLINS INDIA

krishna coriolis
slayer of kamsa
dance of govinda
flute of vrindavan

OTHER WORKS

ramayana series®
prince of ayodhya
siege of mithila
demons of chitrakut
armies of hanuman
bridge of rama
king of ayodhya
omnibus hardcovers
prince of dharma
prince in exile
prince at war

gods of war
vertigo

Dance of Govinda

KRISHNA CORIOLIS – BOOK II

ASHOK K. BANKER

HARPER

First published in India in 2011 by Harper
An imprint of HarperCollins *Publishers*
a joint venture with
The India Today Group

Copyright © Ashok K. Banker 2011

ISBN: 978-93-5029-100-9

2 4 6 8 10 9 7 5 3 1

Ashok K. Banker asserts the moral right
to be identified as the author of this work.

This is a work of fiction and all characters and incidents described in this book are the product of the author's imagination. Any resemblance to actual persons, living or dead, is entirely coincidental.

All rights reserved. No part of this publication may be reproduced,
stored in a retrieval system, or transmitted, in any form or by any means,
electronic, mechanical, photocopying, recording or otherwise,
without the prior permission of the publishers.

HarperCollins *Publishers*
A-53, Sector 57, Noida 201301, India
77-85 Fulham Palace Road, London W6 8JB, United Kingdom
Hazelton Lanes, 55 Avenue Road, Suite 2900, Toronto, Ontario M5R 3L2
and 1995 Markham Road, Scarborough, Ontario M1B 5M8, Canada
25 Ryde Road, Pymble, Sydney, NSW 2073, Australia
31 View Road, Glenfield, Auckland 10, New Zealand
10 East 53rd Street, New York NY 10022, USA

Typeset in 11/ 12.7 Adobe Jenson Pro
InoSoft Systems Noida

Printed and bound at
Thomson Press (India) Ltd.

For Biki and Bithika:
My Radha and my Rukmini.

For Yashka and Ayush Yoda:
My Yashoda.

All you faithful readers
who understand
that these tales
are not about being Hindu
or even about being Indian.
They're simply about being.

In that spirit,
I dedicate this gita-govinda
to the krishnachild in all of us.
For, under these countless
separate skins, there beats
a single eternal heart.

preface

If it takes a community to raise a child, then it surely takes a nation to build an epic.

The itihasa of the subcontinent belongs to no single person. The great epics of our culture – of any culture – may be told and retold infinite times by innumerable poets and writers; yet, no single version is the final one.

The wonderful adventures of the great Lord Krishna are greater than what any story, edition or retelling can possibly encompass. The lila of God Incarnate is beyond the complete comprehension of any one person. We may each perceive some aspects of His greatness, but, like the blind men and the elephant, none of us can ever see everything at once.

It matters not whether you are Hindu or non-Hindu, whether you believe Krishna to be God or just a great historical personage, whether you are Indian or not. The richness and wonder of these tales have outlived countless generations and will outlast many more to come.

My humble attempt here – within these pages and in the volumes to follow – is neither the best nor the last retelling of this great story. I have no extraordinary talent or ability, no special skill or knowledge, no inner sight or visionary gift. What I *do* have is a lifelong exposure to an itihasa so vast, a culture so rich, a nation so great, wise and ancient, that its influence – permeating into one like water through peat over millennia, filtering through from mind to mind, memory to memory, mother to child and to mother again – has suffused every cell of my being, every unit of my consciousness.

And when I use the word 'I', it is meant in the universal. You are 'I'. As I am she. And she is all of us. Krishna's tale lives through each and every one of us. It is yours to tell. His to tell. Hers to tell. Mine as well. For as long as this tale is told, and retold, it lives on.

I have devoted years to the telling, to the crafting of words, sentences, paragraphs, pages, chapters, kaands and volumes. I shall devote more years to come, decades even. Yet, all my effort is not mine alone. It is the fruition of a billion Indians, and the billions who have lived before us. For each person who has known this tale and kept it alive in his heart has been a teller, a reteller, a poet, and an author. I am merely the newest name in a long, endless line of names that has had the honour and distinction of being associated with this great story.

It is my good fortune to be the newest reteller of this ancient saga. It is a distinction I share with all who tell and retell this story: from the grandmother who whispers it as a lullaby to the drowsy child, to the scholar who pores over each syllable of every shloka in an attempt to find an insight that has eluded countless scholars before him.

It is a tale told by me in this version; yet, it is not my tale alone to tell. It is your story. Our story. Her story. His story.

Accept it in this spirit and with all humility and hope. Also know that I did not create this flame, nor did I light the torch that blazes. I merely bore the torch this far. Now I give it to you. Take it from my hand. Pass it on. As it has passed from hand to hand, mind to mind, voice to voice, for unknown millennia.

Turn the page. See the spark catch flame.

Watch Krishna come alive.

author's note

All my books are long in the gestation, some conceived as many as thirty-plus years earlier, none less than a decade. It takes me that long to be sure of a story's longevity and worth and to accumulate the details, notes, research, character development and other tools without which I can't put my fingers to the keyboard. This particular story, Krishna Coriolis, originated in the same 'Big Bang' that was responsible for the creation of my entire Epic India universe – a series of interlinked retellings of all the major myths, legends and itihasa of the Indian subcontinent, set against the backdrop of world history. I'm using the term 'Big Bang' but in fact it was more of a series of carefully controlled delayed-time explosions over the first fifteen to eighteen years of my life.

At that time, the Krishna story was a part of the *Sword of Dharma* section of the Epic India library – which retold the 'dashavatara' storyline with an unusual twist – as well as an integral part of my massively ambitious retelling of the world's greatest epic, the Mahabharata or the Mba. I began work on my Mba immediately after I completed the Ramayana Series in 2004. After about five years of working on my Mba – a period in which most actual MBA students would be firmly established in their careers! – I realized that the series was too massive to be published as it was. I saw that the Krishna storyline, in particular his individual adventures, could stand on its own as a separate series. So I separated the stories into a parallel series which I titled Krishna Coriolis. Naturally, since the story now had to stand on its own, rather than be a part of the larger Mba story, I had to rewrite each book to create an independent entity with a reasonably complete beginning, middle and end. This process took another three years, and resulted finally in the form the series now takes. You're holding the second book of this parallel series in your hands now, titled *Dance of Govinda*.

Dance of Govinda is just the second part of the Krishna Coriolis, which is interlinked with the much larger Mba series, which itself is only one section of my whole Epic India library. Yet, I've laboured to make this book be complete in itself and be a satisfying read. Naturally, it's not complete in the story, since that would require not just the full Krishna storyline but also the larger Mba story and the larger context behind that as well. In that sense, it's just a part of the big picture; but even the longest journey must start with a single step and if you permit, *Dance of Govinda* will take you on a short but eventful trip, one packed with action and magic, terror and adventure. The reason why the book, like the remaining books in the series, is so short, almost half of the length of my earlier Ramayana Series, is because that's the best way the structure works. By that I mean the individual parts of the story and the way in which they fit together. Sure, I could make it longer – or shorter. But this felt like the perfect length. In an ideal world, the entire series would be packaged together as one massive book and published at once – but that's not only impossible in terms of paper thickness and binding and cover price affordability, it's not the right structure for the story. Stories have been split into sections, or volumes, or, in our culture, into parvas, kaands, suras, mandalas and so on, since literature was first written. You might as well ask the same question of Krishna Dweipayana-Vyasa – 'Sir, why did you split the Mahabharata into so many parvas and each parva into smaller sections and so on?' The fact is, a story needs to be structured and the story itself decides which structure works best. That was the case here and I am very pleased with the way *Dance of Govinda* and the other books in the series turned out.

The *Sword of Dharma* mini-series, as I call it now, is also written in first draft and tells us the experiences and adventures of Lord Vishnu in the heavenly realms. It is a direct sequel to the Ramayana Series as well as a bridge story to the Krishna Coriolis and Mahabharata Series. And since it deals with otherworldly events, it exists outside of 'normal' time as we know it, which means it is also a sequel to the Krishna Coriolis and also a prequel to the Ramayana Series. I won't confuse you further: once you read *Sword of Dharma*, you would understand instantly what I mean because the story itself is an action-packed adventure story where questions like 'when is this taking place?' and 'so is this happening before or after such-and-such?' become less important than seeing the curtain parted and the world beyond the curtain revealed in its full glorious detail. No matter how much I may show you in the Ramayana Series, Krishna Coriolis and Mahabharata Series, all these 'mortal' tales are ultimately being affected and altered by events taking place at the 'immortal' level, and only by seeing that story-beyond-the-story can we fully comprehend the epic saga of gods and demons that forms the basis of Hindu mythology in our puranas.

But for now, *Dance of Govinda* marks a crucial turning point in the story of Swayam Bhagwan (as the Bhagwatham calls him). Not only has he survived every attempt to destroy him at birth, he will grow and thrive. By the close of this book, he will have gained the ability to stand on his own two feet – hence the title. And even though just a babe for most of the story, he is capable of far more than most grown heroes – not just more action, but more masthi as well! For that is the beauty of Krishna, he is not just a warrior but also a lovable mischievous tyke. There are as many stories of his infantile pranks as there are tales of his derring-do in this book, for I have tried to be as thorough as possible in mining the rich vein of Shrimad Bhagwatham, the Vishnu Purana and the Harivamsha sections of the Mahabharata in seeking every known recorded incident of Krishna's infancy.

And that too is only part of the much, much larger tale of Krishna, which itself is part of the larger tale of Lord Vishnu, which is only part of the far greater saga of gods and demons. It's an epic saga, but the beauty of it is that each portion is delicious and fulfilling in itself!

Enjoy!

	yadrcchaya copapannah	
	svarga-dvaram apavrtam	
	sukhinah ksatriya partha	
	labhante yuddham idrsam	

Blessed are the warriors
Who are chosen to fight justly;
For the doors to heaven
Shall be opened unto them.

Kaand I

one

The being that had once been Prince Kamsa towered over the city.

He had expanded himself enough to be able to stand and gaze out at all Mathura. He surveyed his domain from a height of several hundred feet. Looming above the low-lying dwellings of the city, even higher than the tallest structure in the capital – his palace – he was able to see to the farthest extremities of the capital. His gargantuan form dwarfed the palace beside him. He was tempted to sit on the vaulting central dome but decided against it: the crack he had caused when he had tried merely to lean against it lightly was still there; sitting might well lead the structure to collapse altogether.

The city exhibited signs of unrest. The smoke curling skywards from sporadic fires and the sound of crowds clashing with his soldiers didn't concern him overly; what irritated him was that his official diktat was being resisted by his people.

Really, Yadavas could be very stubborn at times! Couldn't they understand that he must eliminate any possibility of his slayer still being alive?

It was galling enough that the son of Devaki and Vasudeva had escaped his grasp despite a decade of iron-handed security measures and intense scrutiny. He was still unable to comprehend how that had been accomplished. His sister and bhraatr-in-law had still been in their quarters, confined by manacles and chains, surrounded by his most reliable men, all armed to the teeth. Yet come the time of the birth of the eighth child, they, and everyone else in the entire city, appeared to have … fallen asleep!

It was quite absurd. Vasudeva could hardly have drugged the whole city. Yet, somehow, every living soul had fallen dead asleep during the crucial hours when his nemesis had been birthed. Including himself.

Longing to smash his paw into something, he raised it, but controlled himself with an effort. He would only end up destroying half the city if he did what he really wanted to – lash out. He settled for seething silently as he recalled the frustration he had felt when he had awoken to find that the night of the Slayer's prophesied birth had already ended and the next day begun.

To add insult to injury, by the time he and his aides arrived at Vasudeva's domicile, the true Slayer had been spirited away and replaced with another child, a female babe who, when he attempted to kill it, had slipped out of Kamsa's grasp, floated in mid-air and told him how he had been duped, before laughing and vanishing into thin air.

That was one of the things that troubled him: Why had she told him when the easier way out would have been for her to have him kill the babe, assuming it to be the one spoken of in Narada-muni's prophecy?

By telling him that she was a replacement, she had defeated the very purpose of switching the babies. Now that he knew his prophesied Slayer was still alive somewhere, he had no choice but to ensure its destruction – and his own survival.

Since he didn't know where the real Slayer had been transported, he had ordered all newborn babes to be killed at once.

To be on the safe side, he had also ordered all babes who appeared to have been born in the last ten days to be put to the sword.

That was the reason for the unrest. His soldiers, led by his trusty aides Bana and Canura, had gone from house to house, running their blades through every single newborn – and a few infants too, to be absolutely certain. It was a bloody business, but it had to be done. Surely his people understood that? After all, as his subjects, they ought to have his welfare at heart, shouldn't they? Yet there they were, rioting and protesting violently, even attacking his soldiers who were only going about doing their duty. How insolent!

Now he waited for his army to regroup. The slaughter was done and he was waiting for Bana and Canura to assemble the troops so he could issue his next orders.

Bits of his body dropped off from time to time and lay writhing on the ground. Some fell on the unfortunate soldiers already assembled, and eagerly devoured them, their slithering worm-like forms turning into obscene humps as they swallowed their struggling prey alive. The larger Kamsa got, the larger the assorted parasites in him grew, each individual vermin displaying the same characteristics as its host. Some even had the same mottled purple-faced grin. After all, if a person's pet usually resembled the owner, why not his parasites?

Kamsa lazily raised a foot and squashed a few that were getting out of hand. His supply of soldiers was plentiful but not unlimited, after all. As it is, he tended to kill or maim a fair number of his men – as well as numerous innocent bystanders at times – merely in the course of moving around, or during one of his now-legendary rages.

Which reminded him, he would need new troops soon. It was quite obvious that the present situation was beyond the capacity of normal Andhaka Kshatriyas. For one thing, he suspected that more than a few of them were reluctant to kill their countrymen. That was absurd. A Kshatriya's dharma was to do as he was told, was it not? Then why the moral qualms? Still, they often used words and warnings where the simple slash of a sword or running over by a horse brigade would work more effectively. Too soft for his purposes. He needed tough men who did what they were told without question or hesitation, men as accustomed to killing and as casual about it as a butcher. It was important to rule firmly.

He missed his Mohini Fauj. He had been so proud of that hermaphrodite army ... Not only had they been immaculate at the art of slaughter, they had been a gift from his dear friend, mentor, and pitr-in-law, King Jarasandha of Magadha. But the Mohinis were all gone now, and the damned Vasudeva had been responsible for that, whether directly or indirectly. Yes, Vasudeva had a lot to answer for and he, Kamsa, would see to it that he paid his dues. But first, he had to deal with the job at hand: rooting out and killing Vasudeva's newborn brat before the little fellow grew up to pose a threat to his maternal uncle.

Kamsa heard the tiny sound of hooves and looked down to see Bana and Canura arrive at the head of a bedraggled and weary-looking band of cavalry. His two most trusted aides looked ready to drop.

They dismounted, bowed, and waited for him to reduce himself. He did so, coming down to about thrice his human height. He glared down at them.

'Well, is it all done?'

'Aye, Lord Kamsa,' Bana said. He was so subdued and miserable, he seemed capable of falling over at any moment.

Canura glanced sharply at his companion before speaking

up, 'Aye, sire. The count came to three hundred and eight.' He added, 'Bana's twin sons were the first we killed.'

Kamsa grinned. 'Good, very good.' Then he frowned. 'Three hundred and eight? That's quite a number. Is that the average birth rate?' He glanced doubtfully at the city. 'They do multiply like rabbits, don't they?'

Bana remained as he was, slumped like a man ready to collapse. He stared down at the ground. Canura cleared his throat. 'Actually, my lord. The daimaas said that only twenty-three were born in the past day and night. The rest we killed just to be certain we weren't missing any.'

'Ah,' Kamsa nodded. 'Thorough as usual. Good. Now go back and get the rest.'

Canura stared up at him. 'Get *some* rest, sire?'

'*The* rest. Go kill the remaining children.'

'But, my lord, we killed them all. Newborn babes, as well as those that were born in the past ten days ... even those born in the past fortnight or so, just to be sure!'

Kamsa yawned as he began to expand himself once more. 'Yes, yes, I know that. Now go kill the remaining boys in Mathura.'

Canura craned his neck, raising his voice so that he could be heard; Kamsa rose up above the height of the palace dome and continued to grow. 'Up to what age, my lord?'

Kamsa shrugged. 'All the boys. Kill every son born in Mathura. Each that you consider capable of holding a sword ...' He paused a moment, thinking. Yadava children joined their parents at work at an early age. '... Or a ploughshare or a crook.'

'Every son, sire?' Canura's voice cracked. Kamsa wondered if Canura had sons of his own – yes, he seemed to recall him mentioning having a son or three, a few years ago. 'Even ...'

'OF COURSE,' said Kamsa brusquely, his voice booming now as he towered above the palace again. 'START WITH THE MALE OFFSPRING OF OUR OWN SOLDIERS, THEN WORK YOUR WAY THROUGH THE REST OF THE CITY. AND WHEN YOU ARE DONE WITH MATHURA, CONTINUE THROUGH THE KINGDOM.'

Even from that height, Kamsa could see the incredulity and shock on the minion's face. The man seemed to crumple inwards like a dissolving sand sculpture. 'The ... kingdom?' Kamsa could barely hear Canura's faraway, enfeebled voice.

'YES. BE THOROUGH. DON'T COME BACK TILL YOU'RE DONE.' Kamsa yawned and stretched, and heard his muscles pop and tendons ease. 'I SHALL SLEEP AWHILE ... UNTIL YOU FINISH THE BUTCHERY. THERE'S MUCH WORK AHEAD. I NEED MY REST.'

He glanced down and saw Canura still standing below, staring up, his tiny face and beard barely the size of the toenail on Kamsa's smallest toe. If he flicked his foot even slightly, he would send Canura flying to his death. Bana, it seemed, had collapsed after all. Kamsa nudged the man with the edge of his foot. Something crawled out of an open suppurating sore on his insole and leapt eagerly on Bana's back, moist round mouth opening like a maw to swallow.

'Better drag your friend away before he becomes dinner for that thing. Go on.'

Canura, still looking stunned, glanced down, saw the parasite about to devour Bana's head, dropped to his knees and began beating it off. He cried a little while doing so, which was unusual for Canura. When it was dead, he put his arm around Bana's shoulder and dragged him to his horse which had backed away several yards, nervous around Kamsa's rakshasa stench.

Moments later, followed by the ragged lines of soldiers that comprised the remains of Mathura's once great army, they rode away. From their deathlike silence and the lacklustre manner in which they diminished from his sight, it was evident that their new mission was not to their liking. Deserters were already breaking off from the main column and riding away in different directions, no doubt preferring the death penalty for desertion over participating in further slaughter of their own.

Kamsa slapped at a particularly worrisome mite on his cheek. His claw came away sticky and green. Yes. This sorry-looking bunch wouldn't do any more.

It was time he acquired a new army.

two

Nanda gazed in awe at the being in his wife's arms.

She cradled it reverentially, beaming up at her husband with pride. 'Is he not magnificent?'

Nanda shook his head in disbelief. 'He is God Himself Incarnate, descended on prithviloka to grace and bless us. Let me witness his glory!'

Yashoda peeled back the corners of the swaddling garment to reveal the dusky features of her baby. He slept peacefully, the faintest shadow of an all-knowing smile turning up the corners of his mouth, a chubby fist beside his cheek.

Husband and wife marvelled at the sleeping infant.

'He is perfect in every way,' Nanda said.

'Yes. Even his colour, so dark, beyond black, almost bluish in its hue. It's the exact shade of dusk falling over Gokul on a monsoon eve.'

'Shyam-rang. The colour of dusk. That is what we shall name him.'

'Shyam?'

Nanda smiled. 'That too if you wish. But I meant to call him Krishna.'

'Krishna,' Yashoda repeated, crushing the consonants between her palate and tongue. 'I like it. It describes him so beautifully. He is literally Krishna. The colour of darkness. Beautiful, beatific black.'

'Well said, beloved one. In fact, his colour and aspect bring to my mind that great Bharata ancestor of the Suryavansha Ikshwaku line.'

'You mean Rama Chandra of Ayodhya?'

'Yes. Was he not described as being gifted with this same dark-hued aspect, a complexion so dark it almost glowed bluish in a certain light?'

Yashoda nodded slowly, thinking back to the time she had heard a passing bard recite the tale of Rama and his travels. *Travails, more like it*, she thought, thinking of Rama's banishment with his wife Sita and those last years of sad estrangement. She prayed such sadness would not be the lot of her son. 'Yes, but let us not name him Rama, if you please.'

'No, I did not mean that we name him so, merely that something about his aspect reminded me of how the bards describe Rama Chandra at his birth.'

She smiled. 'I like the name Krishna very much.'

He beamed at her. 'Krishna he shall be, then. King of the dusk, master of twilight, commander of the world between day and night.'

She laughed. 'Nanda, you always did have a gift for bombastic pronouncements!'

She carefully covered the sleeping infant again, tucking in an errant black curl behind his ear; he had surprisingly long hair for a newborn. 'He shall be a gopa, like his father and his father before him, back to the beginning of time. A simple cowherd; and he shall find joy in it. His weapon shall be the flute, to entertain himself through the long solitary hours, and to draw his flock homewards at day's end. He shall command the finest Gokul cows, and rule the milk and butter sheds, and he shall be king of all the dung-heaps in Vraj country if he pleases!'

The couple laughed at that. Nanda put his arm on his wife's shoulder, feeling a great rush of love and affection for her. 'My beloved, you always know how to put me in my place and keep me firmly there. It shall be as you say, subject to the blessings of the Brahmins whose task it is to choose auspicious names. If they agree, this son of ours shall be Krishna the gopa, not Rama the warrior.' His eyes twinkled mischievously as he turned to leave. 'But he shall be king of Gokul, master of the gopas, and commander of the hearts of the gopis!' He winked at her and left the shed with a flourish before she could retort again.

Yashoda chuckled softly, rocking her baby gently. 'That's your father. He has delusions of grandeur and far, far too many cows for a single man!'

Nanda emerged from the shed to find a huge gathering waiting eagerly on the hillside. People were still coming, some even running out of sheer excitement, arriving from all points of the compass, shouting eagerly to one another the news that Nanda–Yashoda had had a son that morning. Nanda straightened his back and raised his hands, asking for silence. The excited murmuring and chattering died down reluctantly. Gokul's gopis and gopas were boisterous, loud, rambunctious people and the words 'quiet' and 'slow' were not part of their limited vocabulary, but they quietened down and stood still for Nanda, their respect for whom was enormous. Though a tribal republic in social structure, Vrajbhoomi did have her chieftains and lords, not in the feudal, patriarchal or zamindari sense but simply as the spokesperson and voice of the people. Nanda was the voice of Gokul and everyone listened when he spoke.

'Yashoda has given birth to a boy! We have chosen to name him Krishna, subject to the approval of the Brahmins.'

A great cheer went up. It was echoed by even those still coming at a running pace – they raised their crooks and yelled as they came.

Nanda waited for the cheers and applause to die down.

'Send for the Brahmins. I shall now retire to perform the

necessary ablutions and prepare for the birth ceremonies. Go forth and spread the word across Vrajbhoomi. There shall be feasting and celebration as never before. All are welcome!'

The hail of joy that greeted this was even greater than the one before. Nanda raised his hand in acknowledgement and turned back to the house. There was much to be done and he would have to oversee it all himself. For once, Yashoda the ever-efficient, ever-perfect mistress of the house would not be able to take care of the arrangements with her customary ease.

However, Yashoda appeared at the doorway before Nanda could reach it. He started to admonish her, then broke off and simply stared.

'You look ... radiant,' he said. 'But you should not be moving about just yet, my love.'

Yashoda smiled. Nanda felt his heart flutter at the sight of that winsome smile, the flash of those perfect teeth. 'I feel as if I birthed ten days ago, not this morning.' She frowned as if seeking words to describe her feelings. 'I feel ... refreshed, rejuvenated. It's quite remarkable. All I did was nurse our son and suddenly I felt energy coursing through me, as if I were years younger and stronger and healthier. I can't explain it.'

Nanda looked down at the wrapped bundle she cradled in one arm. He was still suckling at the breast, but when Nanda tugged back the cloth to gaze at him, he let the nipple pop out of his mouth and stared up brightly. Nanda felt a rush of joy as those beautiful light eyes danced up at him, catching a beam of sunlight that made the little face glow as if lit from within. He felt a surge of energy and love, such a great rush of affection as he had never felt before. He smiled, amazed at his own responses, and, as if in response, the babe gurgled and chuckled softly. 'Uh ... uh-huh!'

He glanced up at Yashoda and saw her watching her infant son as well as her husband with something bordering on awe. 'Is he not too newly made to be responding thus?' he asked uncertainly. He was no expert on babies, still …

She was quiet for a moment, then said, 'There is something about our Krishna that is unlike any other babe, isn't there? I feel it. Do you feel it too?'

He looked down again and saw that the boy was back at the bosom, suckling greedily. But the eyes, so large in that little round face, found his father's face again and despite his mouthful of nourishment, he gurgled happily. 'Uh … *bah!*'

'Yes,' Nanda said in wonderment. 'What you say is true. Our son is unique.'

three

Jarasandha surveyed the results of his campaign from the vantage of a plateau. The flat tableland which had provided an effective command post for his advisors and him during the past few days stretched for almost a tenth of a yojana behind him.

Before him lay a plainsland with a city in the foreground. The city had withstood his army's siege for two full moons, the longest any city had resisted him. While not overlong by usual standards of the age, the siege was unusually long for him personally – he found it hard to believe that the half-demolished, charred and smoking carcass of the once-proud capital city sprawled below was still stubborn enough to withstand his assaults. He mused why this was so even as he pondered how to break the siege once and for all.

Perhaps he had been too complacent in his first approach, sending his usual emissaries with the standard missive advising the king of the land to lay down his arms and accept Magadha's superiority. He had even sent a white ass ahead of the emissary, his own little attempt at humour and commentary on the age-old Arya practice of sending a black horse ahead of an army in the great ashwamedha ceremony. In that Vedic ceremony, the territory that the anointed black horse stepped on became part of the domain of the king who sent forth the stallion. And if the owner of the territory resisted, the king was justified in waging war against the errant king or chieftain until he conceded.

Perhaps it was simply the crusading thrill of the Vedic ritual, or the lust for empire, but every single ashwamedha yagna performed to date had resulted in total triumph for the king performing the ceremony.

Jarasandha wondered if that immaculate record of success had not been kept clean merely by failing to record the occasional instances of failure. After all, since almost all itihasa was recorded, stored, and passed on by Brahmins, it was in their vested interest to project a one hundred per cent success rate for one of their biggest, most lavish and most profitable ceremonies, was it not? Then again, he had to admit his own bias against Brahminical practices. As the leader of the first and only kingdom made up entirely of outcastes and no-castes, he was hardly the most unbiased commentator on the ways of the priestly varna.

In any case, the white ass usually served to confound and confuse the receiving kings and their senapatis. Unable to see the rich dark humour inherent in the joke, they invariably responded with contempt, rejecting the emissary outright and laughing at the seemingly pathetic attempt of a low-caste pretender to imitate the high and mighty horse sacrifice. It was only when the screaming and the fires and the slaughter began – always starting from the back end of the city, which Jarasandha's intrepid Mohinis infiltrated discreetly even as all attention was focussed on the emissary and the ridiculous white ass with its colourful anointments – that they realized the white ass was meant to represent *them*. And if they failed to note the metaphorical significance, Jarasandha was always happy to point it out, emphasizing the fact that he had changed the ceremonial *black* of the ashwamedha stallion to a *white* ass to signify the highest varna of Arya society. The fact that he used an ass to represent them rather than a stallion was quite self-explanatory: the joke was on them!

But none of his usual ploys and tactics had worked on this city. Come to think of it, he didn't even know the name of the damned place. And he didn't intend to find out either. It was just another city, one of hundreds he had conquered, and one of a thousand he would command in a short while. When building an empire, one did not count the fleas on one's ass – or on one's rump either! One simply swatted them to a pulp.

He had tried a siege assault, infiltration, artillery, waves of arrows across the city wall, poisoning the fresh water supply, slaughtering children captured from neighbouring villages that were loyal to the king, and a variety of other devices. The city itself now resembled a ruin rather than the proud, beautiful siege town it had been two moons ago. But the walls still stood, and armed defence met his soldiers when they attempted any assault, and the gates still stood. Battered, broken, bleeding … but still not under his power.

He beckoned. His trusted aides Hansa and Dimvaka, always near, came up at once.

'Give the order to withdraw.'

They stared at him dumbly. Accustomed as they were to obeying him unquestioningly and instantly, he had never known them to be dumbfounded even at his most bizarre or unspeakable command. Yet they stared at him speechless now.

'*Withdraw*, sire?'

'Aye. Pull out all our troops. Leave not so much as a dying man or a chopped limb behind. Take everything. Move out within the day and move on. Continue on the same route as before, until you reach the next location.'

They continued to stare at him, exchanged a brief glance, then nodded slowly, turning to go. He chuckled, giving them an excuse to look back and stare questioningly: 'You're wondering why.'

They stared back impassively. Like all those close to him, they spoke rarely and only as much as was needed. Jarasandha was no Brahmin to depend on words. There were more efficient ways of communication. Swords spoke louder.

'You're thinking that if Jarasandha of Magadha fails to breach even a single city, it will dent my unmarred reputation. Word will spread that the forces of Magadha can be resisted. They will say we are not the demons we claim to be. That we can be stood up to and bested. Then the rout will begin. Even those cities we have already subjugated will rise up against us. And those we have not yet reached will resist us with renewed vigour. We shall have to fight twice as hard and ten times as long to conquer the same territory.'

They did not have to nod to show agreement: Hansa and Dimvaka agreed with everything their lord said or did. It was implicit in their existence. The first thing they disagreed with would be their last. Dogs to this master, there was no room in their cognition for anything other than total obedience.

Jarasandha smiled. 'You are right in thinking these thoughts. I cannot afford to let this city go unsacked and unpillaged. In fact, I must now make an example of it. I must demonstrate to the world what happens when anyone defies me too fiercely and too long. It is one thing to put up the show of a fight or a brief siege in order for the local chief or king to maintain his honour in his people's eyes. That I can accept and condone. But this,' with a contemptuous arm, he indicated the city sprawled five hundred feet below like a scattering of broken toys, 'this is unacceptable. This is open defiance. This is a challenge to the death. And so I shall give them what they ask for. They shall have death. They shall have destruction. I shall raze this city to the ground and no other shall ever take its place. This site shall forever remain barren and blood-stained as a reminder of the price of defying Jarasandha of Magadha.'

He grinned, revealing his teeth in an expression that he knew made even his most trusted generals want to step back uneasily. Rarely did they see their master this angry, this bloodthirsty, but often enough to know well enough to be wary of him, of his power, of what he was capable of unleashing.

'But how will I do this if I command the army to move on? I shall tell you how.'

He clapped his hands around both of them, swinging them around to face the edge of the plateau, the direction he was facing. 'In order to set an example, I have decided not to use the army for this special case. Instead, I shall accomplish this alone.'

Jarasandha sensed the men's powerful shoulders tensing involuntarily beneath his grasp.

'You, sire?' Dimvaka asked. 'You will take the city yourself … alone?'

Jarasandha grinned. 'Yes, I shall do it. Both I and myself.'

four

All was in readiness for the naming ceremony. Nanda was overwhelmed with the turnout. He had barely had time to glance out at the crowds, but they seemed to extend well over the next several hillsides, and the sheer volume of sound suggested that the whole Vraj nation had gathered there.

He supposed the reason was the utter joy of having a rare occasion to celebrate after months of terror and pain, and he was not too modest to acknowledge that his non-partisan standing in the community made it possible for all factions, all tribes, all varnas – in short, everyone – to eat and drink and be merry at his festivities without worrying about the political or social ramifications. The only thing he hoped was that there would be enough food and drink to go around. Vraj Yadavas could be a lusty bunch and from the looks and bustle of the crowd, they would consume as much as any army.

A fleeting thought crossed his mind, an errant question about how much this would cost him, but it was dismissed instantly and forgotten soon. Everything he owned was the community's and everything the community had was his; that was the way it was in Vraj. The pride he felt in the air, those shining eyes and wet cheeks, they were because this child was not his alone, he was Vrajbhoomi's son.

News of the massacre had reached this remote corner of the nation from Mathura, and the sheer horror of the event had penetrated through even his shield of fatherly joy. But as the morning had drawn on, it had actually energized the proceedings. Somehow, the birth of a son to Nanda and Yashoda on this particular night seemed propitious and extraordinarily auspicious. To the thousands, perhaps even tens of thousands for all he knew, assembled here now, it must also feel like a raised fist defying the brutal Prince Kamsa – sorry, *King* Kamsa – and his pogrom against the newborn sons of the Yadava capital. A golden ray of hope in the dark morass of tragedy, shining on despite the odds.

Nanda suspected that many of those celebrating were doing so as an act of defiance, as a means of grieving for the little innocents who had been slaughtered in Mathura the previous night. What better way to mourn the dead newborn sons of their friends, relatives and allies in distant Mathura, crushed under the tyrant's boot heels, than to raise a cup and dance in celebration of one that yet lived, untouched by that monster's killing claws. He could understand his people's eagerness to salute his son's birth as a symbol of fresh hope and freedom from tyranny.

A flurry of excitement rose nearby, alerting him to the arrival of the very personage he had been awaiting. He bowed low before the white-bearded, white-haired yet balding preceptor who approached with halting but determined steps, leaning on two stout brahmacharya youths who more than compensated for their guru's age and gait with their cherubic robustness.

'Pundit Gargamuni!' Nanda exclaimed. 'It is an honour to receive you at my humble domicile.'

Gargamuni's wizened face creased in a thousand folds as he chortled. 'Nanda Maharaja, it is *I* who have the honour today. There is not a Brahmin in all Vrajbhoomi who does not long to be here.'

Nanda performed the ritual ablutions of hospitality as he listened respectfully to the old priest. Gargamuni's bony feet twitched as Nanda washed them gently with water, then milk, and then with water again, as was the custom. 'Your hands are too soft, Nanda … that tickles!'

Nanda smiled discreetly. For an old Brahmin, Gargamuni could be quite a wit at times. He had always enjoyed listening to Gargamuni's stories of his younger days as a Brahmin and the experiences and adventures he had been through. As the guru of the Yadavas, Garga was reverentially known as 'Muni', and the honorific was now a fixed part of his name. Nanda could not recall a time in his life when Gargamuni had *not* been there to offer spiritual advice, succour, oversee ceremonies, or otherwise fulfil a guru's role. Vrajbhoomi was blessed to have his guidance and wisdom.

As he finished wiping the pundit's feet, he heard the sound of a baby crying and looked up, smiling indulgently. His smile faded to a look of puzzlement as he realized the source was not his own son. It was a babe swaddled in the arms of a woman who appeared to be asking Nanda's men to let her pass so she could go to him. One of them, Nanda's younger brother Sannanda, turned to glance enquiringly at him. Nanda raised an arm, gesturing to them to let her pass.

The woman approached with the aspect of one fleeing something or someone. When she reached the spot where Nanda had knelt before Gargamuni, she crouched and bowed. And as she did so, the cloth covering the child slipped, revealing the baby's head and part of one shoulder. The boy – for it was a boy – gurgled and clenched his fist happily, turning his eyes towards Nanda. He appeared to be at least four or five despite being just a year old – it was a meaty shoulder and large fist for an infant; yet the way she carried him suggested a much younger child. He was also exceedingly fair of complexion and handsome of profile – at least that is the impression Nanda got from the little he saw of the child from the angle he was at. Nanda brushed these observations aside as the woman began speaking with great urgency.

'My lord Nanda, Pundit Gargamuni, I beg you for your protection and shelter.'

Nanda glanced at his family priest. The old man's bushy white eyebrows rose several inches, resembling a moth taking flight.

'Who are you, gracious lady? Why do you seek us out thus? And from whom do you need protection and shelter?'

The lady glanced around again, fearfully. 'My name is Rohini—' she began.

'Rohini,' the old pundit said speculatively. 'A fine name. It means one who is filled with a rising tide of bliss. Thereby also the Tall One, and by implication, the Mother of Cows.'

Nanda nodded to acknowledge the preceptor's definition though he did not entirely understand how the guru had come by the three quite different definitions from merely a single word. He then turned his attention to the lady, who – Nanda noticed now that his attention had been drawn to that aspect of her form – was indeed quite tall. 'Rohini-devi, I am Nanda; welcome to my land. What is your purpose here?'

She glanced at the old pundit. 'I wish that Pundit Gargamuni perform my son's naming ceremony.'

'Certainly!' said the old priest, responding so suddenly that he caught Nanda quite by surprise. 'It would give me great pleasure!'

Nanda recovered from his surprise. 'Well, yes, I expect Pundit Gargamuni will be pleased to do so as soon as he performs the ceremony for my son.'

The tall lady shook her head. 'I mean that it must be done together. Both boys must be named together. That is why I have brought him here.'

Nanda was taken aback at this odd insistence but took it in his usual good humour. 'Well … I suppose it could be done. But why this urgency? And what does your talk of protection and shelter mean?'

The woman moved closer so she could speak softly and yet be heard above the din of the surrounding crowd. 'Kamsa's soldiers will come even to this remote district sooner or later. It's imperative that both boys be named before that happens. You must clear these crowds and we must perform the naming ceremony in private, discreetly.'

Nanda wondered briefly if the woman was in her senses. Did she not see the enormous crowd? Did she not feel the spirit of jubilation in the air, a sense of celebration? 'That would be impossible. Besides, I am not sure they ought to be named together. What do you say, Gargamuni?'

Gargamuni nodded his head sagely. 'Together is good, yes.'

Nanda stared at him. Whatever was the matter with Gargamuni? Agreeing so readily? He looked at the lady and shrugged. 'But why is it so important?' he asked. 'I didn't quite follow your—'

Rohini moved closer, grasping the bundle in her arms tighter than before. 'It's a matter of life and death, Nanda Maharaja. Not just for us, but for our newborn sons as well. You see, these two boys are brothers. They must stay together always, for only in one another's company will they find strength enough to face their enemy when the time comes.'

Nanda was speechless for a moment. He cleared his throat and said softly, gently, as if addressing a deranged person, as the woman might well be: 'It is impossible that they are brothers, dear lady. But that aside, who is this enemy you speak of? And why would he desire to harm two infants?'

Rohini Devi leaned forward, her voice hissing as she spoke her next words softly, sibilantly: 'Kamsa …' she said, 'his army already seeks both these boys. He will resort to any means necessary to destroy them. I beg you; protect my son and your own from him.'

five

Protesting the unmitigated abuse endured over the past few years of Kamsa's reign, the enormous palace doors groaned. The palace complex resembled a ruin rather than a king's domicile. Under Kamsa's father Ugrasena, the seat of the Yadava nation had been a place of pride and beauty. Designed and overseen by the great architect Vishwakarma himself on Ugrasena's commission, it had stood as a testament to the high cultural and aesthetic standards of the Andhakas.

But Ugrasena was long gone, dethroned and confined to a sunless dungeon inside his own palace, with only his repentant queen, Padmavati, to keep him rough company – and after the shocking discovery that their son Kamsa was in fact the progeny of a rakshasa who had lain with her and seeded her womb, what comfort could husband and wife have found in one another in those dark confines? Gone as well was the reign of prosperity and joy that had come with the latter half of Ugrasena's rule, which began once he grew to repent his earlier, youthful ardour and war lust and began to dismantle the machinery of violence in favour of laying the foundation for peace. His greatest moment had come when he had crossed rajtarus with King Vasudeva in a historic ceremony after signing a peace pact, heralding a new era.

But Kamsa had demolished all his father's work, even as he had gone about demolishing Mathura itself, and his own palace.

He had started by pulling down the peace treaty, then gone on to destroy more tangible institutions.

Now he intended to take the final step in a long progression. To ascend to the pinnacle of his reign, and build the legacy that he hoped he would be remembered for in years to come ... centuries, millennia even.

Not that historic achievements mattered much to Kamsa. He had killed the court historians a long time ago, at the commencement of his reign in Mathura. The idea of anyone watching his actions, jotting down his words and describing his every deed, then organizing it all into neat Sanskritized packages of verse – shlokas, they called them, after the metric quatrain invented by Valmiki for his adi-kavya epic – was distasteful in the extreme to him. He loathed, feared even, the idea that there were eyes and ears recording his every word and deed and recording *their* version of them for posterity. After hearing one particularly horrendous account of his own ascension to the throne, he had gone about the palace complex rooting out every last munshi – as the scribe sub-varna were called – and had killed them all. Eaten them alive, in fact. It seemed a fitting way to kill a poet. After all, what else was a poet but a person who ate lives and spat out his own version of them for public consumption? So Kamsa had eaten every last court scribe alive. Since then, itihasa had gone unrecorded in Mathura, which was why he could do what he was about to do now without concerning himself with how it might appear to watching eyes.

Kicking one misaligned door hard enough to splinter the yard-thick wood, he shoved the groaning doors of the sabha hall shut, then turned to face his audience.

The sabha hall was filled with Brahmins – pundits, purohits, rishis, munis, sadhus, sanyasis, gurus ... he had invited every Brahmin of note. He intended to give out guru-dakshina, the sacred ceremonial paying of compensation that all Kshatriyas, the warrior varna, owed to their teachers, the Brahmin varna. He had announced a feast such as Mathura had never seen before. That was all that was needed: every Brahmin of note in the city had come eagerly. Now he scanned the hundreds of white-clad, ochre-clad, and even sky-clad Brahmins of every shape and size, and smiled.

He had reduced himself to his human form and size for the occasion. It would not do to scare them away until he had accomplished his goal.

There was no fear on any of the waiting faces. Brahmins rarely feared anyone or anything. Brahmin-hatya, the killing of a Brahmin, was the worst crime any Arya could commit. It deprived one of any possible chance of ever attaining moksha or liberation from the eternal cycle of birth and death, for regardless of one's other actions, no Brahmin would ever perform the samskaras (religious rites necessary for the aatma's ascension to higher planes) on one who had slain a Brahmin. Whatever the provocation, none dared harm a Brahmin – except other Brahmins, of course, and even that was rare. The epic conflict of the great brahmarishis Vishwamitra and Vashishta was perhaps the only recorded instance of such an enmity, and it was an exception so rare, it bordered on mythology.

He held his smirk as he strode towards his audience. They were seated cross-legged in rows, awaiting the promised feast. Brahmins loved to eat, didn't they? And no matter how much they ate, they never seemed to get fat! Well, there were a few exceptions, but generally, Brahmins were rake-thin. He supposed it was all that self-deprivation and long meditation. What did they call it? Ghor tapasya? Why would anyone deprive oneself of the fleshly pleasures for any reason? Surely enlightenment couldn't be better than the physical pleasures of life and the body?

'Your repast shall be served shortly,' he said, and then, seeing the Brahmins craning their necks and cupping their hands theatrically behind their ears, realized that his voice was not loud enough to be heard at the far ends of the hall. 'YOU SHALL BE FED SOON!' he shouted.

Then he began to expand himself. The reaction was instantaneous. Shock. Revulsion. Sneering disapproval. He retained the grin as he grew until his head touched the thirty-foot-high ceiling of the sabha hall, but then continued as he shattered the ceiling, making plaster and debris fall all around, and broke through the roof, rising up, up, up through the air. He stopped when he was about a hundred feet high. That was sufficient for his purposes.

The chaos below amused him. While the Brahmins were agitated and upset at his lapse of protocol, a few even injured due to the falling debris from the hole in the roof, the majority were still seated complacently, waiting to be fed. *Expecting* to be fed. That was what he hated about their varna. The sense of entitlement they possessed. As if all the earth and the remaining two worlds were theirs first to claim and possess and enjoy. As if they need only toss the leftovers to the other varnas.

But they always needed Kshatriyas to do their dirty work. What good were Brahmins without Kshatriyas? They could not protect themselves, could not have fought off rakshasas and other asuras back in the days when the mortal realm was still new and the eternal war between the devas and asuras raged as fiercely on earth as on the other two planes of existence. Brahmins always needed Kshatriyas, and Kshatriyas were the ones who fought, died, struggled, achieved, triumphed; yet Brahmins were the ones who wrote the itihasas, composed the epic poems, recorded the court histories, carried the knowledge of the sacred Vedic verses and rituals, and generally acted as if they were the be-all and end-all.

Well, it was time Brahmins pulled their share of the load. He had made them assemble here to make sure of that.

The growth and transformation to his rakshasa form resulted in its inevitable side-effect: growths and suppurations began at once. He began plucking the sticky and wet abominations off his body. Some squealed loudly as he tore them off. He strode down the long lines of expectant Brahmins, dropping a festering worm-like thing here, another oozing sore there, and so on, all the way down the line. There was ample food to feed every last guest.

The serving done, he turned and watched. The sabha hall had descended into mindless chaos. It pleased him to see the Brahmins finally jolted out of their smugness as they realized that this was a feast of a different kind altogether. He watched with glee as one monstrosity plucked from his body gobbled up half a Brahmin, and its oozing gummy shape merged with that of the human to form a new shape: a bizarre amalgam of man and wart, or whatever it was one called such extrusive growths. The result resembled some grotesque demon from the annals of the First Asura Wars, that age when the demoniac races had broken through from the hellish realms into the mortal plane and run amok before the first great Arya nations had taken up arms against them. A creature that was neither human nor anything else, yet was distinctly humanoid in shape and form, and, as he knew so well by now, nearly indestructible. For how do you kill a living wart? Let alone a wart of a higher varna!

He watched the vast hall filled with writhing gooey shapes settle into a semblance of quietude. Finally, when every last one had been fed, he sighed with satisfaction.

It was always nice to have guests over for lunch and to see them well fed.

Now for dessert…

six

The people of the city rejoiced. It had been over four days since the invaders had departed, taking every last piece of siege machinery, weaponry and possession; not a living being stirred outside the city walls. The siege was over, the threat had ended; they had triumphed! It was an incredible success.

'We withstood the might of Magadha and survived,' said the maatr of the kingdom. Like many Arya nations which still rigorously followed the old Vedic ways, this was a matriarchial society. No male had ever ruled, nor ever would. It was not an issue of which sex was better or superior, simply a practical matter. Women were better at governing, running things, administrating, keeping the peace, maintaining the cities well, and doing all the things that made up the daily business of ruling a kingdom. And if anyone dared to think that men might perhaps, possibly, just maybe, be better at warcraft, the person had certainly not faced the maatrs in battle.

The citizens emerged now, resplendent in their armour, which was specially polished and cleaned for the occasion. During weeks of hard siege and withstanding brutal intrusions and assaults, there had been little time for food or rest, let alone polishing armour. But with the enemy having retreated, and a celebration called for, the maatrs were proud to adorn themselves in their finest robes. And for a maatr, no garb was more resplendent than battle armour. Glimmering with gold, silver and flecks of coloured stone cleverly sown into the chain links of the mail, the metal garb clung becomingly to the Amazonian bodies of the hard-muscled warrior matrons who were the mainstay of the country's army. Nor were they all young specimens; there were grandmothers among them, white-haired and noble in their ageing pride, as well as women scarred and maimed from combat. They were nonetheless resplendent in that moment of glory.

The environs of the city had been scoured thoroughly over the past four days. The moment the last wagons of the last grama-train had departed, fading into a faint trail of dust on the northern horizon, the spasas had been sent forth through underground tunnels to scour the countryside. They went yojanas in every direction, up to the tableland plateau and far beyond the river which was their primary source of life. They found nothing. The enemy had truly withdrawn. It was no ruse. Not a living enemy remained in sight. Except for a few wounded, rotting corpses left in a pile right in front of the city gates. These were the stray soldiers of Magadha who had fallen to the arrows or javelins tossed by the defenders, or been slain in the skirmishes and confrontations over the past weeks.

There were barely a hundred or two of these unfortunate carcasses. As a rule, besiegers rarely suffered even a tenth as many losses as the besieged. Within the city, the toll numbered in the thousands. Those who had not been killed outright by the deadly rain of arrows and boulders hurled by siege machines, and the random javelin showers flung by the powerful shoulders of the Mohini Fauj, had been killed in the direct skirmishes and encounters. Many had been murdered by the infiltrators who managed somehow to sneak into the city on suicide missions, slaying dozens by dint of the element of surprise before being brought down. Others had died of disease from the confinement, of ailments and old age, or were crushed under disintegrating structures felled by the hurtling boulders, or burnt alive in the fires.

Nobody paid heed to the rotting pile of corpses. The maatr gave a command for the corpses to be buried in a single unmarked mass grave – but she admitted it was not a high priority. There were many thousands of their own dead to deal with first, before more serious diseases broke out amongst the living, and these had to be cremated with all due ritual and ceremony, which would consume resources, energy and time, all of which were nearly exhausted by the siege.

The truth was, had the siege gone on, they would have been hard-pressed to last more than another fortnight. Oh, they could have held the city longer, but the cost would have been piteous. In any siege, after a certain point even the most stubborn and proud leader must weigh the cost of letting one's people die or of giving them a chance to survive, however slim that may be, by sallying forth and attacking the enemy while they still had a measure of strength and numbers to do so.

So the celebrations began, and continued even as the inevitable chores were undertaken: rebuilding, cremating the dead, sending hunting parties out for fresh supplies of meat in the nearby forests which were over a day's run away, salvaging what could be salvaged from the ruined, scorched and salted harvest fields on the lower plains beside the riverbank that had been the city's primary source of nourishment, and a hundred other odd jobs and endeavours.

A further three days passed before they got to the pile of enemy corpses.

Due to the inclement weather and cloudy skies, the corpses had not putrefied as badly as they might have. The monsoons were late in coming this year, but they were en route, and the usual cloud build-up had shielded the land from the harsh sun. Still, the dead bodies were maggot-ridden and beginning to fall apart when the delegated team of maatrs came to dispose of them.

As they approached the pile, the volunteers made various sounds of disgust, mostly imitating retching.

'Let's just throw on as much oil as we have and burn the whole lot where it lies,' said one woman warrior, her voice deeply nasal due to her pinching her nose to avoid the stench.

'Can't do that,' said another woman apologetically, wincing as the wind changed, bringing the full richness of the aroma to her nasal glands. 'Maatr's orders are to bury them. Oil supplies are short enough as it is.'

The women looked at the pile doubtfully. 'We could bring dry brush and wood and use that to burn them.'

The maatr-in-charge snorted. 'Do you know how much it would take to burn this lot? A hundred wagonloads! Maybe more. And without oil ... Besides, the smoke and ash would carry across the whole city.' She gestured at the city behind them and indicated the direction of the wind. 'And the outer ones would burn but it would be a putrefying mess on the inside.'

They were all silent for a moment, considering the idea, then, one of her companions said in disgust, 'Oh, thank you, Suverya, for that wonderful thought. Excuse me while I go relieve the contents of my belly.'

'Get to it, then,' the maatr-in-charge ordered. 'Let's start digging a pit. And remember, we have to make it large enough and deep enough to take the whole of this sorry bunch. Maatr intends to plant an orchard over it afterwards.'

'An orchard?' someone asked, incredulous.

'Yes,' said the woman-in-charge sourly. 'To commemorate the siege. Besides, fresh corpses underground give good fruit. Come on, get to work, you lazy bunch!'

It was the afternoon of the next day when they came across the body.

'Maatr!' exclaimed one of the younger women, for all women commanders and rulers were called maatr in their society, 'come take a look at this.'

The maatr-in-charge and several of the others within hearing range came out of curiosity. They looked down at the male body split perfectly into two halves from the centre of the bald crown of its head right down to the waist. The cut was blade-smooth, perfect, as if it was an apple that had been sliced into two halves rather than a grown man.

The maatr-in-charge frowned and wiped the sweat and grime from her brow before asking irritably, 'And what great vision am I supposed to be looking at, Narayani?'

'It's as good as new,' replied the young woman who had discovered the anomaly. 'It hasn't rotted at all. How is that possible?'

And it was true. Apart from the fact that the body was split into two halves, it was pristine. No decay had occurred as yet, nor were any maggots or putrefying flesh visible. The women examined the body curiously and all agreed that apart from the body being cut into two halves, its skin and flesh resembled that of a living man.

'It's almost as if ...' one woman said, then stopped.

'What?' asked the one beside her.

'Well, it's almost as if you could put the two halves together and they would fit perfectly, with barely a seam visible.'

'So speaks the expert seamstress!' sang out another, drawing a burst of laughter. It was good to have something to laugh about after the miseries of the past months.

Out of sheer curiosity, three or four of the women actually picked up the two halves of the severed corpse and placed them together.

'Look! They fit together like a whole body!' said the one who had thought of it.

One of the women holding the halves together felt movement beneath her fingertips. She frowned, assuming she had only felt some reverberation or other movement, and looked down.

The eyes of the severed corpse opened.

The volunteer screamed and let go of the body, backing away, *scrambling* away. She tripped and fell over another body. 'It's alive!' she cried out.

The erstwhile severed corpse got to its feet, causing the other women around it to back away as well. It looked around. The thin red line running down the centre of its bald head all the way down its naked chest and body glowed brightly for an instant, then faded away.

The severed body was now a whole man. A living man. With no trace of a seam, as the wit had remarked.

As they stared on in stunned incomprehension, the maatr-in-charge reached for her sword. 'Kill him!' she cried. 'Kill—'

That was as far as she got. The severed man's tongue shot out of his mouth and lashed out at her with whip-like ferocity, covering a distance of over two yards to strike her across the chest and waist at a diagonal. The maatr-in-charge felt a moment of scalding heat, as if she had been struck by a red-hot whip. Then the acid saliva from Jarasandha's tongue ate through her armour, garb, flesh and bone with instant efficacy, and her body split into two at the diagonal cut. She fell open like a ripe fruit and perished. The two halves of her body hissed and sizzled as they parted, the exposed flesh and organs corroded by the acidic saliva.

Stunned, the other warriors attacked this unexpected enemy who had risen from the dead. But Jarasandha moved amongst them with lightning speed, swinging around in a half-circle to strike cobra-like at the more than half a dozen women in rapid succession. He would be here one instant, his whip-like tongue lashing out to sever one's arm before she could slash out with her sword, then over there in the next, yards away, decapitating another woman's head, and so forth. Many died screaming with agony and without lifting their weapons; others, shocked and stunned, died before they could react.

It was an astonishing display. Within moments, the entire burial crew lay butchered, the dissected bodies of its members steaming and hissing.

Then Jarasandha moved into the city. And then began the slaughter.

He met a great deal of resistance. Relaxed though they were, taken by surprise, caught off guard, and all of that, yet the maatrs were fierce fighters and strong-willed independent Aryas.

But it made absolutely no difference. Jarasandha passed through them all like a force of nature, like a hurricane through a sugarcane field, like a tiger through a flock of geese. He mowed down the entire city within a day and part of a night. By the time he was done, there were many, many more corpses to cremate and commemorate, but nobody left to do the needful.

He left the city that way, every last citizen a rotting corpse, a place fit only for worms, flies and maggots. He left just a single horse alive, mounted it and rode to join his forces. There were many more cities to ravage and kingdoms to subdue.

This was only a sideshow.

The real game was the one unfolding in the Yadava kingdom, under the surmise of his protégé, Kamsa.

seven

From the growing volume of sound outside, Yashoda judged that a great many people were assembling to be part of the naming ceremony of her newborn. It pleased her. She felt it was important that her son be seen by as many as possible. She did not know why she felt so; she simply felt it. As for herself, the sheer joy of having a child was beyond belief. That moment she had seen the newborn life that had issued forth from her womb, the instant she first set eyes on her beautiful tiny daughter, had been the happiest one of her life. The intensity of it had been indescribable, like nothing she had ever felt before.

She frowned.

My beautiful tiny daughter?

Yes, that was what she had just thought, hadn't she? A fleeting recollection of glancing down and seeing ... a girl. Still covered in birth fluids, naked as creation ... and that was one of the first things any mother would notice.

Yashoda looked down now at the dozing tyke nestled against her. She was on her side, lying facing the entrance of the sleeping chamber. The baby was sleeping facing her, snuggled into her warmth and the folds of her sari. She could only make out a tiny clenched fist and part of a minuscule ear. But this was a boy. She had no doubt about that. Then why had she thought she had seen a girl born to her the night before?

She smiled wryly at her own foolishness. Of course, it was a mistake; that was all. She had been so exhausted after the long labour – a full day and almost a whole night of straining and heaving – that seconds after her dear one's birth, she had passed out as completely as if she had never slept a wink all her life. In her exhaustion, she must have taken this little fellow to be a filly. Or perhaps it was her mind, which had been wishing for a girl, that had made her see him as one, if only in her tired mind's eye.

She knew that Nanda would have loved a daughter too, unlike so many other men – to be honest, unlike most men, who would much prefer a son. But she came from a line of maternalistic Yadavas, a family of strong women who stood their own *against* men and *beside* them, and never let their own daughters and granddaughters ever think, even for a moment, that a man could do all that a woman could. A man couldn't, of course. And he always knew it. But either because he couldn't or despite it, he always tried harder. All a woman need do, then, was try equally hard, and she would always win in the end. That was simply nature's way, the way of Prithvi Maa, Mother Earth, for all life on this mortal plane, and the way of Prajapati, the creator in human form. That was the reason why cruel men and despots resorted to violence – because only a sword and savagery could give a man an ephemeral sense of superiority over women, and over other men.

So perhaps she had wanted a daughter so much – had assumed, coming from a long and illustrious line of daughters of daughters of daughters, that her first-born would also surely be a daughter – that she had looked at her child already convinced that she had birthed a girl. A gopi rather than a gopa. Yes, that was surely it.

And then she had fallen dead asleep, waking only that morning. And come to think of it, when she had looked down at this little doll, there had been no surprise or consternation on seeing he was a boy. She had accepted it without question. Indeed, it was only now that, lost in her own thoughts, she had briefly thought she recalled birthing a girl. Just a mistake in memory, that was all.

She put it out of her head. This was no time to think of what-ifs and might-have-beens. This was the day of her newborn son's birth. And, from the noise of the gathering outside, she deduced that the whole of Vrajbhoomi had turned up to view him. It was a day of celebration after many, many days of darkness and grief. The crowd would have been no less if she had had a daughter. If the Vrajvasis were ecstatic that she had a son, it was not because of the usual reasons but because many Yadava sons had died in Mathura at the hands of Kamsa and his marauders. The boy lying by her side was a symbol of freedom from the tyrant's yoke, a sign that the Vrishnis of Vrajbhoomi continued to live free despite the despotic reign of the Childslayer.

Which made her wonder: What had happened to Devaki and Vasudeva's next child? There was some uncertainty about whether this one constituted the seventh or the eighth, the confusion being set off by the apparent miscarriage of their seventh child last year. Rumour had it that it had been no miscarriage, that a deliberate samkarsana procedure had been performed to remove the baby intact and alive from the womb, to be transported to an unknown destination. If that was true, Devaki's present pregnancy would be the eighth. The prophesied one. The long-awaited Slayer of Kamsa.

Yashoda knew that Devaki and her own pregnancy had proceeded apace, which meant that Devaki had either delivered by now or would deliver any day. She shuddered at the thought of the fate that awaited that unfortunate eighth child. No wonder all Vrajbhoomi had collected outside her house today; the Yadavas were here to celebrate the birth of their son – and to ensure his survival. The long arm of Kamsa reached every corner of the kingdom, as so many had learnt to their dismay; but they were determined to celebrate this and save this child.

The baby touched her arm.

Yashoda looked down.

Two dark black eyes looked up at her, as bright as shiny purple grapes. Tiny teeth flashed. It was surprising that the child had been born with a full head of hair, as well as with some teeth. And the way he looked – the way he was looking at her right now, this instant – it was quite something. She almost believed he was actually *looking* at her. *Seeing* her. Sensing her thoughts and feelings. And that he had touched her at that precise moment to comfort her, to assure her that nothing would happen to him, that he would never suffer the fate intended for the unfortunate son of Devaki and Vasudeva.

You will never lose me, Mother.

She could almost hear his voice in her mind, speaking with a chuckling light-heartedness that indicated he knew all there was to know and had seen everything there was to see.

She smiled and caressed his tiny fist lovingly. 'If only you could speak, my little calf. If you could only understand what I am saying. You would know that your father and I would never let any harm come to you.'

Nor would I let any harm come to both of you, Maatr.

She smiled. 'Yes, of course, my son. Some day, you shall be big and strong and protect us all. But until then, your father shall ensure your safety. You need fear nothing and no one.'

I do not fear anything or anyone, Maatr.

'Of course you don't, my little gopa. Listen, all who love you are present around us, ready to defend you with their lives if need be.'

Yes, Maatr. I sense their love and fierce loyalty. It is very reassuring. I am indeed fortunate to be born into such a loyal and loving family.

Yashoda almost laughed. Here she was, talking aloud to her newborn son – and believing he was speaking to her mind! She must be really tired. Perhaps she should call out to her sisters and friends to come in now. They had volunteered to leave her alone for some respite as well as to help greet and attend to the never-ending stream of relatives and well-wishers; she had only to call out loud enough and they would come at once. Or perhaps she ought to call for her maatr and aunts, or even her maatr-in-law. She ought to change her garb before greeting the guests, after all.

Do not be concerned, Maatr. You are quite well. This is not your imagination. I am indeed speaking to you within your mind.

'Devi, protect us!' exclaimed Yashoda.

She stared down at the tightly wrapped bundle on the cot beside her.

He gurgled happily, kicking his feet free of the swaddling cloth, and put a tiny fist into his mouth, sucking on it.

You will pardon me but I only wish to get to know you and our family better. After all, I am now a part of the family too, am I not?

'Yes, of course,' she said, then thought: *Am I really having a conversation with my day-old infant son? How can that be?*

Please remain calm. I would like to use your mind to see them through your memories and senses. At the same time, you shall also be able to see them through my senses. It shall only take a moment ...

'What—?' she began to ask what he meant.

Then suddenly she felt him inside her mind – not just his voice, but his presence itself, like a warm glow in the centre of her brain, emanating outwards, filling her entire being with great calm and quietude, a sense that she was the universe and the universe was her and nothing and nobody could deny her anything she desired.

And then she felt her consciousness spreading, widening to encompass the room, the house itself, then moving outwards beyond the walls of the house, outside the dwelling itself, and into the crowd of assembled people waiting outside ...

eight

So many people!

'Yes, my son, we have a *big* family!' she said, then realized she wasn't actually speaking. Her body was still inside the house, but her consciousness, somehow connected to his, was soaring free of bodily restraints, hovering above the crowd now, then swooping down, moving into ... the mind of a laughing adolescent boy with his mouth open ...

Sucaru!

'Yes, he's my cousin, my uncle Carumukha's son ...'

A flurry of images, thoughts, sensations, feelings, memories, words and inchoate pieces of consciousness whipped past like odours and scents on a dancing wind. Yashoda realized that her son was reading Sucaru's mind, absorbing his every memory, sensation, imbibing his entire life in the wink of an eye.

He is a nice fellow, said Krishna, chuckling with delight. *I like him!*

Before Yashoda could say anything, he was off again, whipping out of Sucaru's mind and into another's consciousness. This time it was Carumukha, Sucaru's father, Yashoda's uncle. The sensation was quite different: the father was naturally more mature, serious, yet the same light-hearted spirit pervaded his mind as well. And the manner in which they perceived the world was so similar, it was quite extraordinary. Yashoda laughed aloud with delight – although she suspected her laughter was silent rather than truly out loud – to see herself among her uncle's memories, as seen through his eyes over time.

Another nice person; I like him very much. I shall learn much from him!

There was no need to speak further, and no time either, as the child whisked them both out of Uncle Carumukha's mind and onward to the next.

Yashodevi, my aunt! Your sister! She is so like you!

The glee was so infectious that Yashoda found herself smiling, laughing, if only metaphorically, as she saw her sister through her child's pure, innocent mind. It was almost like being inside her own consciousness but of course with substantial differences, for the two had different experiences.

She likes to be known as Dadhisara rather than Yashodevi since too many people confuse Yashodevi with Yashoda-devi, which is what they call you out of respect.

And he gurgled with laughter as if he had discovered a wonderful secret.

The next one was Yasasvini, Yashoda's other sister. She also preferred to be known as Havihsara, but for a different reason.

I love my aunts and they love me very much – even though they have yet to know me! How wonderful!

Next came Catu and Batuka, Yashodevi and Yasasvini's husbands respectively. There were slightly embarrassing memories in their minds but her Krishna's innocence meant that he merely absorbed the overall amalgam of sensation and adjudged the essence of the person – *Good! Wonderful! I love him! Such a nice fellow! Good man!* – which, as she learned quickly, was almost always positive.

They seemed to move faster as he went along, almost as if Krishna was learning to use Yashoda's consciousness more efficiently, riffling through the metaphorical leaves of memory faster and faster, until he was literally dancing from one mind to another to yet another – hopping, skipping, laughing, gurgling – like a butterfly from flower to flower to flower. There also seemed to be a pattern to his movements; he went from one mind to the one closest to it in consciousness, then to the next relevant one, and so on.

Aindavi and Kirtida – her best friends – were followed in blurring succession by Bhogini, Sarika, Vatsala, Tarangaksi and Taralika, Medura, Masrna, Krpa, Sankini, Tusti, Anjana, Bimbini, Mitra, Subhaga, Niti, Kusala, Tali, Paksati, Pataka, Pundi, Sutunda, Subhada, Kapila, Prabha, Malika, Angada, Visala, Sallaki, Vena, Vartika, Dhamanidhara, Hingula ... all her remaining friends!

Whee!

Whee indeed. It was breathtaking in the most literal sense of the word. But there was no time to catch breath – or whatever the mental equivalent of that may be – for Krishna was off again, to another group of minds, this time riffling through a dozen at the same rate as he had riffled through a single mind at first. He was getting faster, no doubt about it. Yashoda didn't know whether to be awed by her child's ability or by the encyclopaedia of memories, images and sensations that she was being exposed to. At any rate, it was overwhelming. The child also began to learn the relationships and interrelationships with enviable ease. It seemed incredible that he could do so, but she was already far past the point of suspending disbelief and was merely riding along involuntarily, which made her an entertained spectator.

Sumuka! My grandfather, your father!

And then followed Patala-devi, her mother and his grandmother. And Sumuka's friends and colleagues: Vararoha, Karanda, Kallota, Kila, Antakela, Gonda, Tarisana, Visaroha, Varisana, Purata, Tilata and Krpita.

And then there was Patala-devi's brother Gola who was, of course, her uncle and his great-uncle. Gola's wife Jatila-devi. Gola's sons Yashodhara, Yashodeva and Sudeva. Then her mother's closest friends Danka, Damani, Dindima, Cakkini, Tundi, Sughantika, Ghanta, Ghargara, Bhela, Bharunda, Karala, Mukhara, Ghoni, Dhvankarunti, Dingima, Condika, Pundavanika, Dambi, Cundi, Manjuranika, Handi, Ghora, Karabalika, Jatila and also Patala's closest, dearest friend of all, Mukahara-gopi.

Such sweet, lovely grandaunties I have!

'Krishna—' she began, hoping for a respite. But he was off again, now tearing through memories like a gale-force wind through a row of ashoka trees. All she could do was marvel at his capacity to absorb.

Parjanya Maharaj, her father-in-law. Variyasi-devi, her mother-in-law. Parjanya Maharaj's brothers Urjanya and Rajanya, and sister Suverjana with her husband Gunavira, the last just arrived that minute from Suryakunja, tired but very excited.

Then Anakadundhubi himself as he was known to Yashoda and those closest to him, Nanda Mahajaraja to the world at large, Krishna's father, her husband. Her brothers-in-law Upananda, Abhinanda, Sannanda and Nandana. Upananda's wife was the only one not present, but the other wives were: Pivari-devi, Kuvalaya-devi and Atulya-devi. Her sisters-in-law, Sananda-devi and Nandini-devi. Sananda-devi's husband Mahanila, and Nandini-devi's husband Sunila. Upananda the widower's sons Kandava and Dandava and their friend Subala who was like an adopted son to Upananda. Nanda's Kshatriya cousins Catu and Batuka, with their respective wives Dadhisara and Havihsara.

Nanda's friends by definition would include the whole of Vrajbhoomi but his closest friends were gathered close by and Krishna swooped through the gathering. Pinga, Pattisa, Bhrngaq, Saragha, Kedara, Ankura, Cakranga, Kambala, Harita, Upananda, Harikesa, Supaksa, Maskara, Dhurina, Sauabheya, Pathira, Ghrni, Sankara, Mathura, Mangala, Pingala, Pitha, Sangara, Ghatika, Dandi, Kala, Dhurva, Utpala, Saudha and Hara.

It went on that way, seemingly endlessly, until Yashoda lost sense of time and place and even self-awareness. The world became a blur of minds and memories, and Krishna's infectious gurgle seemed to fill the whole world, echoing across prithviloka and bouncing off the silvery round face of Chandamama, the moon itself, which beamed back like a doting uncle.

nine

Devaki felt as if the moon himself was mocking her. Chandamama seemed bright and cheerful this cloudy Sravan day, beaming down in broad daylight as if taking advantage of the sun's concealment behind a brooding cloudbank. She could almost hear him laughing down at her, chuckling with infantile delight. She sighed and passed a hand across her face. She was tired and heartbroken and beginning to imagine things. She wished Vasudeva were there with her. His presence comforted her.

Mathura was in the grip of insanity. Kamsa's vendetta had grown out of bounds. All morning, the screams of the dying had filled the city. Even in the spot that was the most secluded from the general population – the heart of the royal enclave – Devaki could hear the faint howls of anguish and cries of distress. She shuddered at the very thought. How many infants had died in place of her own son! How many other innocent fathers, mothers, and other proud Yadavas had lost their lives standing up to Kamsa's unjust diktat! It was a pogrom such as the Yadava nations had never witnessed before. And overseeing it all, ensuring that his orders were complied with to the letter, Kamsa himself strode from time to time across the kingdom, his shadow casting a giant pall across the once-great nation. *Like the shadow of Yama-deva, Lord of Death himself*, she thought.

Kamsa was not about at present at least, which was something to be thankful for. He had been sequestered in his palace for hours, doing god knew what. She had heard that the senior-most Brahmins in the kingdom had been summoned by her brother that morning to attend some conference or feast. What there was to celebrate on such a grisly day, she had no idea. But Kamsa's calendar was his own; he seemed to live on a different plane than his fellow Yadavas – if they could even be called his fellow Yadavas any more, that is. After everything that had transpired, she hardly knew whether to think of him as her brother. It was evident that he had never truly been her brother except in name.

But thinking about him only brought the darkness back to her heart. It reminded her of her parents, locked in that sunless dungeon for so many long years. The occasional reports that came to her from time to time assured her that they were alive, but what sort of living was that, buried in a suffocating dungeon without basic facilities or even proper food? How did they survive?

She could barely stand to think of it, or of Kamsa's other atrocities over these past years, not least among which were the heartless slayings of her own offspring. Six children had she delivered from her womb into the world. Six newborn infants, precious and pure, had Vasudeva carried, weeping each time, only to see them grasped roughly by the tyrant and their brains smashed against the wall of Kamsa's chambers. Even now, the very thought threatened to stop her heart, to blind her, to make her want to drop to the ground and never rise again.

But then had come the seventh child. And the eighth. And both had survived. Both lived. And that was what gave her hope. Gave her strength to stand now. To look out from her balcony and attempt to gaze out at the city, or what little of it she could see from her secluded palace. Now that the eighth child had been born, that part of the prophecy fulfilled, Kamsa had permitted Vasudeva and Devaki to move back to her official residence. In any case, the temporary residence where they had been incarcerated over the past decade was virtually obliterated, destroyed by Kamsa's men in that last frantic search for any trace of the Slayer. Her lips curled scornfully. *As if I would have hidden my son in my own home, only to be found eventually and destroyed!*

A sound akin to thunder drew her attention skywards. She glanced up and saw a dark, fearsome cloud rolling her way, seething and churning in the sky, as if about to give birth to some nameless god. She drew back instinctively. Something about the shape of the cloud, the intensity with which it rolled and seethed, attracted her gaze. She found herself unable to take her eyes off it.

As she watched, the cloud drew closer, approaching the Yamuna which she knew was just beyond that hill flanking the city's north road. It continued to roll and seethe with greater intensity than any cloud she had seen before, until she began to wonder if it was indeed a cloud or something quite different.

She glanced around. There was no wind to speak of, nor was even a leaf stirring in sight. The eastern sky was dense with clouds, blocking the sun momentarily, and those were utterly still.

Yet this cloud, the one coming from across the Yamuna – *from the direction of Vrajbhoomi* – was seething and boiling like a living thing!

How was that possible?

It wasn't, of course.

Even allowing for some unique wind which served to blow that single cloud in this opposing direction to the rest, there was still something highly unusual about the mass approaching her.

It wasn't white, of course. But neither was it black. Or even some shade of grey, as monsoon clouds usually were.

It was a shade of blue. So dark it was almost black, but not quite.

She could see light within its centre as it approached steadily, rolling over and over itself like a curling wave. The radiance was intense, deep blue, like a flame within a black-skinned pot.

And like a bolt of lightning out of a clear sky, it came to her.

Ghana, such clouds were called. Dense. Thick.

Shyam-rang was the shade. The colour of dusk. Not day-white, nor night-black, but twilight-blue.

Black with a heart of blue. *Ghana-shyam*. Dense, deep blue.

Again, that gurgling sound in her mind — like a baby's.

The cloud crossed the Yamuna and approached the palace enclave of Mathura. Coming within a kite's flying length of her own palace.

Then, when it was positioned precisely where she could see it perfectly, it stood still in the sky, remaining motionless for several moments.

And gurgled.

Yes, gurgled.

Not thundered. Or boomed. Or gnashed. As monsoon clouds are wont to do.

This cloud gurgled. Like a babe. Like a newborn infant.

And as she watched, disbelieving, yet seeing with her own eyes what she could not deny, the cloud shaped itself, like clay moulding its own contours, assuming a figure that was unmistakable in its shape and curves and features.

The cloud took the shape of a baby.

Not just any baby. Her son. Her eighth child!

Maatr, I am well. I have found a wonderful family. They are very nice people. I shall take very good care of them, each and every one of them; you don't need to worry any more.

'Son?' Her voice caught on the two simple syllables, the emotion in her heart welling into her throat.

Yes, Maatr. Please don't be sad any more. I don't like to see you sad.

'My baby!' she sobbed, and tears spilled down her cheeks, hot and plump.

My brother will join me soon. We shall both be together, safe and sound. You can be at peace now. We shall take care of everything from now on.

Devaki had no more words to offer. What could one say to a cloud that spoke with one's son's voice?

Maatr, please don't cry any more. I know it has been hard for you. But the dark days are about to end. I am happy. Please be happy with me!

'Yes!' she cried. And cried one final tear, a tear of joy.

A tear rolled down the face of the cloud-baby as well, matching her own. It rolled off the face of the cloud-baby, and started falling down, down, until it landed on the balcony beside her, with a soft plop, and lay on the floor at her feet.

See! Now you made me cry. Now I shall cry, and cry a lot!

'No, my son. Don't!'

A rich gurgling chuckle. The kind only a baby can make.

I am teasing you, Maatr. I cry only because I need to do so. Our land has been stricken by drought for far too long. It is time for the rain to return. That's all I meant!

She covered her mouth with her hand, stifling her gasp. Was it true? Was this really happening? Was this really her baby, her eighth child?

Yes, Maatr. Who else would it be? I cannot promise to come to you often, as you-know-who is watching, but you may keep my tear as a token of my love for you and Pitr. Please give him my love as well. And know that I shall do my part. Everything will change now. Be happy. Smile! Bring back the spring and summer you have kept hidden all these years; let the sunlight into your heart once more. I shall be present in every ray of sunshine, every drop of rain, every bird cry ... I am watching over you.

As he said these final words, the cloud drew away, dissipating as quickly as it had approached, unfurling, uncurling, like a wave retreating and diminishing, until, barely a moment later, it was gone, leaving nothing but a shadowy wisp in the sky. Like the ghost of a memory.

Devaki looked down and saw the cloud-tear that had fallen at her feet. She bent to pick it up – and gasped. It had turned to stone. To smooth polished marble, so dark it seemed black at first, but when it caught the light, she saw that it was in fact deep blue, the same colour as the cloud, the colour of her beloved son. It was roughly the shape and form of a newborn babe, as if naturally formed rather than shaped by the hands of man.

'Ghanashyam,' she said, feeling her heart lighten even as she lifted the heavy bust and carried it into the chamber. 'I shall name you Ghanashyam.'

And she laughed aloud with genuine pleasure for what seemed like the first time in years. Outside, thunder cracked and the sweet scent of first rain came to her on a soft wind as the drought over Vrajbhoomi ended at last. It was accompanied by the faint gurgling laughter of a baby.

ten

'Lord Kamsa?'

He awoke from a dream of being smothered by a monsoon cloud – a gigantic thundercloud, fat with rain, that glowed dark blue when lightning flashed deep within its watery depths – and thrashed wildly for a moment. Then he realized there was no cloud. He was not large enough for his head to reach the clouds. He had reduced to man-height once again and was sitting on his rear, sprawled in the debris of his palace sabha hall, anga-vastra stained with what seemed to be his own vomit, and lower garments soiled as well. He sat up groggily, feeling the world spin and spin again – counter-clockwise. He shook his head only to feel a sensation akin to his brain being shattered to shards and his skull rattling with the fragments. He shuddered mightily, retched, felt his vision blur to blinding whiteness, then struggled back to consciousness.

'Mighty prince, can you rise?'

Rise? Had he not risen already? He was the king of the Andhakas, was he not? And a far greater king than his father had ever been! Who dared ask him such a bold question?

He struggled to his feet, lost his balance and fell, sprawling on his back. The ceiling above was broken and through the jagged hole he saw a cloud passing overhead. Something about the cloud caught his attention. He lay on his back, staring up, transfixed.

It seemed like a typical thundercloud at first sight, but as he continued to stare, it seemed to change shape. Not in the genial way that clouds alter their form slightly as they drift by, but instantly, like a boiling cloud erupting from a fire – except that this cloud boiled and erupted *downwards*, directly towards *him*! And the shape, it was the shape of a newborn babe – chubby, cherubic, with puffed-out cheeks and big round eyes that seemed to take up half its face, a waggling double chin, short plump arms, torso and legs kicking out behind as it swam down towards him. Impossible! It was the very cloud from his dream. Right there, right then, in the flesh ... or in the smoke ... or whatever one called the stuff that clouds were made of.

'Lord Kamsa? Are you well? Shall we—?'

The world around receded to a blurry buzzing in the distant background. Only the cloud existed, right above him, and it was coming down. He blinked, snorted to clear his sinuses, but the cloud was still there, still boiling down, still approaching him with naked aggression. Its colour was a dense deep blue, the colour of twilight sky. And that face, while cherubic, was also terrible in its determination and utter self-conviction. It stretched out one chubby short hand; the little fat fingers were grasping, reaching for him—

Kamsa screamed.

The sound startled him more than it startled anyone else. It broke his stupor and, hands slipping on who knew what stickiness and mushiness, he scrambled to his feet and ran across the sabha hall, leaping and skipping across bits of fallen ceiling, shattered furniture and the remnants of what appeared to be the Andhaka throne – *My beautiful new throne, part of the new palace and the new Mathura that I have designed* – until he was at the far end of the vast chamber, his back to the wall, in the

shadiest corner available. Away from the hole in the ceiling ...
And the cloud, the cloud!

'KEEP IT AWAY FROM ME, KEEP IT AWAY!' he screamed.

He stood breathing heavily, gasping from time to time to take in more air.

Several moments passed.

Nothing happened.

Slowly, he began to register the presence of others around him. Soldiers clad in vaguely familiar uniforms, others in more familiar garb, faces he knew quite well but could not place at the moment – faces that were turned to him with visible concern and incredulity. Had he not banned all coloured uniforms and garb in Mathura? How then were these people ... A shadow flitted across the floor, directly beneath the hole, and he lost his thread. After a moment or two, Kamsa glanced this way, then that – his gaze passing cursorily across those surrounding him, barely noting a single one – then his eyes swept back to the hole in the ceiling. From this angle, he could see nothing but an irregularly shaped piece of the sky.

But from the shadows passing across the debris-strewn floor beneath the hole, he could tell that clouds were still passing overhead.

Not clouds. *The* cloud. *That one!*

'Lord Kamsa?' The man approaching him, clad in the armour and accoutrement of a high-ranking warrior, seemed less concerned than puzzled. 'What is it that troubles you? Why do you skulk thus in this shadowy corner? No sign of threat is to be seen anywhere. You are among your own here.'

Kamsa shook his head firmly, not taking his eyes off the hole in the ceiling. *There! Shadows! Moving!* His vision blurred, then swam back into focus, purple and green motes marching merrily from right to left and back again in perfectly arrayed rows.

'Perhaps you do not recognize me. I am—'

'Shhhh!'

Kamsa's hissing carried across the sabha hall, silencing the whispered conversations that had sprung up among those standing around, staring at him. He reacted as well, surprised at the impact his shushing had made – he had intended to be very soft. 'Be silent! It may hear you and attack again!'

The man standing before him stared blankly. '*It*? What is it you fear, great prince? There is nothing here that can harm you.'

Kamsa shushed the man again, fiercely, and gestured towards the ceiling, even as he tried to conceal his gesturing by turning partly away and looking the other way. 'It's watching. I must be careful. Must!'

The man turned and looked around, glanced back at Kamsa, then looked again. This time, he seemed to follow the direction of Kamsa's gesturing – which had become more frenetic and nervous by now – and looked up and saw the hole in the ceiling.

He strode back to the middle of the sabha hall, directly beneath the offensive hole in question. Kamsa stopped gesturing and stuffed his fist into his mouth, biting down hard enough to scrape a layer of skin off his knuckles. *The fool! It will get him now!*

'Careful!' he whispered hoarsely.

A few soldiers within earshot glanced at each other.

The fools, Kamsa thought, *they don't know it's up there. The minute that idiot general or whoever he is looks up, it will swoop down and gobble him up alive. It's just waiting up there!*

The man with the familiar face and the high-ranking warrior's uniform looked up, peering skywards. Something changed in the light streaming down from the open hole in the sky and he exclaimed.

'Look!' he said. 'I have never seen the likes of it before!'

At once, several others drew closer to him, to see for themselves what he was referring to. In a moment, most of those standing around in the ruined sabha hall were staring up through the hole of the ceiling.

'Fools!' Kamsa cried. But what he had intended to be a shout emerged only as a hoarse whisper.

'My lord Kamsa,' said another man, a familiar voice and face that he knew vaguely but could not place at the moment. 'Quick! Come and see. It's quite extraordinary!'

Kamsa suddenly realized that everyone was staring at him. Several of his men had begun whispering amongst themselves again, with expressions that suggested that he was either insane or worse. *A coward, they think me to be a coward. The fools!*

A sudden flash of his customary rage shot through him, shaking him out of his stupor. But the instant he began to rear up, to start roaring at them in denial, the shadows on the floor began moving frenetically, as if the cloud was waiting above, waiting and watching, and any move he made, it would match and out-match. He subsided at once, quivering.

'Lord Kamsa?' said the man.

Who is he anyway? What the devil is he doing here? Who are all these people? And why the hell are they still staring at me and whispering – some are even smirking discreetly now – as if I am the crazy one?

Kamsa realized he would have to show them *he* was sane, and *they* the crazy cowards. He would have to draw the cloud's attention to himself, and when it swooped down again, he would have to run, furiously, to get away. Let them be eaten by it. Or worse. What did he care? But it was important that he disprove this absurd notion of him being a coward. Nonsense! He was the bravest Yadava that ever lived, since the days of his forebear Yadu himself.

Shivering, trembling uncontrollably, he forced himself to go forward. He stumbled slowly through the debris and sticky wet waste that lay over everything like a coating until he reached the spot below the hole again.

'Look, my lord. Can you see it now? Is it not wonderful?'

Kamsa forced himself to look up.

Just a quick glance and then he would run like blazes again. Just one glance.

He looked up. And gasped a deep sigh of disbelief. His legs buckled, threatening to give away with relief.

The cloud was gone.

In its place was a sky roiling over with rain clouds, passing overhead in a stately procession, pregnant with rain, even as a bright sun shone from a clear blue sky.

'Is it not remarkable, my lord?' said the strange warrior cheerfully. *Bahuka*, Kamsa remembered at once, his name was Bahuka. 'The drought has broken and rain clouds appear out of a clear blue sunshine sky. A rare phenomenon indeed. It is a significant omen.'

eleven

The day of the naming ceremony dawned bright and clear. Nanda's estate was a mela of celebration. The crowds that had begun to arrive to celebrate Krishna's birth had only swollen over the past ten days. In a sense, the celebration that had begun that day had not ended yet. With the cowherd community of Gokul going all out in its pouring forth of joy and exultation at the birth of their clan-leader's first child, the merriment reached a peak. Word of the child's beauty and uniqueness had spread far and wide; everyone gaped at the ghanashyam colouring of the child, the deep blue smoky skin, big jewel-bright eyes, pouting mouth, dimpled cheeks, and curls that hung low over the large forehead.

Hair festooned with fresh blossoms and saffron, ears dangling jewelled ornaments, necks bedecked with jewels that clinked and hung low with the weight of the precious metal, the gopas and gopis – male and female cowherds – were dressed in their finest garb. Many played musical instruments as they came. The brilliant colours of Vrajbhoomi clothing outmatched the shades of even the rainbow arcing across the Sravan sky. It had rained every evening since the day of Krishna's birth, and the drought that had plagued entire swathes of Yadava farmlands and grazing pastures had officially and decisively ended. Already, the cows and bulls had begun enjoying the fresh green shoots that had begun pushing their way out of the richly watered earth.

The cattle too were adorned: the bulls with gleaming nose rings and gold-capped horns, the cows in silvery streamers and braided festooning, the calves with wreaths. All were washed in the river, and then smeared with oil and turmeric; the prime ones were decorated with garlands of gold and wreaths of peacock tail feathers. Around them ran the children, dressed like their parents and playing the part of gopas and gopis perfectly, right down to the gaily coloured turbans and polished mukuts.

Mango leaves had been strung across the courtyard of Nanda Maharaja's house; the ground and interior of the house had been swept clean and lined with freshly stacked cow-dung patties, with sandalwood paste mixed in to give off a sweet scent. Great shining brass pots were lined up in the centre of the aangan, around the altar of the sacred tulsi plant. The gateways of the estate were adorned with various ritual leaves, strips of gaily coloured fabric, banners and flags. The sound of kettledrums and conch shells filled the air for yojanas around.

Preceptor Gargacharya's arrival was heralded by a flourish of conches and the ritual greetings, exchanges, ablutions and appropriate ceremony. His mood was further enhanced by Nanda Maharaja's warm and generous greetings and adherence to all the necessary injunctions of Vedic ritual.

Nanda gifted 200,000 decorated cows to Gargacharya and the procession of Brahmins that accompanied him. In addition, seven enormous mounds of sesame, as was the custom, were gifted to the pundits, along with fantastic stores of gold cloth and rivulets of precious jewels and mineral stones. Though born of a magnanimous heart and generous spirit, Nanda's joy at his beautiful son and the propitious arrival of the best monsoon in a decade had opened the coffers of his generosity further. He had reason to celebrate, and wealth to spread. Even the Sutas – the travelling poets – and the Kusalavya bards who recorded the itihasa of such events, composed poems about them, wrote and sang songs and earned a modest living singing the tales of each occurrence, were delighted to receive lavish gifts of ornaments, garlands and cows. No distinction was made between Sutas of different varnas – Suta proper, Vandi, Kusalavya or even Magadha bards – all were treated equally, fed richly and given the same set of gifts.

'The child's name should begin with the syllable *Ka*!' announced the happy instructor of the clan. 'As befits his dark colouring and in keeping with the wishes of his pitr and maatr, he shall be named Krishna!'

A roar of approval greeted the announcement. Everyone already thought of the boy as Krishna, and even if the acharya had recommended a different name, the boy would have been given that nickname. Either that or Kali – the two names that were customarily given to any Arya child who was as densely black skinned. They were in fact the most common names in the Arya world, most Aryas being subject to countless millennia of exposure to the harsh sun of their native land.

Unknown to the immense crowds celebrating Krishna's naming day, another boy had also been named at the same time. Seated only yards away from Yashoda and Krishna were Rohini and her yearling son who were discreetly but strategically placed in the shade of the aangan's awning. This arrangement had been devised by Gargacharya.

'But who is this honourable lady?' Nanda had asked, concerned, soon after her unexpected appearance and self-introduction.

'She is none other than the wife of Vasudeva, secretly wed precisely for this purpose,' said the ageing pundit with a twinkle in his eye.'And the son she brings is none other than Vasudeva and Devaki's seventh child, spirited away by godly forces to be raised by her in secrecy, far from the evil gaze of Kamsa and his minions. I sanctified the wedding myself, under equally stern terms of secrecy. Rohini is legitimately the boy's foster mother now.'

Nanda stared at his guru, astonished. He had not known. 'So you knew about this, Gurudev?'

Gargacharya chortled. 'There are many things you are not aware of, Nanda. And that you need not trouble your mind with. It is enough that your son and her child are brothers; that is all you need to know.'

'Brothers?' Nanda asked, even more baffled.

Gargacharya scratched his balding pate and glanced around, as if wondering if he had said too much.'You are a clan-brother to Vasudeva, are you not? In fact, you are even known as Vasudeva yourself. Vasu, because as lord of the gopas and gopis of Vrajbhoomi your spirit pervades all who live here, and Deva, because you are godlike to your people. So Rohini's son is Vasudeva's son, which means he is like your own son, therefore Rohini's son and Krishna are brothers!'

Nanda's head reeled. But he implicitly trusted his guru's judgement and wisdom; he bowed and touched the guru's feet with his forehead and asked no more questions.

So when the time to name little Krishna came, Gargacharya also performed the ritual for the other boy, Rohini's son. Except that he recited the verses for the other boy softly and his associate repeated them within the house, from his position beside Rohini and the boy, and applied the various items of the ceremony to mother and child as required. Thus did

Gargacharya perform the namakarans of two boys even though the world saw him perform only one.

When he had named Krishna, and the crowd roared exultantly, Gargacharya quickly took advantage of the roar to name Rohini's son as well.

'His name must begin with the syllable *Ba*,' he announced.

Nanda and Yashoda turned to glance inside the shade of the awning, to see what Rohini replied. Little Krishna turned his round head and gazed inside too, his dark bright eyes gleaming as a mischievous smile played around his puckered lips. The boy sitting inside on his mother's lap leaned forward, his face leaving the shade of the awning and cutting into a beam of sunlight that had somehow found its way through the large fronds of a banana tree. His eyes found Krishna's unerringly and both infants looked at one another no less intently than two kings locking their gaze. The contrast was striking: the older boy was as milky white as Krishna was night black. Yet, beneath the veneer of the marbled whiteness that was his skin, there was a faint bluish hue. The same deep shade of blue that was Krishna's colouring, but like a blue light hidden within a white bushel instead of a black one. In that instant, as Nanda and Yashoda looked from one child to the other, there could be no doubt that they were blood brothers, from the same womb. Rohini's and Yashoda's eyes met as well, and both women smiled, sharing a happy secret. Nanda sighed and shook his head, not knowing what to make of it all, but trusting in the powers that were and the wisdom of his guru.

'Balarama,' said Rohini softly, only speaking loud enough to be heard by the Brahmin beside her. The Brahmin nodded and continued rocking to and fro in his cross-legged position, reciting the appropriate shlokas that confirmed the name as the given appellation of the child. Gargacharya added his own benediction to the ritual and it was done.

Krishna threw his head back and laughed his rich gurgling laugh. Yashoda looked down, amazed at how soon the boy was able to hold up his head. It was much faster than any baby; most took at least a few months, and none did it in less than several weeks. Yet here was Krishna, barely ten days old and able to hold his head, turn and look any way he pleased – up, down, left, right. Truly, he was a precocious one.

Across the estate and the adjoining pasture fields, the crowds were dancing and singing with joy. Gopas played roughly and fiercely, pushing one another over, splashing buckets of water, ghee, milk, curds and buttermilk on one another, lapping up the food as well as wallowing in it! Music exploded as a thousand musicians played at once, all somehow finding the same syncopation and matching one another perfectly, in the harmony that came only of a lifetime of generational togetherness.

'Sadhu! Sadhu! Sadhu!' went one refrain, announcing the auspiciousness of the occasion.

'Krishna! Krishna! Krishna!' sang another chorus, celebrating the birth of Vraj's newest and most honoured son.

The feasting continued all through the day and night, with not a single being, be it animal, human or bird, turned away unfed. The poorest of the poor were welcomed with open arms, embraced, given gifts and fed lavishly. The richest of the rich were treated with rough joy, drenched in ghee, buttermilk, curd, butter or plain milk – any one of the products of the sacred goumata that was their livelihood and indeed, their life itself.

And through it all, as he lay beside his newly found brother Balarama, little Krishna laughed and clapped his chubby palms together. The older boy, able to stand and walk with halting but firm steps on strong little legs, stood watch over Krishna as intently as a sentry over a prince. When some of the gopas came closer to try and tease the newborn, Balarama stood blocking their way and glared at them so fiercely, they changed their minds and backed away.

Krishna only chortled and clapped his hands again, kicking his chubby legs merrily. His gurgling laughter seemed to fill the air, echoing from one end of the land to the other. Yashoda, tired and sleepy but happy beyond description, lay in the arms of her beloved Nanda and wondered idly if Krishna's laughter could be heard as far as Mathura.

twelve

The warrior's name was Bahuka. He was an ageing veteran of more wars and conflicts than even he could count; so many that at one time or the other, he had fought for virtually every major faction in Aryavarta, with the result that it had happened quite often that he was on a certain side in one war and on the opposing side in the next. He had killed former comrades, former leaders, been hired by the scions of kings he had killed, and had enjoyed such a chequered career that he was feared by one and all. The consequence of all this battle experience and notoriety was to make him a man completely without airs. He feared nobody and nothing on earth. He said what he pleased, to whomsoever he pleased. The same applied to his behaviour and actions. For the past few years, he had aligned himself with Jarasandha, and this, he claimed, was the first alliance he had made not for wealth or power but because he believed in the cause that the king espoused. 'Which,' as he added wryly, 'is what will probably get me killed.'

He was overseeing Kamsa's toilet. After the meltdown in the sabha hall, he had insisted that Kamsa ought to look like a king in order to earn the respect of a king from his subjects and followers. So he had ordered a bath drawn and was now ensconced in a comfortable seat while Kamsa was being scrubbed, rubbed, bathed and perfumed by a host of female attendants.

He is still wearing his battle armour and sword, Kamsa noted sourly, which was explicitly against Kamsa's own long-standing orders and a breach of protocol in any king's private chambers. But he was Jarasandha's man, and Kamsa knew better than to say anything to him. He had no doubt that the man was there to report to Jarasandha and was probably spying out everything he could possibly spot as quickly as possible. Once he had all the dirt he wanted, he would ride back on a fast horse to his master and fill his ears with poison about Kamsa being afraid of clouds and whatnot.

Kamsa felt like reaching out and yanking the man down into the bubbling hot bathing pool, where he could beat him to a bloody pulp and drown him. But he couldn't do that, of course. The sooner the man finished his spying and reported back to Jarasandha the better. That was probably why the man stayed fully dressed, Kamsa realized – because he intended to be ready to leave at any moment.

That realization brought a tiny smile to his face. He grinned involuntarily and the grizzled veteran glanced at him, cocking a bushy white brow.

'Are the bathing beauties soaping the right spots?'

Kamsa stared at him dully for a moment, then realized the man was making a lewd comment. He scowled. 'No. Of course not. I was just thinking, that's all.'

'Of your beloved wives? Your beautiful, loving, devoted wives who await you back home?'

Back home? *Mathura* was his home. Didn't the old fool know that? Aloud, he had to be more diplomatic.

'My father-in-law is very generous. He has given me a grand palace to reside in. However, pressing matters require me to stay here in Mathura.'

Bahuka nodded. Another bathing attendant entered, bringing more scented oils. The elderly man watched her scantily clad form approach with a keenness that suggested that age had not dulled his virility. 'He is somewhat surprised that your stay has lasted this long.'

Kamsa was dipping his head into the warm, scented water at that time, to rid his scalp of the unguents the attendants had massaged into his hair, and Bahuka's words caused him to involuntarily swallow a little water. He emerged coughing and spat out a mouthful of water, almost far enough to land on the veteran's road-dusty boots. 'I confess ...' He hacked a few more times and watched as a bubble popped out of one nostril and drifted away nonchalantly. 'I confess it has taken a mite longer than expected. But only because there is so much more work to be done here.'

Bahuka looked at him speculatively. There was something about the old man that suggested he had looked at rabbits in the field in just the same way, moments before bringing them down with a slingshot stone to their flanks. His grey eyes gleamed in the diya-lit incandescence of the steamy air. Whorls of steam and mist drifted around him as the barely dressed attendants passed by, making him seem out of place, like a rusted lance in a cupboard of soft silks.

'It has been a decade, Kamsa,' he said quietly. 'A little more than a decade, in fact. Is that what you call a *mite* longer?'

Kamsa did not fail to notice the lack of an honorofic before his name. Nobody had addressed him simply by his first name in ... a long time. And the veteran's tone, while quietly polite, had a deathly steel edge to it as well. He was sending a subtext with the words – that he was speaking for Jarasandha himself, and Jarasandha wanted to know why the hell Kamsa was still in Mathura.

'I...' Kamsa flailed his arms in an attempt to pretend he was still busy bathing. Water splashed everywhere. 'I am sure Jarasandha has come across cities that have proven stubborn or resistant to him, from time to time? Surely they have taken him a mite ... somewhat longer to overcome than other cities?'

Scratching his crotch vigorously, Bahuka glanced down at the soapy wet floor between his feet and chuckled. 'Not *ten* years, Kamsa! I doubt Lord Jarasandha has taken more than ten weeks to overcome even the most stubborn opponent to date!' He stood slowly, pointing a gloved finger down at the bath. 'I don't think you have earned the right to even compare yourself with your illustrious father-in-law yet, boy. So it's best you answer me like a man, and stop making excuses. That way, it might go better for you.'

Kamsa stared up at the warrior. Who did this fellow think he was, speaking to him this way? 'Mind your tongue, Bahuka. Remember you speak to the king of the Yadava nation!'

Bahuka hawked and spat – right into the pool. Kamsa felt some of the spittle hit his bare chest and was shocked. 'Boy, from what my spasas tell me, you aren't king of your own house! Let alone the entire Yadu nation.'

Kamsa was so shocked, he found his anger slow in coming. How could anyone behave thus in front of him – and expect to live! 'Be careful what you say next, general. They may be the last words you speak.'

The veteran put his hands on his hips and laughed, throwing his head back to reveal a mesh of ugly white scar tissue on his throat. Evidently, someone had tried to cut the man's gullet with a not-too-sharp blade and had sawed the rough blade to and fro several times to achieve the desired result. And quite clearly, the victim had somehow survived the attempt. Kamsa felt his skin crawl. What sort of man survived having his throat vigorously sawed open? Definitely not a cowardly one.

Bahuka finished laughing and shook his head sympathetically as he looked at Kamsa again. 'You have been tinpot dictator of your own little playground too long, young fellow. Lord Jarasandha was right to send me here – as he is always right. You have lost touch with reality, with the world around you, even with your own limitations. I suspected it from the reports my spasas kept bringing me, and which I passed on each time to Lord Jarasandha with my recommendations, but when I saw you this morning, lying in your own residues in that wreck of a sabha hall, surrounded by the debris of a failed regime, I knew you had completely lost it altogether.'

Kamsa growled. It was the best he could do. He did not want to speak any words that he might regret later. Expressing himself through words had never been particularly satisfying to him. Growling communicated his feelings more effectively. The bathing attendants began to scream and whimper and retreated to the far ends of the bathing pool, some clambering out to be lost instantly in the steamy mist.

'I was merely tired and resting after a hard night's work,' Kamsa said, unable to control the sulk in his voice. 'I had just finished infecting all the senior Brahmins in the city.'

Bahuka cocked a head with renewed interest. 'Is that so? And when did you do that?'

'Because the Brahmins hold the people together. By reassuring the people that this damn Slayer myth is true, they give them hope to continue to rebel against me. By infecting the

Brahmins and turning them into my own creatures, I wanted to break that final wall of resistance.'

Kamsa climbed out of the bathing pool, careful not to let himself slip. He knew that Bahuka was watching him like a predator and would strike at any sign of weakness. Besides, if he couldn't tell the man what he felt, he could at least show him his naked backside as he climbed out. Actions always spoke louder than words.

'Really?' Bahuka asked. 'So *that* was your great plan? But I didn't ask you *why* you did it, I asked you *when* you did it.'

Kamsa rubbed himself down, frowning. The attendants had all fled, no doubt afraid that he was going to erupt in another of his nearly daily rages and slaughter them all, or worse. In fact, he couldn't understand why he was unable to expand himself. Despite growing angry several times since the interaction with Bahuka had begun, he was still the same human size. Why?

He turned around, scowling. 'What do you mean *when* I did it! You mean, when did I infect the Brahmins? Why, yesterday, of course.'

Bahuka stared at him curiously, then frowned, stared some more, then finally chuckled. He shook his head, clicking his tongue sympathetically. 'It's worse than I thought. You are now losing time along with your mind.'

Kamsa stared at him uncomprehendingly. What was the man babbling about now? What did he mean by 'losing time'?

Bahuka laughed. 'Your little act with the Brahmins was months ago, immediately after the birth of the Slayer and his slippery disappearance from right under your nose. You were lying senseless in that ruin of a sabha hall for several weeks. Nobody dared go in and wake you for fear of your wrath.'

Kamsa stared at him in disbelief. This could not be true, could it?

'Besides, your ploy with the Brahmins was useless. They all do that very day as a result of your stupid attempt. What else do you think was all that gooey mess you were lying in, splashed around the sabha hall the day I arrived? That was all that was left of them, you fool!'

Kamsa turned and hurled the contents of his morning meal, eaten just before bathing, into the scented pool.

thirteen

Soon after the namakaran of the two boys, Gargamuni visited Mathura.

An old and renowned preceptor of the Yadava nation, none dared question his comings and goings, not even Kamsa's most brutal marauders. The reason for this was more likely their own superstitious and religious beliefs rather than any lack of fear of their self-crowned king. There was also the very compelling fact that Brahmins carried no arms and never resorted to violence, even to defend themselves, and therefore posed no threat.

Gargamuni's destination was the princess' palace.

Vasudeva and Devaki greeted him with warmth and due ceremony. They assumed he was there as usual to enquire after their well-being as well as to pass on news of the Vrishni clans. Brahmins were the primary source of news and information, after all. And the older the Brahmin, the sharper his ears for the choicest titbits!

What he had to say that day was quite extraordinary and wholly unexpected.

'The Slayer is alive and well in Gokul, deep in the heart of Vrajbhoomi.'

Vasudeva sank to the ground, his knees giving way with relief. Devaki was already seated on the ground in front of the muni. They clasped hands as tears of joy rolled down their faces. Gargacharya beamed at them.

'I have come from the home of Nanda Maharaja, lord of the gopas and gopis of that region. He and his wife Yashoda believe the boy, Krishna, to be their own and love him passionately. They will raise him as well as you would have.'

Devaki lowered her head in sadness at the thought of never being able to watch her son grow, to watch him take his first steps, speak his first words ... but she also felt a great sense of relief and joy that he would be so well cared for. *As well as Vasu and I would have raised him ourselves – were we but given the chance.* She wiped her tears and nodded at the muni's words. Vasudeva's arm squeezed her shoulder, comforting her. The emotions coursing through both of them were the result of ten years of persecution, pain, constant stress and fear. To hear that their son was finally safe and far from Kamsa's bloody claws was immensely liberating.

'There is more good news,' Gargamuni said, his eyes twinkling beneath his bushy white hooded brows. He leaned forward and said in a conspiratorial whisper for dramatic effect: 'Your seventh child is also safe and well.'

Devaki gasped with delight. She looked at Vasudeva who was staring at Gargamuni with an equally delighted expression.

'His name is Balarama,' the old acharya said. 'He is a fine strapping young boy, just over a year old. And he is being raised by Rohini, the wife you took on my advice last year.'

Vasudeva nodded, glancing at Devaki who was looking at him, then looking at Gargamuni. 'I did as you said, Gurudev. And truly, your advice was wisely given. Or that boy would be dead now as well.'

Devaki nodded slowly, thoughtfully. 'So *this* was the secret that you said you could not divulge to me at the time.'

'Yes,' replied Vasudeva, 'for Gargamuni warned me that to speak of it even amongst ourselves might have led to Kamsa's spasas latching on to the truth. Are you upset with me for not telling you that I took another wife?'

Devaki shook her head, smiling. 'Do you even have to ask? I am happy beyond words. Our son is alive! *Two* of our sons! It is the happiest day of my life!'

Vasudeva smiled with relief. Although a man could have as many wives as he desired, it was customary to consult the older wife before remarrying. In fact, in Arya society, the older wife was usually the one who chose the new wife, for the new entrant into the household would spend as much or more time with her than with the husband. It was as important for the wives of a man to be able to live harmoniously – to be friends, even – as it was for the man and woman to appreciate one another. Vasudeva had had no choice in the matter, even though the marriage to Rohini was conducted by Gargamuni from afar and no actual marital interchange ever occurred between them; but he still felt responsible. There were many types of relationships, marital and otherwise, but the bond he shared with Devaki was unique. His loyalty to her was complete and uncompromised. Rohini had known this, Gargamuni had assured Vasudeva before the wedding, and was willing to undertake the task of raising a child on her own without naming the father publicly – a daunting task for any woman in any age. The mere knowledge that she was aiding in the survival of Vasudeva and Devaki's son and ensuring that the Slayer foretold of in the prophecies would live as a result was sufficient for her.

'Balarama,' Devaki said, raising her head to look up at the sky visible between the pillars of her chamber. 'It is a beautiful name. Almost as beautiful as Krishna.'

Then she remembered the figurine and felt she must show it to them.

She brought it out of its hiding place in a corner of her private chamber where she had wrapped it carefully in a red ochre cloth. She unwrapped it now, as reverentially as if it were a scroll containing the writings of the sacred Vedas, repository of all Arya learning and wisdom. Gargamuni and Vasudeva admired the polished blue marble, wondering at its smoothness and its perfectly formed replication of a newborn babe.

'You say this formed from a single drop of rain left by a rain cloud?' Gargamuni said. 'Sadhu! Sadhu! That was no rain cloud; it was your son Krishna himself, who had come to inform you that the long terrible drought had ended, and the time of seeding and harvest was back for the Yadava people. It was a sign that the reign of Kamsa will end soon.'

But Devaki was busy staring at the statue and blinking in disbelief. 'It has changed shape since I last looked at it.' She touched the stone gently in wonderment. 'At first it was only a rough blob, the features barely visible. But now ...'

They looked at it closely. The piece of blue marble — a hue that none had ever seen in any sample of that particular stone — was shaped perfectly to resemble a newborn infant in every last detail. It could not have been more perfect had it been crafted by a master artisan. The baby lay on his back — legs and hands raised upwards in the classic pose, as if reaching for his mother — his cherubic face captured in a posture of laughter, an errant lock of hair fallen over his broad forehead. Unable to help herself, Devaki gently touched the forehead as she would a real child, as if to brush back the lock of hair from his eyes.

She felt real warm flesh beneath her hands and the shape of the forehead changed in front of their eyes, the lock of hair moving back and settling slowly on the hairline, resting neatly on the scalp now.

The sound of a baby's gurgling laughter filled the palace. Even the serving girls paused in their work and looked up, wondering. And the sentries posted below, though loyal to Kamsa, glanced around and at each other fearfully, wondering what the sound meant. The news that the Slayer had been born and had escaped Kamsa's clutches despite his best efforts had spread across the kingdom. It had adversely affected the morale of those still loyal to the usurper king. After all, if the Slayer was out there and would some day destroy their master, what might he not do to them, Kamsa's minions?

Devaki gasped in surprise. 'It lives!'

But when she touched the statue again, it was only smooth marble – not cold, however, as marble ought to have been, but firm and unyielding as stone nevertheless. She sighed, disappointed.

'You speak truly, Devaki-devi,' Garga said. 'Krishna himself has ensured that you shall not be deprived of the joy of his presence. He is with you in every sense.' Garga glanced around, not because he feared being overheard, but to make his point theatrically. 'But you must be certain not to let anyone know of this token of his love, nor what it represents.'

Devaki swallowed, nodding vigorously. 'I call it Ghanashyam for that reason.'

'Ghanashyam,' Gargamuni mused. 'How apt. And in fact, the scriptures said he could be named with the syllable *Ka*, but *Gha* and *Cha* were permissible too! How apt indeed.'

The old preceptor rose to go. 'Oh, one last thing,' he said, 'it almost slipped my ageing memory, yet it is more important than anything else I have told you until now.'

Vasudeva wondered what could be more important than knowing that two of their children were alive and had successfully survived Kamsa's murderous clutches, but held his silence.

As if knowing Vasudeva's thoughts, the old Brahmin wagged a bony finger with white hair growing sparsely between the knuckles at him. 'Kamsa has failed to inform you of this but I have learnt of it through my sources. An invitation arrived for you yesterday from Hastinapura.'

'From Hastinapura?' Vasudeva's heart skipped a beat. 'My sister Pritha, is she well?'

'Indeed. You need not worry on her account. She is quite well, though troubled, of course. There is great unrest in that fine kingdom of the Purus.'

Vasudeva nodded, relieved that nothing had befallen his sister. They had been very close before Kamsa's madness had made even normal social interaction impossible. 'I have heard there is unrest there as well. And of course that Jarasandha is raging at their borders.'

Gargamuni nodded grimly. Despite his age and benevolent paternal features, at moments like these, the steel within him was clearly visible. 'Jarasandha is one of the reasons why this meeting has been called. They have called on you formally, using the pre-agreed code to indicate extreme distress. It is certainly a crisis.'

'Then I must go to Hastinapura!' Vasudeva said, rising. 'If my Puru brethren need my help …'

'Nay, my son, nay.' Gargacharya put a hand on his shoulder, firmly keeping him seated. The strength in the old man's arms surprised Vasudeva. 'If you leave, Kamsa's spasas will know the purpose and destination of your journey and he or his representatives shall surely race you to Hastinapura. By right, Kamsa is now king of the Yadava nation, even if self-declared. And if he goes to Hastinapura, the Purus would have no choice but to greet him formally and acknowledge him as such, and that is something they are loath to do. Through clever statecraft, Pitamah Bhishma has successfully avoided recognizing Kamsa's sovereignty for all these years, without dishonouring the Puru nation's ties with us Yadavas. If you go, you will render all that statecraft wasted.'

'Then what would you advise me to do?'

Gargamuni nodded, indicating that he had given the matter some thought. 'Lord Akrur must go in your place, as your spokesperson and friend, but not as an official envoy.'

Vasudeva was frustrated at not being able to go himself, but nodded at the old guru's wisdom. 'It is a wise choice. I trust Akrur to speak as if he were me personified. But if he goes to Hastinapura, might not Kamsa still attempt to outplay him by arriving there as well?'

Gargamuni's eyes twinkled as he wagged a finger. 'That is why I have requested that the meeting not take place in Hastinapura or Mathura but on neutral ground.'

Vasudeva nodded approvingly. 'Where is it to be, then? I shall instruct Akrur accordingly.'

'It is a remote fishing hamlet deep in the heart of the Yamuna's valley, where the Dasa fisherfolk live.'

Vasudeva nodded, frowning. 'I am vaguely aware of the place but more precise directions would help.'

'Your friend need only follow the Yamuna. She herself shall lead him to his destination. A boat shall be waiting for him there. It shall carry him across the river to the island.'

'An island?'

'Yes, an island in the midst of the river. It is named Pachmani. But the local fisherfolk call it Manchodri. It is there that the meeting shall take place. None but you and Akrur should know of this meeting.'

Gargamuni told Vasudeva the date of the meeting, then said his goodbyes, shuffling away with a deceptively shambling walk. Absorbed in thought, Vasudeva watched him go.

fourteen

Kamsa's sleep was plagued by a fevered dream of him reduced to the size of a gnat flying across a cornfield as a gigantic monsoon cloud – the same anthropomorphic deep blue cloud he had seen in the sabha hall – attempted to strike him down with bolts of lightning. The jagged bolts crashed down to the left and right of his scorched flanks, resulting in blinding white explosions. Flying in a zig-zagging motion was all he could do to stay inches away from each new assault. As one final bolt seared its way towards him, he knew this was the one that would strike him dead, blazing him into a vaporous puff on impact. He screamed with abject terror.

He awoke thrashing on the floor of his bedchamber. He croaked, calling to his attendants, but nobody came. After several moments of struggling to regain his wits, he got to his feet and was about to throw a tantrum, perhaps bite off the heads of a few of his more recalcitrant attendants, when he heard the unmistakable sounds of marching from outside his balcony. Looking out, he saw more activity in the courtyard than ought to have been at this time of night. He didn't bother to dress, and left his chamber in just the white langot in which he slept, wishing yet again that he could expand himself as easily as he used to. Had he been able to do so, he would have simply expanded himself to five or ten times man-size and leapt off the balcony, the few dozen yards to the ground posing no more difficulty than leaping down a short flight of stairs.

But for some inscrutable reason, he just couldn't grow any further than this normal man-height, no matter how hard he tried. It was frustrating in the extreme. For one thing, throwing a tantrum was not quite as effective as it used to be: his people just weren't that scared any more. In fact, he suspected that they secretly laughed at him behind his back, as if the behaviour that had been so terrifying when he was a giant's size now seemed ridiculous and feeble. And it probably was. He felt so himself.

He emerged into the courtyard, and was struck at once by a blast of cold breeze that made him acutely aware of how little he was wearing; he wished he had taken a moment to throw on something. But this was the monsoon season, surely, and he hadn't expected the temperature to be this low outside.

'WHAT IS GOING ON HERE?' he bellowed. Or rather, attempted to bellow. What he produced instead was a squeaky croak that tapered off into a whimper as a fresh gust of icy cold breeze blew across the open courtyard. Kamsa shivered and, teeth chattering at the unexpected change in temperature, was forced to cover his bare torso with both arms crossed. He struggled to overcome his reaction and stand straight, to command respect and instil fear. The problem was, he was so accustomed to eliciting these responses through sheer force, power, size and intimidation that he had no idea how to gain them through normal means. Appearing in his langot in the early hours of the morning of a chilly day, while his soldiers marched and stood around in immaculate uniforms and ranks, he ended up looking absurd.

'What are you men doing?' he demanded, wheezing. 'I called no turning out of ranks this morning!'

'I asked them to,' said a laconic voice from behind him.

Kamsa turned to see the lanky form of Bahuka striding leisurely up to him. Contrasting with the darkness of the courtyard, the veteran's hoary head of hair glowed with a penumbra of light from the palace behind him, which threw his features into shadow and lent him an air of almost supernatural menace. Kamsa shivered again, wishing like hell he had draped on an anga-vastra at least. But who could have expected a monsoon morning to be this chilly?

'You?' he stuttered through chattering teeth.

'Aye,' said Bahuka arrogantly. 'In case you forget, Prince Kamsa, I command the army now. By your own writ.'

By my *writ? Since when?* 'I am your king,' Kamsa replied angrily, feeling some heat finally surge through his freezing body. 'Address me with my proper title. And I recall signing no such writ. I am supreme commander of our armed forces.'

Bahuka moved slightly in the shadowy darkness of the courtyard, gravel crunching under his boots. He was only leaning over to speak softly to Kamsa but for a split second he appeared to be attacking and Kamsa involuntarily took a step back.

'You reverted to "prince regent" when you declared Lord Jarasandha to be de facto ruler of Mathura and the other Yadava nations,' he said softly, yet not so softly that the ranks nearest to them did not hear every word.

I did? When was that? Kamsa racked his brains furiously but could remember doing no such thing. Yet he could hardly say so aloud. It would only make him look like a fool again in case Bahuka produced a signed scroll with Kamsa's seal on it. And in a sense, Bahuka was only saying aloud what Kamsa had always agreed to do. After all, that was the arrangement he had had with Jarasandha: to take over his father's kingdom and rule it independently, but under fealty to Jarasandha – which could be interpreted legally as making Jarasandha the de facto ruler.

Receiving no response from Kamsa, Bahuka went on, a little louder this time: 'As for the army, you yourself announced my appointment as commander of the forces. At a very dignified martial ceremony in the new palace.'

'The new palace?' Kamsa replied idiotically. *What ceremony? What appointment?*

Bahuka reached out, startling Kamsa yet again, placed a heavy gloved hand on the apparently erstwhile young king's bare neck, and gripping it in exactly the kind of hold required to break a man's neck with a single twist – Kamsa had done it often enough himself – turned Kamsa's neck just enough to make him look in the other direction, diagonally. In the distance, he saw the looming shape of a structure he did not recognize having seen before, right where his old palace – which was in fact his *new* palace when he took over Mathura – had stood. He could see a steady flow of men carrying heavy objects coming out and depositing the load to a line of waiting uks carts.

'There,' Bahuka said in a low tone that was almost a growl.

'Oh,' Kamsa said, 'I see.'

But he did not see at all. How could a new – or a new-new – palace have risen overnight without his noticing it? And why was it that he could recall none of it?

Boot heels clicking on the flagstones, then crunching across the gravel, a man came running from the direction of his private residence. He carried a large garment of some kind and bowed low as he approached. He handed the piece of clothing to Kamsa who stared at it stupidly.

After a long moment, the man said querulously, 'My lord? Your garment? To guard you from the cold winter wind?'

Kamsa started. 'Who is that? What is your name?'

The man glanced at Bahuka who nodded. He then rose to his full height and approached a little closer. 'Lord Kamsa, it is I, Pralamba, your chief advisor.'

Kamsa stared at the unfamiliar face. He had never seen the man before. Pralamba held out the garment again.

Kamsa attempted to laugh in derision, but it came out as a coughing fit. 'It is only mid-monsoon. This is barely a passing rain breeze. I do not need any garment.'

Bahuka cleared his throat. 'Prince Kamsa, being occupied with statecraft, you seem to have failed to notice the passing of the seasons. The monsoons have passed, as has autumn. It is now early winter. Perhaps you should take the garment after all. We wouldn't want you to freeze to death.'

Kamsa stared at Bahuka's silhouetted profile, dimly visible in the light from the distant chambers. Nearby, he thought he heard a soldier in the ranks snicker. Face burning with shame, he took the proffered garment and put it on, admitting that the clothing did provide welcome protection. He had been freezing to death; that was no monsoon wind. But when had the seasons changed? It had only been a day or two since Bahuka had arrived in Mathura. How had so much happened so soon?

Another man marched up to them, walking with the quick stride of a military man. He stopped short and saluted smartly.

'Captain Pradyota, report,' Bahuka said with the ease of a general giving orders to a long-serving junior.

'Sire, we are ready to move out. Awaiting your command.'

'Very well, Captain, stand by a moment at your ease.'

Captain Pradyota saluted again and stood at ease, awaiting further orders.

Bahuka turned to Kamsa. 'You do remember Pradyota, do you not? He is captain of the guard.'

Kamsa frowned, still trying to get warm, almost ecstatic at being covered by the warm woollen garment. 'What about Bana and Canura? Where are they?'

'You dismissed them. Pending further intimation.'

Not sure what to say next, Kamsa swallowed nervously. There appeared to be a whole parallel timeline in which all manner of events had taken place without his being aware of them. He no longer knew what was what. 'I see. And Pradyota is now captain? What is the mission that requires assembling at this early hour?'

Bahuka cocked his head with an attitude of interest, as if surprised at Kamsa's ability to make any observation of intelligence. 'Why, it is part of your ongoing programme, my lord.'

Kamsa chose his words carefully. 'Remind me, which programme are we speaking of?'

'The one that you decided upon after the alleged Slayer was supposedly born and escaped your grasp.'

'Yes, yes. But spell it out, man. Explain it to me again.' Kamsa was struck by sudden inspiration: 'I wish to hear you say it so I know that my plan is being followed to the letter.'

He saw Bahuka's teeth flash in a reluctant grin. *Take that, you old blade.* 'Certainly, sire. When even the pogrom of slaughter of the newborns and children did not produce results, you decided that the problem lay with the people's faith in this mythic Slayer.'

'Their faith?' Kamsa repeated, thoughtfully.

'Aye. And that faith was bolstered and encouraged by the Brahmins, of course. The keepers and teachers of dharma. You knew that the Brahmins were encouraging belief in the non-existent Slayer and giving the people confidence to rebel against you. Short of wiping out the entire population and restarting the Yadava race anew with your own seed – a possibility you did consider for a while – there was only one other option available to you to quell this defiance.'

'Only one other option,' Kamsa repeated. He had zero recollection of all this, of course.

'To destroy the people's dharma itself. As well as the Brahmins' sense of dharma.'

'Destroy their dharma. Yes, of course,' was Kamsa's dazed response. He had no idea what that meant, but it sounded promising. Not the kind of elaborate philosophical thinking he would usually indulge in, but interesting nonetheless.

'And so you opened the coffers of Mathura.'

'The coffers?' he frowned.

'Yes, the royal treasure chest, accumulated by you, your father, and the kings of Mathura before him back to the beginning of the Andhaka nation. A considerable store of wealth indeed.'

As Bahuka continued, Kamsa's attention turned back to the quads of men he had noticed earlier. They were emerging from the palace – the new-new palace – carrying what appeared to be treasure chests, he now realized, and loading them onto the long line of waiting uks carts. There were a great many carts and a great many chests and, judging by the fact that it took four strong-backed men to carry each one and all four men were bent over and straining to carry the weight, they seemed very heavy.

'And by giving all that wealth away to the people, starting with the Brahmins and then onto the other varnas in proportion ...'

'You did say "giving it away", did you not?' Kamsa asked.

'Aye, Prince Kamsa. By showing such unparalleled generosity, you would not only win back the hearts of the entire populace, and make them feel well and thoroughly compensated for any hardships they might have endured during the long difficult years of drought which unfortunately coincided with your own regime, but you would also give them an opportunity to afford such pleasures as they had only dreamt of before.'

Kamsa was silent. He was too stunned to say anything. Bahuka went on, barely able to disguise the smugness in his voice.

'And so you ushered in a new age of hedonism in Mathura. You gave away so much wealth that not a single citizen needs to work another day in his life. Farmers have stopped tilling their fields, cowherds care about their flock no more, women don't make butter or ghee to sell in the market any more and children have stopped learning. Everyone has been too busy enjoying the new-found wealth. Drinking, eating and pleasure have become the new way of life. Wine has begun to flow as readily as the first good monsoon which coincided with your surge of generosity. Basically, over the past several months, your plan has begun to show results.'

'It has?' Kamsa croaked.

'Indeed! It worked brilliantly. The people of Mathura are like fattened calves now. They are too busy indulging themselves to bother with resistance. Even Brahmins have taken to ungodly indulgences! All talk of dharma has died out, for when there are such rich spoils to be enjoyed, nobody wants to listen to the voice of one's conscience. Every citizen has become your confidant. The flow of information is free and rich; cooperation is absolute; rebellion is non-existent.'

And Bahuka clapped a powerful hand on Kamsa's shoulder, almost breaking his clavicle. 'Truly, your plan was brilliant, Prince Kamsa. You have changed the entire character of Mathura in a few short months! And all it took was the bulk of your ancestral wealth. Splendidly done, my lord. Splendidly done!'

fifteen

Akrur emerged from the darkness of the forest into the clear, cold light of a winter evening. He gazed with relief at the river coursing under the overhang, reflecting the light of the setting sun. 'Yamuna-maa, to see you is always a blessing. Today, it is also a relief.'

He made his way carefully down to the riverside, following the pebbled shale bank further. He had started out following the river as instructed, but when he had reached a point where the bank rose too high and was too densely forested to follow, he had had no choice but to go around. It was a great relief to finally be in sight of the river again, for these were unfamiliar woods and he did not know what dangers lurked within them.

He smiled again, with great pleasure this time, when he came around a bend and saw the boat moored to the bank up ahead. He quickened his pace as best as he could.

A dark form unfolded its limbs and rose to meet him as he approached the boat.

'Lord Akrur?' asked a voice with the inflection of the fisherfolk of the river.

'Yes,' Akrur replied.

'Pray, step aboard,' the man responded, busying himself with untying the boat's mooring. 'It is almost night and they are all assembled and waiting. You are the last to arrive.'

The man was silent as he pushed the boat free of the shore using a long pole. Akrur thought it best not to disturb the boatman. The river was flowing at a goodly speed and the fisherman was poling them upriver, a task that demanded all of the man's considerable strength and dexterity. Akrur would have been glad to help but there was only the one pole and he was not sure he knew how to pole a boat in that manner. He watched the man work, powerful back muscles heaving as the light dimmed and a silvery sheen – rippling like the tendons of the fisherman's arms and thighs – lay on the river's surface. The man was much older than he had seemed at first glance. It was hard to tell in this faint light, but Akrur thought he spied a shock of white hair under the cloth that the boatman had tied around his head. Other than that, and the whites of his eyes and teeth, the man was blackness itself, a shadow lost among the shadows of the growing darkness.

'Where are we going?' Akrur asked out of curiosity. He could see now that their destination was not the far side of the river as he had assumed at first.

The man jerked his head once, never missing a beat in his rhythmic poling.

Akrur peered in that direction but saw nothing at first. He waited patiently, and as they worked their way steadily upstream, he began to discern a place where the faint gleam of the river was absent – a roughly oblong patch in the middle of the river's course. Finally, they were close enough for him to make out that the patch was an island. Of course, he had been told that the meeting was on an island.

'Pachmani, is it not?' he asked tentatively.

'We call it Manchodri,' the man answered shortly. 'It is my home.'

As they approached, Akrur realized the brilliance of the choice of rendezvous. Not only was the island not easily visible from the riverbank, it was nearly impossible to reach. From the way the water roared a little way upstream, he could tell that there were large rocks that would make a downriver approach extremely treacherous if not impossible. And the effort and skill it would take to pole a boat upstream in this fashion ... well, it would prove daunting to almost any enemy.

As they reached the island proper, his sharp, alert gaze saw the unmistakeable shadows of men moving about on the shore, carrying long stick-like objects that he knew at once to be longbows of the kind favoured by riverfolk. An enemy that did manage to pole its way upstream would have to contend with a hail of deadly greetings. *As secure as any fortress.*

He leapt out on shore, then turned to thank the boatman. To his surprise, he found that the man had handed over the boat to one of the waiting bow men and was following him.

'This way,' said the fisherman, passing him and showing him the way. 'The lights are guarded to avoid alerting anyone who might be watching. Even fish have eyes, after all.'

Akrur was led up a winding path that he would never have been able to navigate unguided in the dark. When they finally arrived at the cottage, he was able to discern the faint glow of shielded lamp light. It had not been visible even a few dozen yards back.

The door of the cabin creaked as the fisherman opened it. 'He is here,' he said softly to those within, then stood by to let Akrur pass.

Vasudeva's trusted aide entered the cabin, glad for the warmth of the fire, even though it was shielded and banked to avoid producing too much light and smoke. The fisherman shut the door behind him, and they stood, looking around at the occupants already there and awaiting them both.

The first person he recognized by sight was a tall stately form. 'Pritha!' he said warmly, offering the appropriate greetings and gestures, 'it is so good to see you again!'

Vasudeva's sister greeted him with matching warmth. 'Well met, good Akrur. You are truly a sight for sore eyes.'

'And you,' he said, although he was disturbed to see how thin and wan she looked. Perhaps it was just the dim light? No, there was a distinctly haggard look about her beautiful features. He asked quietly, 'Is all well with you?'

She sighed. 'I have my health. It is more than most can say.' She turned to include the others. 'Allow me to introduce you.' She led him around the small group of figures seated or standing around the cabin.

She paused in front of a tall imposing giant of a man with a shock of white hair and ageing features that did nothing to diminish his sheer power and personality. 'This is Pitamah Bhishma, he is like a father to us all. His given name is Gangeya, after his mother Ganga-devi, but we call him Bhishma on account of the terrible vow he took.'

'A vow he took on my behalf,' said a woman's voice from across the room. Akrur turned to see a woman about the age of his own mother but possessed of such striking beauty that the instant he laid eyes on her, he was riveted. The fisherman who had brought him to the island had gone to stand by her, and seeing them together, side by side, the resemblance was unmistakable. From the difference in their ages, he discerned that they must be father and daughter. 'And on the insistence of my father here,' the woman continued bitterly, 'who made Bhishma swear that he would never sire a child as long as he lived in order to preclude his offspring from claiming a right to the throne of Hastinapura and depriving my own children of that privilege.' She laughed bitterly. 'And what good did it do? Both my sons are dead. And Hastinapura languishes on the brink of disaster, with no one to carry the Puru legacy onward.'

'This is Satyavati,' Kunti said, introducing Akrur with due formality. 'She is foster-mother to Bhishma and widow to the late Shantanu, king of the Purus. Shantanu had already sired Gangeya when he met Satyavati and desired to marry her. But her adoptive father Dasaraja,' here Kunti introduced the fisherman who nodded curtly in greeting, 'insisted that they could wed only if Shantanu swore that only Satyavati's children would have the right to claim the Puru throne.'

Dasaraja shrugged. 'Kings often desire beautiful fisherwomen or other women of lower stature. They rarely wed them, and even when they do, they rarely give their other children the right to kingship. It is the way of the world since time immemorial. I was only ensuring that my daughter would not be loved and then forgotten like so many other women of our community. The vow he took was entirely Gangeya's choice. I did not ask for it. Nor did I impose it as rigidly as he himself does even now.'

Kunti turned back to Akrur. 'Shantanu had countered Dasaraja's condition saying that he could not deprive his lawful son of his rightful place in succession and had returned home to Hastinapura in great sorrow, for he truly loved Satyavati and desired her more than anything else. But Gangeya came to know of his father's sadness and came to meet Dasaraja himself.'

The ageing fisherman shrugged. 'He swore to me in sight of the river – his mother's sister – and in the gaze of all the devas that he would not spill his seed so long as he lived. If he never sired a child, there could be no question of anyone but Satyavati's children ascending to the throne.'

Marvelling at the sheer audacity of the vow, Akrur turned his gaze back to the proud aquiline profile of Bhishma Pitamah who stood impassively staring ahead. To never know the touch of a woman or the pleasure of coition for his entire life! No wonder he was known as He Of The Terrible Vow ... *Bhishma* indeed!

Kunti went on: 'Satyavati's sons were Chitrangada and Vichitravirya. They were schooled by Bhishma Pitamah himself, and were great princes and legendary warriors. But their lives were cut short prematurely through circumstance. Shantanu was already long dead by that time. This left only Bhishma Pitamah to father more children in order to further the Puru race—'

'Which of course, he would not do on pain of death,' Satyavati cut in sorrowfully, and Akrur saw that her bitterness was directed not at Bhishma personally but at the strange turn of fortune that had brought them to this juncture. 'So I called upon a son I had birthed from an earlier encounter with the great Sage Parashara ...'

'Which story I shall tell you at some other time,' Kunti went on, 'for it is a strange and lovely tale in itself. But for now, meet Satyavati's son that she speaks of, the great mind that separated and organized the sacred verses of the Vedas, and who was known thenceforth as Ved Vyasa for this achievement, but whom we all know by his given birth name, Krishna Dweipayana, or simply Krishna for short.'

Akrur turned to look at the man who had, all this while, been staring out of the window at the dark night. He was struck by the intense, piercing gaze of the tall, pitch-dark man with formidable features. He swallowed and performed the necessary formalities of greeting a great sage, for there were few greater than this one. 'Pranaam, Gurudev.'

Ved Vyasa, as he was known by legend and reputation, simply nodded in greeting.

Kunti continued, 'Krishna Dweipayana, as Satyavati's son, albeit by an earlier union, was legitimately her heir. And so, after Bhishma refused to break his vow and sire an heir to the Kuru dynasty, she called upon Krishna Dweipayana to do so. He agreed on certain conditions. Satyavati agreed to all his conditions, but her daughters-in-law were unprepared and unable to accept a personality so striking as the great sage. As a result, one bore a child who was born blind.'

'Dhritarashtra,' added Satyavati sadly.

'And the other bore a son who was born devoid of skin pigmentation and with all the attendant complications caused by that condition.'

'Pandu – the white one,' Satyavati added. 'Ved Vyasa had a third son, named Vidura. A wonderful, perfect boy, but sired upon a maid and therefore ineligible to ascend to the throne.'

Akrur nodded slowly. 'You are married to Pandu,' he said to Kunti.

'Yes, and my husband is capable of producing an heir,' she said with a trace of bitter sadness in her voice, 'but he has been cursed. I will go into the details of that tale as well. Suffice it to say that he cannot sire a child on me or upon my sister queen Madri without dying instantly.'

Akrur rubbed his forehead. 'So if Pandu cannot sire an heir upon his wives due to the curse, Dhritarashtra must do so.'

Kunti sighed. 'Yes. But Dhritarashtra's wife Gandhari has been pregnant for well over a year now and hasn't given birth.

All the elders are agreed that her child has withered away in her womb.'

Bhishma Pitamah spoke up. 'Now tell the good Lord Akrur what all this has to do with him and his people. For while the tales and tragedies of the Kuru race are no doubt compelling, he was not called all this way at such great risk simply to hear the unfortunate story of our inability to further our great dynasty.'

Kunti inclined her head respectfully in agreement. She turned to Akrur: 'As in any Arya dynasty, when an heir is lacking, it creates a void. In this case, the void is a great one, for the Kuru dynasty has built a great and powerful kingdom, possessed of unmatched wealth and prime resources. We are the direct heirs of the great Bharata and his forebear Sudas, after all, who fought the legendary Dasarajna war that first established our line upon this subcontinent. To rule Hastinapura is to dominate all Aryavarta, for our kingdom's borders mark the point of ingress into this part of the world and enclose the richest rivers and lands. The king who sits on the throne of Hastinapura, capital of Hastinapura and the seat of the Kuru dynasty, is undoubtedly the most powerful in this part of the world, if not the world entire.'

Akrur nodded. 'I cannot argue with that. But how does the lack of heirs figure into the present political situation, unless you mean ...' He trailed off, gazing at the fireplace as he accessed his own store of knowledge and came to the inevitable conclusion. 'Jarasandha,' he said at last.

'Yes,' Kunti said, tensing at the name. 'His campaign of acquisition has ravaged the length and breadth of the land. The only kingdom large enough to oppose him now, as well as the choicest jewel in his crown of conquest, is Hastinapura. And in a scenario where we are without a legitimate heir to the throne, if Jarasandha were to stake a claim to our great holdings, even our most docile neighbours might well be tempted into joining him and waging all-out war against us.'

Akrur slammed his left fist into his right palm. 'The Yadava nations shall not stand by meekly and let that happen. We shall stand by the Puru nation against Jarasandha and his allies.'

At these words, the great white-haired sage turned away from his window and looked at the visitor. His eyes bore into Akrur with such intensity that the young man had to make an effort not to step back in consternation. 'Bravely spoken, but naively said. For the Yadava nations are no longer their own master. They are in the grip of Kamsa the Usurper. And he is nothing more than Jarasandha's tool, placed in Mathura merely to ensure that the joining of Yadava forces does not come to pass.'

sixteen

Kamsa found himself riding a horse. He had no recollection of getting on the horse, or even of getting out of bed that morning. By now, he had become unhappily accustomed to these abrupt 'jumps' in consciousness. In the past few days he appeared to have leapt forward by several months, sometimes losing mere days at a time, at other times losing entire weeks or months. He had no explanation to offer, nor did anyone else. Indeed, the few times he had attempted to explain his malady to Pralamba, the advisor visibly balked or stared blankly at him. He had deduced by now that he did not simply disappear from existence during these long absences. Indeed, to those around him, he apparently continued living and working and eating and talking and continuing the everyday business of his life, but to himself, it was as if he had gone to sleep, and woken up days, weeks, or months later, each time without any recollection of what had transpired during the intervening period. To describe it unsettling would be a euphemism; it made him feel vomitous and nervous all the time.

He had lost all confidence. The fact that he appeared to have lost his supernatural abilities only compounded his misery. Not only was he unable to expand himself, he had lost his superhuman strength as well. Reduced to the stature of just a normal mortal man – or as normal as he could be – hemmed in on every side by Jarasandha's henchmen and spasas, and unable to even *live* consciously through every day, he felt as if he had become a foot-soldier in some elaborate game of chaupat, the dice-game of military strategy favoured by kings and generals.

He had never cared for the game, partly because anything that required concentrating too hard and too long frustrated him as a boy, but also because his father enjoyed it a lot and was very good at it; so of course he had had to hate it intensely. He had broken his father's most prized chaupat set once, grinning with malicious joy as he shattered the ivory pieces and dice to fragments under his boot heels. He still remembered how happy that made him at the time – thinking of how upset his father would be when he found the destroyed game – happy enough to not care about the thrashing he was sure to receive from Ugrasena later.

Now, he shuddered as he rode round a large field towards the royal stables, and couldn't help glancing up at the sky – he almost expected to see a giant boot heel coming down to smash him to pulp.

There was no boot heel in the sky but from the clear cerulean blue upturned bowl above him and the warmth of the sun on his face and neck, he deduced that it was late spring or early summer now. How much time had he lost this time? A few weeks? More than that? He dreaded finding out, just as he dreaded knowing what had happened in the 'lost time'.

Handing his mount to a syce, he re-entered the palace precincts through the stable gate. Construction was still in progress in some parts, but he was struck by how much Bahuka had been able to rebuild during his blackouts. On the long walk to the palace proper, he was confronted at every turn by new statuary, shrubbery, gardens, temples – *temples!* – and other artistic and cultural flourishes that had been absent during the decade of his rule. It angered him to see all the very things he had ordered destroyed, or had demolished himself, reconstructed in even grander finery than had existed before he, Kamsa, took the reins of power in his granite fists.

Once within the palace, he was struck by the architectural and interior changes. Gone were the alterations and amendments he had made to extinguish his father's Mathura. Of course, he was partly responsible for destroying his own renovations – he did recall being somewhat out of control during the past year or four, or perhaps even all through the decade. And why not? He had been liberated from the yoke of his father's tyranny. The domestic despot had been unseated, the captive prince released at last. It had been a decade of celebration.

He almost smiled, recalling the havoc he had wreaked, the wanton destruction he had unleashed, the sheer scale of demolition! Ah, but they were great years. He would do anything to continue that celebration – forever! Damn that Bahuka and the master he served. Jarasandha might be emperor of the mortal realm or even of all three realms for all he cared, but here in Mathura, Kamsa was still king. And it was time he demonstrated that. What else was Bahuka but Jarasandha's glorified spasa, stationed to spy on Kamsa and exercise control over him? The same went for the new cronies that Bahuka had carefully placed around him – all spasas of Jarasandha, no question about it. Today he would put that spasa and his cronies in their place once and for all. He would show them who was king of the Andhaka nation.

He entered the royal enclave and stopped short at once. The three courtyards – each of which was high-walled and accessed by only a single lowered gate, Bahuka's newfangled design again – were packed to the brim with soldiers.

Not *mere* soldiers. These were members of the Mohini Fauj. Prime specimens of Jarasandha's eunuch gladiators, birthed, castrated, bred and trained for havoc. It had been a while since he had confronted them, and coming upon them unexpectedly brought home the extent to which he had changed since that fateful day many moons past when he had gone into the heart of Magadha in search of Jarasandha, and had wrestled and slain that marauding king's choicest champions without working up much of a sweat.

A hundred pairs of eyes turned to look at him – eyes that seemed as distant as the stars that were coldly fixed in their firmament and as unseeing of anything that might occur on earth. Blood spilled, muscle rent to shreds, bones cracked and marrow drawn, sinew and gristle bared, glistening and gristly innards strung out , babies speared and mothers butchered ... nothing would draw a response from these cold eyes. They were merely windows through which machine-like minds viewed the world in two stark extremes: Enemy and Potential Enemy. Black and Not-yet Black. Everything and everyone was black or a shade of grey.

Examined, identified and assessed, he was dismissed as roundly as if he were a stray cur that had wandered into the grazing grounds of a pride of lions – lions that yawned and carried on with their existence and did not deem it fit to dignify his entrance with their attention. That was how he was spurned by the Hijras now. They simply turned away, even those closest to him showing their backs to him, and continued whatever it was they were doing, which, judging by the eerie silence that pervaded the enclave and the relatively relaxed postures in which they stood around, appeared to be simply waiting. Even when resting or waiting idly, Jarasandha's Mohinis did not simply lounge or sprawl sloppily; they remained at ease but in positions of preparedness, ready for any threat or command. This discipline of eternal readiness was partly what made them such formidable opponents.

Kamsa began moving through the close-packed press. It was hard going. Clad as they were in leather skirts and vests, with chain-link armour sown into the leather, Kamsa did not wish to brush against their garb and risk scraping the skin of his arms or legs. Yet they did not offer to move aside or even budge an inch from where they stood. Indeed, after that initial inspection, it was as if he had ceased to exist. The lions couldn't care less what the cur did next: slunk away or stayed and risked his mangy life further.

He could have raised his voice and commanded them to move aside and make way for him. After all, he was Jarasandha's son-in-law and as good as his heir and second-in-command. Or so he had believed. But that would have seemed unmanly to these half-men, who compensated for their lack of sexual identity by sheer willpower, discipline, training and mastery of martial skills.

Had he possessed his own supernatural powers, he would simply have batted, swatted, kicked and shunted them aside like so many clay puppets and barged through. But his powers were gone – he had reluctantly and with great frustration come to accept that fact – and all he had were his normal human strength and skill. He used them as best as he could, shouldering the Hijras aside and moving through slender gaps. The going was not easy, and often a casually distended javelin, or sword hilt, or even a leg or an arm, would be in his way and he would have to physically push it aside – yet not too forcefully for fear of starting a fight he could not possibly hope to finish successfully. By the time he reached the second courtyard, his shoulders were bruised, the backs of his forearms skinned and bleeding in several places, and his legs felt as if they had been rubbed raw on the outside.

He was hugely relieved to see a familiar face.

'Pradyota!' he croaked, seeing the captain of the guards in conversation with the chief of the Hijra Fauj battalion.

Neither the captain nor the Hijra paid heed to him; they were engrossed in their talk.

Someone snickered and a whisper as soft as wind rustled nearby, with a distinctly mocking tone that he knew well from the time he had spent with Jarasandha's army and with his own Mohini Fauj contingent.

He cleared his throat and said in a louder, more commanding tone: 'Captain Pradyota?'

The captain frowned and looked around, forehead creased with irritation at being interrupted.

Kamsa was forced to wave a hand. He had to stand on tiptoe to be sure he was seen, because the Hijras around him were all at least a foot or more taller than him.

'Over here, Captain.'

Captain Pradyota saw him and reacted with a peculiar mixture of scorn and derision. Then he strode forward, somehow walking easily and without impediment through the same crush of Hijra soldiers. Kamsa knew then that the crowd of Mohinis he had passed through had deliberately obstructed him in subtle ways, just enough to skin and bruise him but not enough to provoke an all-out fight. He swallowed, glad that they hadn't pressed for a skirmish. In his present state, there was no doubt who would have ended up the victor.

'Prince Regent Kamsa,' said the new captain of the guards, the one that Kamsa did not remember appointing yet Bahuka insisted he had. 'What are you doing here, sire? You were expected in the sabha hall several hours earlier.'

He said it in the tone one would use when addressing a child who returns late from play: Where have you been? Didn't you hear your maatr calling you? Supper was hours ago!

Kamsa tried hard to ignore Pradyota's insulting tone and manner. 'In that case, do your damned job. Kindly escort me to the sabha hall!'

If I had my powers, I would have crushed you between my thumb and forefinger like a little rodent, you fool! How dare you speak to me thus?

Captain Pradyota nodded laconically, the sneer still lingering on his face. 'Certainly, sire.' He glanced at Kamsa's shoulders and arms. 'Did you have difficulty making your way on your own through the courtyard?'

Kamsa resisted the impulse to smash his fist into the man's face.

'You did say I was expected, did you not? Let us waste no more time then.' He wanted that to come out fierce and threatening, and was somewhat disappointed that it merely sounded curt.

The captain chuckled brazenly. He inclined his head towards the Mohini chief who nodded back. Kamsa recognized the chief. He had ridden with him and they had slaughtered together, burnt homes, eaten in each other's company, bedded beside one another, and the Hijra had treated him with utmost respect as was warranted by one so close to Emperor Jarasandha himself, even before Kamsa married Jarasandha's daughters. But now, when Kamsa was at a position where he ought to be saluted, bowed to and indeed be given a formal salutation from the whole contingent, he was being treated like some mlechcha! It was infuriating and humiliating but there was little he could do about it.

The Hijra chief glanced at him coldly as he passed by. *Not so much as a flicker of recognition or acknowledgement on the lout's face!* Kamsa trembled with suppressed fury but walked on. He had almost reached the façade of the royal entrance when a particularly large Mohini strolled casually across his path, jostling him without even glancing aside. The giant was over seven feet tall and bulky enough to weigh two hundred kilos with a third more weight from his armour and sheathed weapons; the jolt was hard enough to send Kamsa sprawling, but he was anticipating some further mischief and took it on his shoulder, gritting his teeth. His shoulder was wrenched agonizingly with the force but he did not cry out or let the pain show. He merely walked on without even a backward glance, went up the marbled stairs and entered the palace of his ancestors where he now ruled as king in name only.

The crowd in the sabha hall surprised him. This was a full-session court! Only he as king could summon such an assembly and preside over it. Kamsa caught sight of Bahuka on the royal dais and strode forward, determined to put the man in his place once and for all. This was going too far! It was one thing to undermine his authority on a daily basis and to virtually use him as a puppet crown-figure, but to exclude him from the administration of his own kingdom was unacceptable!

He was almost at the dais when he noticed that a figure was seated on the Andhaka throne as well. That was treason! No one was permitted to even *approach* the empty throne! Who dared actually sit on it in full assembly? Whoever it was, the person had made a fatal error. Kamsa had taken enough humiliation for one day – for an entire lifetime, in fact – and he knew that this transgression needed no soldierly display of manliness. He had but to command and the fool who had sat on the seat of Andhaka governance would be food for the kitchen dogs.

He raised his arm and opened his mouth to shout, to bellow, to set the entire sabha ablaze with fear and intimidation, as he had done so often before. He needed no giant form, nor supernatural strength to do this, merely his authority as king of the Andhaka Sura nation.

Then he saw who it was that sat on the throne.

And all his bluster, anger and frustration were capped as quickly as the flame of a candle is extinguished by a brass snuffing cap.

And were replaced by stark, naked terror.

seventeen

After the last man arrived, was discreetly checked by the diligent sentries and permitted to enter the barn, the enormous wooden door was shut and bolted, and uks carts rolled before it. A few bales of hay, an uks or two put to munching on soft green shoots, and it appeared as if the barn had never been opened or entered that day. The sentries pretended to lounge on the hay and the cart, chatting endlessly in the loquacious way of Yadavas, while secretly alert and watchful of any stranger's approach.

The last man to enter heard the bolting of the barn doors and knew that the place was now secure. He undid the turban cloth he had wound tightly around his head and which covered most of his face as well, ostensibly to keep him warm from the chilly spring breeze on the journey by uks cart. The others gathered around the large hay-strewn barn did likewise, untying scarves and headcloths to reveal their faces. In turn, each one nodded to the last arrival, greeting him with the respect and awe reserved for the very great or very noble. To use the Sanskrit word, *arya*. The highest of the high. Truly, the dark complexioned, gracefully maturing man who stood inside the barn doors was arya indeed.

Vasudeva nodded back, glad to see those familiar faces. It had been so long since he had been able to set eyes on them, he had almost feared he might never do so. He inhaled the odours of stale feed and fresh cow manure and sighed. His days of being a simple cowherd were far back in the past now, yet he sometimes wished he had never been called to do anything but tend to cows. He knew that Devaki felt the same way. Nothing would give them both greater joy than to leave behind the luxury and comfort of palace and city living and reside in rustic quietude. *I'm no king*, he thought, *nor do I want to be one. Let my sons rule. I am content to be let out to pasture even now.*

But as some great ancient Kusalavya bard had once sung, life was what happened to you when you were busy making other plans.

And so here he was again. Presiding over the Yadava Sangha.

'Well met, old friends,' he said quietly. 'You cannot imagine how much it pleases me to see each one of your faces today. Simply to be alive and to inhale this sweet scent of cow patties.'

Uddhava chuckled softly. Vasudeva noted that his old friend had streaks of grey in his hair and a beard that had not been there the last time they had met. Then again, that occasion had been over a decade ago.

'Would you like to sniff them a little closer, Vasu? That can be arranged!' Uddhava's eyes twinkled mischievously. The others laughed softly. Gopas were known to have cow patty fights at times, and each of them had flung and received his share of freshly patted cow dung in his youth.

Vasudeva laughed loudly, the sound surprising him as it echoed among the high rafters. 'I think our age for supping on such things has passed, would you not agree, old Kratha?' He addressed the question to an ageing man who leaned on a shepherd's crook as if his life depended on it: which it probably did.

Kratha surprised him by raising his bald head and waggling a shaky forefinger in the air. 'Speak for yourself, Vasu. Old *you* may be. I'm ready to take on any man in a cow patty fight. Right here. Right now!'

That brought laughter to everyone's lips. Even serious Chitraketu's mouth cracked open to reveal his teeth. It made Vasudeva realize how long it had been since he had jested and shared such rough good-natured humour with his fellow Yadavas and caused him to curse the reign of Kamsa for the umpteenth time.

At least today we shall finally be able to do something to end that reign, he thought grimly as he went around embracing his clansmen in turn. Tears filled his eyes by the time he was done and he had to swipe at his face more than once. The strongest emotion came when he faced a young man whom he recognized at once owing to the strong resemblance he bore to his father.

'Brihadbala the Younger,' he said, gripping the young man's shoulders.

Brihadbala nodded slowly and bowed his head to Vasudeva. 'Bhagwan, show us the way. For too long have I told myself that my father did not die in vain. That Kamsa the Usurper did not murder my sire and so many other blameless Vrishnis for no cause at all. Now lead us forward to our salvation from this menace, lord.'

Vasudeva wiped the tears from his eyes. 'Would that I could, my child. But that honour does not fall on me. It falls on the Slayer.'

Many heads nodded. Several exclaimed quietly, reverentially. The legend of the Slayer was a formidable one, albeit not spoken of aloud in public. It was the sole source of hope and inspiration to a troubled nation. Many lived only for the day when the Slayer would finally destroy the Usurper and not merely restore the Yadavas to their once-proud glory but take them beyond into a new age of milk and honey wine, as the prophecy claimed.

'Bhraatr, we understand your plight,' said Chitraketu. 'You and your goddess-like wife Devaki have suffered immeasurably. We are proud and honoured to be graced even by your presence at this sangha.'

Vasudeva shook his head. 'Do not speak to me as if I am some visiting lord or purohit, Chitra. I am just a gopa at heart, like all of you. I endure because that has been our way since the days of our great forebear Yadu himself. We learned this from the most beautiful and sacred creature of all on Sri's holy prithviloka, goumata. As the humble cow endures through all seasons and all climes, so do we.'

'True,' said the chief of the Kannars. 'True indeed. But there comes a time when we, as mere mortals, can endure no more. Some would even say we passed that point long ago. What good will enduring do now? It will only enable Kamsa's soldiers to continue slaughtering our newborn babes unopposed.'

Uddhava raised a hand in a calming gesture. 'The slaughter has ceased. Things have changed greatly in Mathura. The army itself has been reorganized. Those two butchers of Kamsa, Bana and Canura, have disappeared to places unknown. The new guard that now runs Mathura is a different beast altogether. It is nowhere near as bloodthirsty and mindless as the White Marauders.'

'Or that awful Hijra Fauj,' said another councillor, shuddering at the memory. 'What Uddhava says is true. Things do appear to be changing. For one thing, instead of sword blades and lance points, Mathura seems to be attempting to win us over with gold and silver!'

'Beware,' said old Kratha shakily, leaning on his crook. 'Gold and silver can cut a man as sharply as bronze and iron. Kamsa's new advisors are shrewd as yaksas. They seek to buy our loyalty with coins. But where do you think those riches come from? From the coffers of Ugrasena! They are depleting the stored wealth of generations of Yadava kings.'

'Perhaps they are only seeking to make reparation for all the damage and killing of the past ten years,' suggested someone. It was instantly shouted down with noises of friendly disagreement.

'Nothing like that! Their goal is to weaken the Yadava people by spreading wealth and luxury around. When you beat a dog for days and then suddenly begin feeding and petting it lovingly, it becomes willing to do anything to earn your affection. *That* is the tactic they are employing!'

Kratha pointed a shaking finger. 'The Kannar chief speaks wisely. Everything Mathura does is but a tactic or a part of some larger plan. Beware!'

Satvata shook his head, looking confused and angry. 'None of this can be disputed. But the question still remains, what are we to do? For now, the giant sleeps, or is listening to different advisors who have convinced him to try new tactics that are apparently peaceful but are in fact devious. So be it. But we cannot wait for another cycle of slaughter and genocide to begin. We must take action *now*, while Mathura is still quiet and non-combative. This is the time to raise an army and march towards the capital! And who better to lead us than Lord Vasudeva himself!'

Cheers and yells of approval met this last comment.

With an effort, Vasudeva shushed and silenced them so that he could be heard. 'We have a plan of our own.'

The murmurs died down at once, and every pair of eyes turned to him, attentive.

'All of you are right in saying that it is time to act. What is more, I agree that the present lull is little more than a ploy on the part of Mathura. There are strange rumours afloat in the royal enclave. Rumours too frequent and similar to be mere gossip. These have been confirmed by my own observations over a period of time.' He paused, looking around at each one. He had their complete attention now. 'For one thing, Kamsa has changed.'

'How?' asked the Kannar chieftain whose farmlands were too distant for accurate reports from Mathura to reach often.

'He appears to have lost his demoniac powers,' Vasudeva said.

The peace of the barn was disrupted at once.

'Please,' Vasudeva said patiently, 'hear me out. I know what all of you are thinking, that if Kamsa is no longer capable of supernatural feats such as expanding himself to the size of a giant or rampaging across entire cities, what better time to attack? But there is a story behind his newfound vulnerability and that story is of great concern to us.'

The gathered Yadavas listened without interrupting Vasudeva.

'I suspect his food and drink are being doctored. Or perhaps some potent mixture or compound is being fed to him without his knowledge. Perhaps in his food, or drink, or some other way ... it does not matter what method is being used. But this diminution of his powers is deliberate.'

'Who do you think is doing it?' asked Chitraketu, with open-mouthed wonderment. None of them had as close a view of the inner workings of Mathura's administration as Vasudeva.

Apart from the godlike adulation they had for him, he also had the best ringside view of the inner circle. What they heard as rumours or gossip weeks, even months after, he saw occurring before his very eyes every day.

'Jarasandha,' Vasudeva replied simply. 'For it is an open secret now that he controls Kamsa and that my brother-in-law is but a tool in the hands of the Magadhan king.'

'He calls himself emperor of Bharat-varsha now,' Uddhava said derisively.

Satvata made a rude gesture and sound. 'He isn't fit to be emperor of my toilet.'

'Even so,' Vasudeva continued, 'his control over Kamsa is now complete. I suspect that for too many years, he was busy with his other campaigns of conquest and it is only now that he has found the time to take a personal interest in the affairs of the Yadava nations.'

'Why doesn't he simply march in and invade us as he has so many other nations?' asked Brihadbala.

They all grew sombre at this. Each one of them had heard the horrific stories of Jarasandha's campaigns of conquest across the Aryavarta subcontinent. The thought of him unleashing his brand of devilry was a sobering one; more frightening than even the worst excesses of Kamsa and his White Marauders a decade earlier.

'Because he wants the Yadavas intact,' Vasudeva said simply. 'We are great in number and strong in spirit. Our combined armies are a formidable force in the world. If we were not facing these internal strifes, or even despite these strifes, we could very well resist Jarasandha's forces to the point where they get decimated trying to defeat us, or we might even win out over them altogether.'

There was no response to this explanation. It made sense as a well-thought-out strategy of the Magadhan emperor, or any emperor for that matter. Destroying the biggest workforce and military force in a region did not exactly make sense from a strategic point of view. Even the most rapacious emperor wanted to leave something to rule over when he was done conquering. And the Yadavas, despite being peace-loving, cow-herding people who were more fond of music and dance and laughter and honey wine than anything else, were fierce when provoked.

'But if he thinks he can set Kamsa up to subjugate us, he is wrong,' said Chitraketu, his red-rimmed eyes – not reddened by drink or emotion, but by a condition he had had since childhood – flashing. 'We shall rebel against the Usurper until the end of our days.'

'Exactly,' responded Vasudeva. 'But the question is, how should we rebel? For the greatest number of able warriors are engaged as cowherds and farmers. If every gopa and gopi leaves aside his or her work, drops the crook and the plough and takes up the sword and the bow instead, all of Vrajbhoomi shall be turned into a battlefield. All the Yadava kingdoms shall be set ablaze in the subsequent conflict. Our lands, our herds, our families, our future ... it shall all be forfeited in the madness of war.'

The gathering fell silent again, considering this equally unpalatable vision.

Old Kratha, who had been listening to the discussion with closed eyes, now opened them and shook his crook at Vasudeva querulously: 'You say that Jarasandha will not invade us. And that we ought not to rebel against his stool pigeon Kamsa. Then what *should* we do? Nothing?'

Vasudeva went over to the old man, lowered his crook gently and placed the wrinkled bony hands upon it again. 'No, old father. The time for waiting and watching and doing nothing is long past. The hour is grown late and the wolf is already in the herd. We must act before Jarasandha does. And we must have a long-term plan and strategy. That is the only way to win this war.'

He turned to the others. 'We cannot fight here on our lands for fear of destroying our entire livelihood. And I do not believe Jarasandha will bring his armies here to invade us and risk everything he has gained over the past decade. This leaves only one final option if we are to fight this menace and root it out from the heart of our nation.'

The congregation waited, listening with a rapt expression.

'We must go into exile,' Vasudeva said, 'and draw the enemy to us, so that we may fight him on our own terms and at places and times of our choosing, not his. If we cannot chase the wolf out of the herd, we must move the herd itself to another pasture, forcing the wolf to expose himself to our attack. And when he is exposed, we shall attack him in unexpected and unthought-of ways, with the help of our new allies.'

'Allies?' interjected Uddhava. 'What allies do you speak of? Which Arya nation dares challenge the might of Jarasandha's Magadhan Empire today? And even if there are some stray recalcitrants, why would they support us if we go into exile and rebel against the seat of our own nation?'

Vasudeva smiled. 'These are all excellent questions. But I am not the one to answer them.' He gestured to a dark figure standing in the shadows. Everyone gasped as the new face emerged into the light. None had realized that one man had arrived long before the others and waited silently through the sangha's discussions for the moment when he would be called out by Vasudeva.

'Akrur!' they said, recognizing their countryman at once, clapping hands on his shoulders and back as he joined them.

'Akrur will tell you of these allies and how our plan of exile and rebellion also ties into their long-term strategy of keeping Jarasandha at bay.' He gestured to Akrur to take up the thread of the discussion.

Akrur nodded and turned to the sangha. 'In one word, Hastinapura. The seat of Hastinapura itself wishes to align with us and aid us in our rebellion against Jarasandha. Taking into consideration Hastinapura's offer of cooperation and by taking a long-term view, I too believe as Vasudeva does, that we shall eventually achieve our goal – of ridding the Yadava nations of the menace of Kamsa the Usurper as well as his puppet-master, the so-called "Emperor" Jarasandha himself.'

eighteen

Jarasandha coolly occupied the throne of Mathura. He looked relaxed, calm, as if he belonged there and had been sitting upon this very seat of power for years. Arrayed around him were several other familiar faces that Kamsa recognized. Hansa and Dimvaka were on either side, as always, like pillars framing the royal personage. Bana and Canura were there as well, standing behind the throne and off to one side. They avoided meeting Kamsa's gaze though Hansa and Dimvaka had no compunctions about staring arrogantly back at him. A few others he knew were Trnavarta, Agha, Vatsa, Baka, Dhenu, his own chief advisor Pralamba, a woman he recognized as the wife of the captain of the guards Pradyota, and of course, the recent thorn in his backside, Bahuka.

Bahuka did exactly what he had been doing these past several months – he told Kamsa what to do.

'Prince Regent Kamsa,' he said in a voice loud enough to carry across the sabha hall and to be heard by every one of the most powerful and wealthy nobles of not just Mathura, but of the entire Yadava race assembled there, 'will you not show your allegiance to your benefactor and mentor, who also happens to be your illustrious father-in-law, the honourable god emperor of all Bharat-varsha, Aryavarta and prithviloka?'

God emperor? Bharat-varsha, Aryavarta and *prithviloka? The subcontinent, the Bharata nations who resided on that subcontinent* and *the entire mortal realm as well? It would need a 'god emperor' indeed to govern that ambitious a principality!*

By exhorting him in front of every last person whose opinion – and power – mattered in this part of the world, the shrewd old tactician had outwitted him once again. He had compelled Kamsa to adhere to protocol since not doing so would be seen as being churlish and rebellious, if not outright insulting. Kamsa knew Jarasandha's methods too well; tolerating insubordination or insults was not part of the Magadhan lord's world view. He had seen him kill men closer to him than Kamsa for lesser infractions.

Seething inwardly with pent-up frustration and fury, he bowed and bent his knee in obeisance. *Bowing before my own throne, here's a royal irony!*

'My lord,' he said. That was as much as he was willing to do. If Jarasandha expected any more, he could come kiss his royal seat.

Instead, Jarasandha surprised him by leaving the throne and coming down the dais steps with arms outstretched in an attitude of dramatic majesty.

'My son!' he cried with redoubtable sincerity. 'Kamsa, my eyes have ached to look upon you these past years. Too long have you kept yourself from me. My heart languishes without your youthful exuberance and energy. Come, embrace me.'

Kamsa let his former friend enfold him in the same lean yet whip-taut arms that he recalled from a decade ago. Jarasandha looked as if he hadn't aged a day since. The grip that held him was powerful enough to snap his back easily, and the squeeze Kamsa received was clearly a reminder of that. He half expected Jarasandha to pull him close and whisper some snarling threat that could not be caught by the rest of the sabha. But the 'god emperor' did no such thing. He behaved as if he were genuinely pleased to see Kamsa again after their long separation. Kamsa recalled his wives, Jarasandha's daughters, with a vague twinge of not-quite-guilt. It had been a fair time since he had seen them last. Perhaps there was as much of the father-in-law's sentiments of wrath and reluctant tolerance in Jarasandha's attitude to him as that of a conqueror seeking new territories. It also gave Kamsa a sense of righteous indignation: Jarasandha should be treating him with more respect than he was at present!

Jarasandha regained his seat upon the throne, gesturing to Kamsa to be seated on another silk-cushioned gold-limned stool that was quickly brought forward by attendants and placed close to Jarasandha's – yet slightly behind it and much lower in height. He gestured to other waiting serving staff.

'Come, partake of refreshment with me. You must be tired after your tax-collecting trip. If you will excuse me, I shall finish dealing with some minor administrative matters.'

Tax collecting? Was that where he was to have been? Perhaps he had been expected to collect the manure the horse had dropped on the field – was that the 'tax' Jarasandha had in mind? Horse droppings?

Kamsa sat with a goblet of honey wine in his hand as Jarasandha issued a few formal proclamations, signed several agreements, armistices, trade deals and other such 'minor administrative matters' with efficient ease.

Go on, thought Kamsa sourly as he watched over the rim of his brass goblet, *be comfortable, dearest father-in-law. Consider this your own kingdom.* It was also clear that all these deals and agreements were the culmination of months of diplomacy, negotiations and tough talk. He glanced at Bahuka who was supervising the formalization of each scroll, instructing the munshis and generally overseeing the whole process. Bahuka sensed him looking in his direction and glanced up, grinning broadly. Kamsa looked down, disgusted.

At one point, Jarasandha looked over at him with a shrewd, knowing glance. He turned to look at Bahuka, then Hansa and Dimvaka and finally included his other cronies and associates in his cryptic glance. Some silent communication passed between them as all of them turned to look at Kamsa. Then, as one man, they all burst out laughing. Jarasandha looked at Kamsa again, his thin lips pursed, eyes half-lidded, a faint shadow of a smile sketched on his sharply malevolent features.

Kamsa fought mightily the desire to dash the goblet of wine at the 'god emperor' and throw himself at the man who had reduced him from a king of kings to a mere puppet figure and a laughing stock in his own court.

Jarasandha saw the change come across his features and read Kamsa's mood accurately.

'Does something trouble you overmuch, my son?' he asked, taking a sip from his goblet. 'I trust you will not mind my calling you son? After all, a son-in-law is like a second son in our culture.'

'Not at all, father dearest,' Kamsa said, seething within but smiling pleasantly. 'I was merely wondering what our plans are?'

Jarasandha nodded in response to some query whispered in his ear by Pralamba before glancing casually at Kamsa again. 'What plans do you refer to, Kamsa?'

'For Mathura, of course,' said Kamsa, using every ounce of his willpower to keep himself from shouting and throwing things. He wanted to, but with merely mortal strength and body, he knew that he would be crushed in a moment. But there were other weapons in his armoury. *So if it's talk and public displays you want, let's do it your way, mighty 'god emperor'!*

'Mathura is *your* kingdom, Kamsa,' Jarasandha said condescendingly. 'Surely you know what your own plans are?'

'Of course,' Kamsa agreed. 'But your overview and grasp of the entire socio-political climate is so much superior to my own, I would be foolish not to ask you to lend your expertise to the welfare of my people.'

Jarasandha looked out across the lake of upturned faces. The backchat in the sabha hall had risen to a gentle lulling background noise while Jarasandha was sealing the treaties and attending to other formalities, but now it had died out altogether. Clearly, the court sensed some animosity between father- and son-in-law and was eager to see what transpired. There was also the fact that Kamsa's reign of terror had not yet been completely forgotten and from the looks he received daily, he knew that everyone was expecting him to return to that old demoniac form at any moment. Perhaps they even thought that this human and vulnerable Kamsa was but a ploy, some tactic designed to appease and lull the citizenry. They were rich and powerful, lazy and self-indulgent, but not fools. And Jarasandha's own reputation preceded him across the length and breadth of the civilized world – and beyond; his cruelty was renowned, his own demoniac origins legendary. A clash between these two titans would be a sight to see, and the rich always enjoyed spectacles, especially the gory, brutally violent kind. *Here we are now*, said the rapt silence of the hallful of nobles, *entertain us!*

Kamsa saw from Jarasandha's face that he too had read tension in the room, and come to the same conclusion. The cool grey eyes remained placid, the attitude stayed nonchalant.

'Perhaps it may be more pertinent if you were to ask me specific questions, so I could answer to the point.' Jarasandha gestured to the chamber at large. 'One would not wish to bore the entire nobility of the kingdom, after all.'

'Of course,' Kamsa responded, carefully mirroring rather than mimicking Jarasandha's polite coolness. The game was on.

Kamsa rose to his feet and stepped a few yards ahead. Jarasandha's coterie instantly grew suspicious and alert: from the corners of his eyes, Kamsa glimpsed hands reaching for sword hilts, feet muscles clenching, eyes narrowing. He kept his movements casual and relaxed, even as he walked to and fro in front of the throne as he spoke. It was unorthodox in the extreme, could even be considered an affront to the throne, but after all he was the prince regent, was he not? And he was speaking not only to the 'god emperor' but also to his father-in-law. The informality could hardly be constructed as an insult when Jarasandha himself had encouraged the casual attitude and emphasized their personal tie!

'What steps do you intend to take to find this so-called Slayer?' Kamsa asked. It was important to start with a hard-hitting question, to gain the upper hand from the very outset. The collective nobility of the kingdom was watching, after all. He would ram question after question up Jarasandha's slender throat, until the so-called god emperor's gullet was too full for him to even take a breath! Then he would go in for the kill and tear the man's innards out with a single slashing accusation. So much for dear loving father-in-law. Before this sabha session ended, he, Kamsa, the rightful king, would be on the throne of the Andhaka nation once more.

However, a faint niggling doubt reared its head in his conscience, suggesting that perhaps he ought to tread carefully.

After all, irrespective of his arrogant treatment of him, Jarasandha was one of the most powerful warlords in the world at present, as well as a harsh and unforgiving enemy. It might perhaps be wise not to antagonize him completely.

But he had already dealt the first punch and now waited to see his opponent reel and rock.

Jarasandha smiled and spread his hands, frowning as he did so. 'What slayer?' he asked with convincing perplexity.

Kamsa resisted the urge to snort. Somehow, without living beings dropping from one's nostrils, snorting and sneezing were no longer as much fun. 'The prophesied Slayer of Kamsa, of course! The one told of by Sage Narada so many years past, and whose coming has been awaited by his people for over a decade.'

Jarasandha chuckled. 'Rumours. Gossip. Idle chatter. Nothing more.'

Kamsa stared at him, dumbfounded. 'You would question the prophecy of a deva-rishi? Brahmarishi Narada himself stated that—'

'Stated to whom?'

Kamsa blinked, unused to being interrupted. 'What?'

Jarasandha smiled indulgently, as if addressing a feeble friend. 'You say this Narada stated this alleged prophecy. To whom did he state it?'

Kamsa looked around, wondering what was happening. 'What do you mean to whom he stated it! Everyone knows about the prophecy. The whole kingdom has been clamouring for the "Deliverer" to be born and now they say he has been born and that my days on earth are numbered! Everyone knows this! Where have you been, Jarasandha? How do you *not* know of the Slayer? I thought you knew everything!'

Careful, don't get carried away. Winning petty points here won't help your score in the final quarter of this game. This was Kamsa's inner voice of conscience and good sense, advising him again. He ignored it. It felt far too good to be slapping the great 'god emperor' around. His larger, dominating, demoniac side might not have been able to display itself through the use of power and force, but it could still unleash some much-needed anger: *Take that, Jarasandha! Yes!*

Jarasandha looked as calm as Kamsa felt angry. 'Where have I been? Consolidating a hundred divided tribal principalities and minor kingdoms into a cohesive collective. Building an empire, in other words. Possibly the greatest empire ever assembled in this subcontinent, if not the world.' Then he smiled disarmingly, as if embarrassed at the sheer scale of his own achievement. 'But let's stick to the point, shall we? This Slayer you speak of, am I to understand that only *you* heard this alleged prophecy being pronounced? Didn't anyone else see this Narada-muni when he is said to have made this outrageous claim of a deliverer being born, etc, etc? A serving girl, perhaps? Or a sarathi on his way to the stables? A cook, a thief, his wife, her lover? None of the above? How odd!'

Titters of amusement rippled through the sabha hall.

Kamsa looked around, furious. '*Silence when the king speaks!*' he roared.

He turned back to Jarasandha, arm outstretched, finger pointing accusingly. 'Stop trying to twist this around. What difference does it make whether Narada-muni made the prophecy to one man or a hundred thousand? The point is, he prophesied that the Slayer would be born, that he would be the eighth son of my sister Devaki by her husband Vasudeva. And that prophecy has in fact come to pass! The Slayer has been born! What I want to know is what the bleeding hell you intend to do about it! Answer me, Father-in-law dearest!'

The last title was emphasized with more than a little contempt. In fact, Kamsa said it with a sneer so pronounced, it was almost nasally intoned.

Jarasandha sat back on the throne, crossed one leg over the other, and rested his elbows on his thighs, then put the tips of his fingers together. It was the posture of a man in complete control of his faculties, calmly contemplating before speaking his mind.

Utter silence prevailed in the sabha hall.

Kamsa realized that he had openly confronted Jarasandha now. That last outburst had verged dangerously close to a challenge. He felt sweat pop from the crown of his head and trickle down copiously from his skull. The nape of his neck prickled with a sense of impending threat. *You've pushed him too far now, you fool,* warned his sensible side. So be it, laughed the demoniac side scornfully. *Let's have it out right here and now!*

There was little doubt about which side ruled Jarasandha. The Magadhan replied with unctuous calm: 'I intend to do absolutely nothing, Son-in-law.'

Kamsa laughed. The sound rang shockingly hollow in the vastness of the sabha hall. 'Nothing? That's all I expected of you!'

'But I expected far more of you, Kamsa,' Jarasandha went on. Now he stood, slowly and with great dignity, moved with fluid grace to the end of his dais, then paused to face outwards towards the spellbound audience. 'When I sent you here to Mathura ten years ago, I expected you to take a very different course of action. Instead, what did you do?'

Kamsa stared up at him, puzzled. What was the man talking about? What was this new ploy? Kamsa had just outwitted him by making him admit he could do nothing to stop the Slayer! He had won, dammit! Why wouldn't Jarasandha shut up, or at least apologize and offer his regrets to him now? Why couldn't he just lose gracefully?

'You usurped your father's throne, imprisoning the great King Ugrasena, perhaps the greatest ruler of this nation since the great Yadu himself.'

Excited murmurs coursed through the court at this unexpected praise of the nation's rightful king. 'Then, under the pretext of an alleged "Slayer" that you claimed had been prophesied, you embarked on a mindless rampage of death and destruction for over a decade. But who was this Slayer intended to kill? You, of course! Because as an immature, thoughtless, patricidal and matricidal boy, you assumed that you were the most important person in the whole universe! So you created this myth of a fictional Slayer who would rise one day from your sister's womb and destroy you, and through the perpetuation of this myth, you brought this proud kingdom almost to its knees.'

Jarasandha gestured to the audience with one hand, as if asking, is it not so? Kamsa glanced around with startled eyes and saw several heads bobbing, faces rapt with admiration for Jarasandha's brilliant politicking and shrewd calculation. The erstwhile king and supreme commander of Mathura could not believe this was actually happening. Yet it must be, for there were several hundred witnesses to it!

Jarasandha acknowledged his audience's response and stepped down from the dais. For a moment, Kamsa saw his intent set eyes and felt sure that this was the moment in which his father-in-law would attack and kill him without compunction. But Jarasandha opened his arms in a clear gesture of peace and conciliation as he descended each successive step, choosing his words carefully and delivering them to match his actions in rhythm and pace: 'Now it is time for you to put this mad delusion out of your head, my son. There is no Slayer of Kamsa! It is a product of your fevered imagination. You were in the grip of demoniac forces all these years and they worked their will through you. But I have released you from their grip. You have been exorcised by Bahuka and his powerful ayurveda. The results are there for all to see.'

Jarasandha reached the bottom of the dais and gestured at Kamsa, showing him off to the court. 'What was once monstrous and bestial is a man once more. Celebrate your return to humanity, Kamsa! Once I have fulfilled my promise to your late pitr and completed my work here, I shall leave Mathura to continue my imperial expansions and consolidation. As it is, I am neglecting my own empire to aid my friends, the Yadava nations here. I am an outsider and will soon be gone. You, however, are a son of this nation, a lord of this great court, master of the Yadus. You are the rightful heir to the Andhaka throne and a potential ruler of all the Yadava kingdoms. History is yours for the making. Give up these foolish delusions, these fruitless quests for this mythical Slayer. There is no Slayer! The people desire a deliverer, that is true. They are weary of the constant rebellions and uprisings by various Yadava factions. It is time to breathe life back to and complete the great initiative to which your father devoted his last years before his unfortunate demise, and to consolidate this great race into a united coalition. The very republic that Yadu envisaged! You can be king of that nation, Kamsa. You can be the deliverer they desire. Be a man, step up and grasp your future with both hands. The world awaits you.'

And in a gesture that Kamsa could never have expected or foreseen had he lived a thousand lifetimes, Jarasandha gripped Kamsa's shoulder tightly with an iron fist and pointed the lean fingers of the other towards the dais, at the Andhaka throne itself. 'Go on, my son. Seat yourself in your rightful place. Yesterday, you were cursed as a demon. Today, you are a man again. It is time you became the king you are destined to be.'

The roar of approval that met the end of Jarasandha's speech drowned out everything else for the next several minutes.

Jarasandha smiled at Kamsa, his brow lowered in that peculiar way he had of looking down while looking up at the same time; between his slightly parted lips, the tip of a divided tongue flickered and snapped as tautly as a whip.

Kamsa stared into the translucent grey eyes of his father-in-law and realized with awe and more than a little admiration that he had just been outwitted brilliantly by the cleverest politician on earth.

He also realized that he had only two choices left now: to bow gracefully to Jarasandha, acknowledge him as the superior man and accept his magnanimous 'gift' of Kamsa's own throne and crown; or attack, attempt to kill Jarasandha, and most likely die in the attempt. He had only a split second to make the choice, but in a sense that had already been made the day he left Mathura in search of the man who would become his guru and his guide. The events of today and of the past several months were merely a seal of authority placed upon that choice he had made. A formalization. It was only his own seething rebelliousness that insisted he could still choose between the two options available to him: bow. Or die.

He bowed.

Kaand II

one

Yashoda admired each tiny well-oiled limb as she massaged it firmly but gently, pulling and exerting just the right amount of force needed to strengthen the baby's muscles without straining the tender flesh. Krishna giggled and squirmed as she massaged his belly and moved her hands up and down against his sides, and squealed uncontrollably when she touched his underarms.

Tickles you, does it? she thought, smiling. She had realized that there was no need to speak the words aloud, and that the bond between them went far deeper than words could express.

Yes, Maatr. But it also feels very nice. Please don't stop.

She smiled and continued.

Beside her, Gargamuni and his entourage of Brahmins continued the padapad recitation of the mantras appropriate to the occasion of the bathing ceremony. Around her were the women of the family. Rohini and Balarama were not present of course, for the pretence of the two boys being just friends rather than brothers had to be maintained. Just because Mathura had changed its political approach of late did not mean that everything was well again. The Usurper still sat upon the Andhaka throne. Word was that Jarasandha the Magadhan controlled Kamsa's every word, action and decree, and that he and his allies had some elaborate game plan that was yet to be revealed. The year of peace had lulled most of the aristocracy and nobility into believing that the worst was past, and being rich and powerful and therefore detached from the woes of the common people, they had formed alliances and bartered deals with the Magadhan and his demon dog in human form, as Kamsa was often called.

But the people continued to resist Mathura's overtures, and of all the Yadavas, the Vrishnis were the most stubborn. They could simply not forget the atrocities that Kamsa and his marauders had visited upon them and their fellow Yadava tribes and clans in the past decades, nor could they forgive those horrors. As far as they were concerned, there could be no real peace until Kamsa was removed and Ugrasena restored to the throne and, managed by Akrur in Vasudeva's name, the rebellion continued to grow secretly. Nanda supported the rebels covertly as best as he could, but was hampered by the knowledge that he harboured the Deliverer in his own house. As Yashoda had often reminded him, he could not afford to do anything that might draw attention to Gokul. As it is, he had been trying to convince her to go with him to Mathura and let Devaki and Vasudeva meet their sons, if only for a brief moment. She had been horrified by the very thought. To take their infant child into the lair of the beast itself? Never! What sacrifices had been made, what terrible slaughter unleashed, how many innocent babes butchered, all so this one child, the one she was now massaging so lovingly, could survive. How could they risk all that? Much as she understood the longing of a mother and father separated from their own flesh, she was not willing to risk Krishna's life in order to give them that pleasure.

If you do not will it, I shall not go, Maatr.

She almost laughed aloud. *Of course you shall not go, my impudent son. You have not yet learnt to walk! I don't expect you to go strolling off to Mathura on your own!*

His cherubic dark face, glistening with the massage oil, wrinkled briefly. He touched one chubby finger to his chin, considering seriously.

It is true I cannot walk yet in this form, Maatr. But I can always fly if I desire.

She turned him over briskly, setting him on her outstretched legs, and slapped him lightly on his buttocks. They jiggled.

'Whether you desire or not is not the question. I am your maatr and I forbid it expressly.'

Behind her, her sisters Dadhisara and Yasasvini glanced curiously at one another, wondering what Yashoda was up to. She heard Yasasvini lean over and whisper to Dadhisara, 'There she goes again, talking to Krishna.'

'As if he can hear her,' Dadhisara replied.

They giggled.

Yashoda smiled. If only she could enlighten her sisters about how wrong they were! But of course, none must know of the true identity of her beloved son. The moment word spread that the Slayer was in Yashoda-devi's house, the whole world would beat a pathway to her threshold.

Yes, Maatr, her child's voice replied sombrely in her head. *It shall be as you will. But you do understand that sooner or later, I shall have to go to Mathura.*

She sighed, her heart leaping inside her breast at the thought of this little bundle of life facing the demon of Mathura. *Not for a good many years yet, I pray. You must grow up to be a man before you face him.*

I do not mean my confrontation with Kams-mama. That is not due for a few more years. I mean going to meet Vasudeva-pitr and Devaki-maatr. I shall have to go soon, and Balarama shall also have to come with me.

She stopped massaging the tiny body. '*What?*' she said aloud. Hearing her voice rise above the litany of the Brahmins, she corrected herself. Continuing to massage his back and shoulders, she articulated the rest of her communication silently. *What do you mean, go soon? Why would you need to go to Mathura?*

For the same reason Nanda-pitr wishes us to go. To see Vasudeva-pitr and Devaki-maatr.

Yashoda glanced around, wishing she was alone with her child so that she could speak to him aloud instead of framing each word in her mind. It was difficult to control the outrush of emotions that flooded her mind along with the words this way, and she feared what she might communicate without meaning to by using this method. After all, he was but a babe.

Not just a babe, Maatr. I have a larger purpose here on prithviloka. You of all people must know that.

Yes, yes, of course, she responded. But her heart said, *No, no, no, never.*

Do not fret, Maatr. Remember, because of who I am, you need never fear any harm. Even while I am gone to Mathura, no one dare harm you in any way.

'Me?' she said. Then continued mentally: *It is not I who fear I might come to harm, my little gopa! It is* you *I am concerned about. You as well as your brother Balarama.*

He chuckled. **Balarama is quite capable of looking after himself as well as me, his kid brother. After all, he is Shesha, you know.**

She had no idea what he meant. Shesha? Wasn't that the great serpent in the ocean of milk upon which sat some great deva ... was it Vishnu?

Krishna gurgled and burped noisily beneath her working hands. And he followed it up with a sharp exudation that made her wrinkle her nose. She slapped his oiled bottoms again, affectionately. *Don't get cheeky with me, little fellow. You may be the Slayer of Kamsa, but you're still my little Krishna.*

Yes, Maatr, he said in a suspiciously serious tone.

The ceremony ended soon after, and Yashoda had to see to the rest of the ritual formalities. Her sisters told her to lay Krishna down and assured her that they would watch over him. She didn't want to put the babe down in the open because the sun was too strong, and so decided to place him with his blanket and toys beneath an un-yoked uks cart that was resting nearby. She positioned him securely in the shadow of the cart and surrounded him with cushions on all sides so that he would not roll over and bang his head or injure himself in any way. Fortunately, he had not begun to sit up yet, so there was no question of him hitting the underside of the cart. She tucked him in firmly so that he would not kick out and hurt his feet on the wagon wheels. The cart was loaded down with metal pots containing various liquid items of nourishment needed for the feast, and its wheels had been chocked with stones to prevent it from budging even an inch. So she didn't have to worry about the vehicle moving while Krishna was under it. She finished tucking him in and kissed him gently on the cheek.

Too tight, he complained. But his voice was already sleepy.

'Tight is safe,' she said, leaning over and kissing him on his forehead. He smelt of oil and milk and something else that she could not put a name to – a smell he always had and which she had never smelt on any babe before. Nobody was around just then, and so she could speak to him normally. 'I will be right here in this field. I will check on you at all times. Don't worry. And don't go anywhere.'

I might decide to take a walk to Mathura, he replied cheekily.

'I doubt that very much,' she said, looking at him solemnly. 'You haven't had your late morning feed of milk yet.'

He chuckled sleepily, then sighed, yawned big and wide, and turned his head away, into the cosy darkness of the underside of the cart.

She smiled and left him.

It was a while later, when she was busy ensuring that every last Brahmin, guest and relative had been fed full to bursting, that she heard the sound. It was customary among Yadavas to not simply feed their guests on formal occasions but to ensure that they were incapable of ingesting a single morsel more or taking a single sip of water for several hours. Nobody knew how this tradition had begun, but it had its origins in some ancient puranic tale of the pitrs, the mythic ancestors about whom there always seemed to be an appropriate story to illustrate every moral and regale every gathering. No doubt some ancient pitr had once eaten his fill at a ceremonial feast, but not *more* than his fill, and not long after, on his way home, he had met a friend on the road and that friend had invited him to come to his home to celebrate some occasion. And when he had done so, and returned home much later that same day or night, his wife or brother or mother or uncle had asked him if he had eaten yet and he had replied, 'Yes, twice, in fact. Once at so-and-so's feast, the second time at such-and-such's celebration.' And the wife (or brother, mother, uncle, etc.) had thought, *So-and-so's feast can't have been very good if he was still hungry enough to eat afterwards!* And soon, word got around that so-and-so's feast hadn't been enough to fill that pitr's belly, so much so that he had to go to a friend's house later to satiate his hunger. And of course, the story had then grown swiftly into an entire legend about how little food there was at so-and-so's feast and how people went home hungry and had to knock at their friends' doors to ask to be fed since they hadn't prepared any food at home that day on account of the feast. And over time, nobody would deign it wise to attend a feast at so-and-so's place, of course!

Whatever the reason, the fact was that Yadavas had to be fed to the gills. It was even considered preferable that a guest throw up from overindulgence – provided that he be fed yet again before leaving!

Yashoda was handing out the sweet dish herself to make sure that every Brahmin got more than enough. She knew how much Brahmins loved their sweets, and had prepared the ones to be served at the feast herself. They were sweet potatoes, cooked in her special preparation designed to bring out the flavour of the yam, soften the tender flesh, and enhance the sweetness. As each Brahmin unwrapped his portion of sweet potato from its enclosing banana leaf and popped it in his mouth, she had the satisfaction of seeing his face alter dramatically in response. She glanced down the row and saw a whole range of similar expressions as each purohit rolled his eyes and head as he mashed the delectable sweet between his palate and tongue. Even her own mouth watered at the sight. As the maatr of the boy whose bathing ritual was being conducted, she had had to fast since the previous night. She would eat only after the last guest had departed after being fed to bursting.

It was then that she heard the sound. It resonated in the field like a loud THWACK!

For a moment, she mistook it for the sound of children playing the danda game. The one where they took a short, thick cudgel-like stick and a smaller piece of wood, laid the small piece on the ground and rapped it hard in such a way that it rose up in the air – and then they hit it sideways, sending it flying to the point of their choice. The aim was to hit the piece into a certain spot each time. It tended to be played mostly by boys, who seemed to love cracking and hitting sticks, and she had seen a group of them playing on the south end of the field. The thought that the sound might have something to do with her Krishna didn't even occur to her. But she did look up and marvel at the loudness of the sound. That must be a very big stick, or a very powerful hitter.

Then she remembered that some of the men had finished eating and they loved playing danda just as much as the boys. No doubt they had started a game of their own and someone had just cracked the thickest danda in half, causing that sound. She saw her sisters and friends looking around quizzically too. Nobody seemed to know what had caused the loud report, but none seemed too worried either. They went back to doing what they were doing.

Eager to be done and to eat her own food, Yashoda bent to place another portion of sweet potato upon the last purohit's banana-leaf plate. Krishna would awaken any time and want to be fed, if he wasn't already awake, that is. And it would be nice if she could eat before feeding him. It enriched the milk, she knew.

A moment later, another sound echoed across the field. This one was even louder than the first, and wholly different. Not merely wood striking wood, but a distinctly metallic thud, as if some firm metal object was being crumpled under a great impact. Then a screaming, screeching metallic sound as if the same metal object were being struck again and again, on an anvil. There were other sounds mingled in this as well, wet sounds, wooden cracking sounds and a third kind of noise that she could not easily decipher, but which made her heart race and her eyes widen.

Everyone was looking around, alert and afraid. The noise was loud enough to be heard through the length and breadth of the field, and hundreds of people had stopped whatever they had been doing to look in the direction ... of the south field!

That's where I left my Krishna!

And with that thought, Yashoda needed to hear no further sounds, noises or urging.

She dropped the metal platter of sweet potatoes, letting the precious sweets tumble into the dirt and not caring, and raced towards the place where she had left her sleeping son.

two

Yashoda reached the south end of the field to find a great commotion. Most of the guests who had finished eating were lounging about there, sitting around in groups and talking, some singing folk songs, others playing games, a few flirting and romancing in the time-honoured way of light-hearted Yadavas. When she came running from the north end, the crowd had taken to its feet and was peering in the direction of the sound – *The place where I left my baby under the cart!* – and the invitees to the feast were chattering anxiously amongst themselves as if some calamity had befallen.

She had to push her way through the crowd, requesting to be let through. 'Please let me pass; my Krishna is there.'

But as the crowd grew denser and the babble louder, she had to resort to shouting, '*Let me through, please!*'

Once the gathering saw that it was Yashoda-devi, the hostess herself, it parted at once, but it still took several agonizing moments for her to pass through the throng, moments during which all sorts of awful images flashed through her mind. Her anxiety made her take in her breath at a faster rate and she felt herself growing light-headed with fear.

Finally, she broke through and stumbled into the open patch at the southern end of the field. The crowd had formed a rough semicircle there, as if held back behind an invisible line. Her sisters were among the crowd, looking as dazed as everyone else.

Yashoda looked around and saw that there was a reason why they were reluctant to go beyond that point. There were things lying around in the way: pieces of wood, shattered blocks, what looked like a mangled piece of metal, and other odd objects that she gradually began to associate as parts of what had once been …

'*The cart!*' she shrieked, clapping her hands to her cheeks.

She looked at the spot where she had left Krishna, where the uks cart had been stationed, near the sala tree.

There was no cart there any more.

She ran the last few yards, passing the unmistakeable remains of the cart's axle, apparently shattered to fragments, two half-broken wheels, and other assorted debris.

In the midst of the wreckage, scattered about were the garments in which she had wrapped Krishna and tucked him in so carefully.

Of Krishna himself, there was no sight at all.

Her heart threatened to freeze with fear.

Her first and only thought was that Kamsa or his demoniacal minions had somehow found her boy – had learnt that one newborn boy who had begun life that fateful night of the prophecy had somehow escaped the spear points of his soldiers – and he or his child-murdering men had come and killed her baby. She didn't understand how the cart had been shattered, or why; only that such destruction could only be the work of a malevolent agent. And who else would attack a child so viciously but the Childslayer himself? Yes, it had to have been Kamsa! And from the appearance of the debris strewn all around her and Krishna's garments, it was evident that he had slain her beloved infant.

'No!' she whispered. 'Not my baby. Please, Lord!'

Maatr.

The single word was a drop of water into a calm pool. It rippled in her consciousness, spreading outwards. As it spread, it quenched the fires of fear and doubt and anger that were brewing in her mind and senses, and replaced those fiery emotions with soothing calm assurance. But she was very troubled and resisted.

I am well. Why do you cry? You have no reason to fear for my well-being. Calm thyself.

'Krishna?' she cried out, in her mind as well as with her lips. 'Where are you, my son? Show yourself!'

Here, Maatr.

She spun around. The watching crowd stepped back, uncertain of what was possessing Yashoda in this moment of anguish. The people had leapt to the same inevitable conclusion: that somehow the agents of Kamsa had found the infant and had killed him in some demoniacal fashion. They didn't need to know or guess at anything further – Kamsa's men had killed children regardless of their birthdate at times, and though the killings had ceased a while ago, nobody trusted the apparent period of peace that had followed the season of mayhem and slaughter. Kamsa was capable of anything.

'Where?' she all but screamed. 'I cannot see you, my son!'

As she uttered this, she saw the expressions on the faces of the watching guests who were staring at her with a mixture of pity, sorrow and sympathy. Several even offered their hands to her, asking her to come to them, speaking words of solace for her loss.

'No, you don't understand,' she said in agitation, 'my Krishna is fine. I just have to find him. Where are you, my son! Show yourself!'

At this, the looks of sympathy intensified and several in the gathering began shaking their heads and clicking their tongues in commiseration. She saw her sisters, mother and friends all approaching, concern writ large on their faces. And off to the other side, she glimpsed Nanda's head bobbing as he made his way through the crowd, his brothers and other associates following him as well.

Krishna giggled. The sound echoed in Yashoda's ears, as clear as a brass temple bell. But she still could not spot him anywhere. There was nothing but debris to be seen for several dozen yards in every direction.

'Krishna! Stop teasing me and show yourself this very minute!' she said sternly, not caring that everyone could hear her. She was growing desperate with anxiety.

I am right here, in front of you, Maatr, keep walking this way ...

'Here?' she asked, moving carefully through the bits and pieces of the cart and its contents lying around, stepping with extra caution as she scoured every square inch. She could see no sign of her boy.

A little to your right, further this way, now turn partly to your left. Yes, look down now ... no, under the big cross-shaped piece of wood stuck in the ground. Yes, Maatr. Can you see me now?

She knelt down on the ground which was churned up a bit in that area as if worked over unevenly by a plough. A ragged block of wood and metal was embedded in the ground. She realized that it was part of the cart's axle, broken off by some great impact and stuck in the ground at a tilt. She could not imagine what force could have shattered something that sturdy, for she knew something about carts and ploughs herself, but she did not care about that just now. It was what lay *behind* it that concerned her. She peered carefully over the jagged metal-and-wood shard sticking out of the ground and her heart leapt with joy as she saw the familiar cherubic face of her baby.

'Krishna!'

He was sitting on a remnant of the blanket in which she had wrapped him, playing with a toy cart with a plough fixed behind it. Studying the way the plough churned up the ground with rapt interest, the infant was bending over and pushing it back and forth in the ground. Nanda had made the toy with his own hands; he had a talent for whittling wood and making toys and decorative objects. Their house was filled with such curiosities, some quite elaborate and ingenious.

Yashoda scooped her baby in her arms, clenching him to her breast tightly enough to stop her own breath.

Maatr! You spoiled the field I was ploughing!

Tears spilled copiously from her eyes as she hugged and kissed and stroked and caressed her child, reassuring herself that he was indeed alive and well. She could not believe it, so frightening the sight of the strewn debris had been, and so certain had she been that something awful had happened to him.

Do not cry, Maatr. It makes me feel like crying as well. And if I cry, it will bring rain and spoil your lovely feast.

She almost laughed out loud. Spoil the feast? She didn't care about the feast. It was only a ritual ceremonial feeding to celebrate his bathing ceremony. It was *he* that she cared about. 'You, and only you, my beloved son!'

I understand, Maatr. But you are crushing me! Kindly let go of me and put me down.

She heard sounds and voices behind her, approaching cautiously. Nanda's voice was among them. She could hear the puzzlement in his tone.

'What happened here, my little Shyam-rang? How was the cart broken? Did someone come and do this? Did they have elephants with them?'

Elephants? Ah, I would like to have elephants to play with, Maatr. May I? Please say yes!

'Krishna, answer my question. How did all this destruction happen? What was that terrible cracking sound I heard earlier?'

I like elephants, Maatr. They remind me of Vakratunda. I wish I could see Vakratunda as well. I recall visiting him to bless him – at his naming ceremony on Mount Kailasa and on other such occasions. I could not frolic with him as it would seem unseemly at my age. But he would make a fine playmate for me now! I wish I could summon him here.

'Krishna! Answer me!'

It is nothing, really. The cart broke, that's all. I didn't mean for it to break. But it did.

Yashoda heard Nanda's voice say from close by: 'Oh, thank the devas, he is alive and well! It is a miracle.'

'But how did it break, Krishna? *Who* broke it?'

If I tell you who did it, Maatr, will you be cross with me?

'No, my baby, I just want to know who did this to you. Was it Kamsa and his men?'

Kams-mama? No, he has nothing to do with this! It was just me, Maatr. I kicked the cart.

'You?' She stared at the child, holding him a little away from her body so she could see him better.

Yes, Maatr. I only meant to push it away a little, that's all. But it cracked and broke and everything started to fall down and all those pots would have spilled on me and I didn't want that, so the second time I kicked it a little harder to push the whole thing away, and everything went flying. I didn't mean to destroy anything, Maatr. I just wanted a little more space so I could sit up to play with my little plough-cart.

Unable to take in the full import of what he was saying, she blinked rapidly. 'I don't understand. How could *you* have broken the whole cart? That's impossible!'

Behind her, she heard Nanda speak gently: 'Yashoda, my dearest, is he quite well, our little Krishna?'

'Yes, he is, praise be to Devi,' she said, turning to glance over her shoulder.

I didn't mean to break it, Maatr. Please don't be upset with me.

'I'm not upset, Son,' she said, then remembered that Nanda was within hearing range, as were his companions. *I just can't understand it. Surely your little foot could not have kicked over the whole cart and shattered it to bits in this manner?*

I just wanted to sit up, that's all! I wanted to sit up and play with my little plough. I like ploughing. Some day I shall do it with a big plough as Pitr does.

So you shall. But I still cannot understand how you broke the big cart. Are you sure that was all that happened? You can tell me the truth, my son.

I only tell you the truth, Maatr. What else would I tell you?

'Yashoda?' Nanda asked again, concern audible in his voice. 'What has happened here? Has there been an attempt on Krishna's life? Or was it a strike of lightning?'

Can you explain it to your father as well? So he can know from your own mind what happened?

I wish I could, Maatr. But it would not be wise of me to talk to Pitr the way I do to you. It would make him vulnerable if he encounters certain demons who may be able to read his mind.

She balked at the thought of Nanda encountering mind-reading demons, but put her fears aside to be dealt with later. *And you are sure this is exactly what happened?*

Yes, Maatr. There was a trace of weariness in the child's tone now.

She turned to face Nanda. He looked more concerned than she had seen him in a long time. Behind him, their anxious and curious relatives and friends as well as the larger crowd of other guests looked on expectantly, pointing happily at little Krishna in her arms even as they muttered and whispered amongst themselves.

'He is well,' she said. 'There is nothing to fear. I admit I was anxious too. But it was a false alarm. Our son is quite safe and hale and hearty.'

Nanda sighed audibly. He turned and raised both hands to the crowd: '*He is well!*'

A great murmur of relief rippled across the guests. As the news reached the ones at the far end, a smattering of applause and cries of commiseration broke out, breaking the mood of tension that had engulfed them.

Nanda turned back to Yashoda. 'What happened here? Was it an elephant in masti?'

'We have no elephants in this part of the country, Nanda. You know that,' she said. 'No, it was simply our little Krishna. He kicked out too hard and broke the cart. That is all.'

Nanda looked at her for a long moment, the muscles on his face flickering as they tried to summon up the right expression. 'It was lightning then, was it? It isn't altogether unheard-of, after all, for lightning to strike down unexpectedly at times.' He glanced up at the clear azure sky. 'Although it isn't the monsoon season and there isn't a cloud in sight …'

She smiled, shaking her head gently. 'No, dear husband. As I said earlier, it was just our little Krishna.'

Nanda stared at her again. Then he looked around at the wreckage, at the large block of jaggedly splintered wood embedded in the ground. 'I don't understand,' he said. 'Is this a jest of some sort? How could our baby son break a whole cart laden with heavy metal vessels? It is simply not possible!'

She sighed. *What do I do? He does not believe me.*

There is nothing you can do, Maatr. Such things must be taken on faith alone. Besides, you are telling the truth. Nothing else matters.

If only it were that simple, my son. Aloud she said: 'That is what happened. Our son is quite extraordinary, you know. He possesses abilities beyond his age.'

Nanda smiled quizzically. 'Beyond his *age*? At what age does any human – man, woman or child – possess the strength to demolish a laden uks cart with a single kick? Not even after a hundred years of training and exercise, I would say!'

'Yet he did, my beloved. Please, just accept it and let us continue our lives.'

Nanda shook his head gently. 'Why are you insisting on this absurd explanation, Yashode? You were not here when the incident occurred. You cannot possibly know what happened!'

'I know, because Krishna told me.'

Now he stared at her with renewed surprise. 'He *told* you? Yashoda, our son cannot sit up or stand, let alone speak whole words!'

'He communicates with me through the mind. He projects his thoughts into my mind where only I can hear his voice. I can do the same with him.'

Nanda laughed. Then he shook his head and sighed again. 'You have been fasting and working too hard, my love. Come, be seated and rest a while.'

Is Pitr upset with me for breaking the cart? I don't want him to be upset with me.

Pitr is merely ... confused, she tried to explain. *He cannot understand how the cart could have been broken by a human child as young as you.*

Is that all? I can remedy that quite easily.

She frowned. *How—?* then stopped.

Around her, the field exploded with cries of consternation, shock, disbelief and other sundry expressions of amazement.

'Devas protect us!' Nanda exclaimed, staring at something behind Yashoda.

In her arms, Krishna giggled happily, bringing his chubby palms together.

There! Is that better? I made it all well again. Now Pitr and you can be happy again!

Yashoda turned and looked.

All the debris strewn across the field had vanished. From everyone's reaction, she guessed that it had all disappeared in the wink of an eye – Krishna's eye!

Not a trace remained of the scattered pieces of broken wood and mangled metal.

Instead, the uks cart with its entire load of metal vessels had been reassembled exactly as it had been before, untouched, unbroken. Perfectly whole.

It was as if the cart had never been broken.

See? I put it back the way it was. Are you happy now, Maatr? I want you and Pitr to always be happy!

And little Krishna grabbed her sari tight, drooling all over her in his apparent attempt to raise himself and kiss his mother.

Please, Maatr. Can I have my milk now? I'm very very hungry! Playing is such thirsty work.

three

Kamsa was in a state of shocked bemusement. Shocked because he could not begin to fathom the machinations of Jarasandha's politicking – his mind was not built to comprehend such things. Bemused since he didn't know what to expect next from his father-in-law. The confrontation in the sabha hall and Jarasandha's masterful handling of the event had turned his head around and spun it like a top until his entire world view was blurry.

The time leaps he experienced further addled his brain. He never knew if he would be able to complete a conversation or finish eating a mouthful of food before he was overtaken by the lack of consciousness. The irregular pattern confused him even more. Sometimes he lost months, and just a week or three on other occasions. But some leaps were only a few minutes or even a few hours long, leaving him in a constant state of disorientation and readjustment. He went through his days feeling as if he had not slept or eaten or rested properly, meeting palace staff who greeted him with condescending familiarity while he had no recollection of ever having met them before. Even the stable dogs who had always feared and respected him now barked and bared their teeth to threaten him; one even attacked him viciously, mauling his arm as the watching guards only looked on and laughed as he cried out for them to put the damn beast down.

Within hours of the end of the sabha session in which Jarasandha had so graciously granted Kamsa his own throne back, the sham of that show had been obvious. The real power was still wielded by Jarasandha and his cronies, and Kamsa was barely tolerated as the pale silhouette of a king. Through Chief Minister Pralamba, and using Captain Pradyota to maintain law and order, it was Bahuka who ran the day-to-day affairs of the kingdom now. There was an elaborate hierarchy filled entirely by new faces loyal only to Jarasandha. And Bahuka was little more than a spare tongue and pair of hands for Jarasandha.

The only faint flicker of hope was the public announcement by the 'god emperor' that he would be departing shortly, coupled with the messages that arrived each day, usually requiring Jarasandha's urgent attention. Kamsa realized that sooner or later, Jarasandha would have to leave Mathura to join his armies and continue his campaign or risk losing the valuable ground he had gained. But until such time, each day was sheer agony to Kamsa. The manner in which the Magadhan king wilfully excluded Kamsa from any discussion or decision of importance, while continuing to be patronizing and demonstrating his fatherly affections was infuriating.

Nights and nights he lay awake on his silken sheets, ripping them apart with frustration as he tried to think of a way out of his predicament. How had he lost so much power so quickly? Or perhaps he had never had the power. Perhaps he had always been just Jarasandha's stooge, but hadn't realized it. He had heard of puppet kings and child-emperors whose kingdoms were actually run by shrewd ministers, mothers or preceptors. But a father-in-law? Well, why not. One backroom kingmaker was as likely as any other.

What truly maddened him was his lack of power.

Rather than tolerate this treatment, the old Kamsa would have simply torn apart buildings, even taken on the whole Hijra Fauj, or Jarasandha's entire army. But *this* Kamsa couldn't even face Bahuka or Agha or any one of Jarasandha's lieutenants or allies, let alone risk incurring the wrath of Jarasandha himself in an all-out physical confrontation.

He had no friends or supporters who could foment and stoke a revolt or coup of some kind either. His decade of debauchery and butchery had made him the most reviled ruler of Mathura – and the most disregarded now. Imprisoning his father and mother, placing his sister and her husband under house arrest, murdering their first seven children and slaughtering countless other infants in the kingdom, and making even his most trusted aides and soldiers kill their own newborns had rendered his alienation complete. His campaign against the Slayer had resulted in his trusting nobody and allowing no one to come close to him. His desperate quest to prevent the birth of the Slayer had cost him everything.

And ultimately, as he fretted and fumed and tossed and turned, one thought came to him over and over again: the Slayer was the one responsible for his plight.

If not for the prophecy, he would have ruled Mathura with an iron hand, had a great time indulging each of his lusts as well as his love of violence, and eventually won the grudging and fearful respect of the Yadavas. A dictator was better befriended than antagonized; even he knew that much about politics. And he would have made a great dictator.

In due course, once the Yadavas were united and in his grasp, he would have allied openly with Jarasandha and aided his father-in-law in his campaign of conquest. Together, they could have ravaged not just the subcontinent but other parts of the world as well. If Jarasandha sought to be 'god emperor', Kamsa could certainly have been 'demi-god emperor' alongside him. Like father-in-law, like son-in-law.

But that damned prophecy had forced him to change his list of priorities.

Because of his fear of the Slayer – a fear that wretched Narada had instilled in his heart – he had devoted most of his reign to the persecution of his sister and bhraatr-in-law and their supporters, leaving him with little time for or awareness of anything else. And what had he accomplished in the end? Nothing! The Slayer had still been born and was out there somewhere. Jarasandha could say anything he pleased, but Kamsa knew the Slayer existed, was real, and was growing in strength and manhood. One day he would be strong enough and powerful enough to come and destroy Kamsa. And in this all-too-pitiful mortal state, Kamsa would not stand a chance of survival.

At times, he even wondered whether Jarasandha had wanted the Slayer to be born, and to escape unharmed. Then he dismissed that possibility as absurd. Whatever else Jarasandha might be, he was no fool.

The Slayer was responsible for everything. Kamsa's decline had begun the very day he had been born. He was also the Deliverer. That meant he would champion the rights of the people. And if the people did not want Kamsa to rule them, they desired Jarasandha even less. Kamsa knew he was not very shrewd or politic, but of this much he was certain: the Slayer was as much Jarasandha's enemy as he was Kamsa's nemesis. And once he was done with Kamsa, he would go after Jarasandha. And if he was powerful enough to escape Kamsa even while yet a newborn, how much more powerful would he be once fully grown?

Kamsa did not know how long he had before the Slayer came for him. But he was certain it would not be very long.

He had to act soon. Somehow, he had to find and assassinate the Slayer while he was still an infant, before he gained his full power.

But how? He had no power himself!

There is a way. But it shall require Jarasandha's assistance.

Kamsa started from his bed. 'Who's that?'

A shadowy figure moved through his darkened chamber. He could see it only by the way it cut the faint moonlight that came in through the verandah, but he could not see the person.

It is I, Narada.

'You!' He almost lunged across the chamber in anger. 'You ruined my life! Your prophecy—'

—saved your life. Had I not forewarned you of the coming of the Slayer, you would have been destroyed by now.

Kamsa had reached for a weapon. He had lost confidence to such an extent that he no longer bothered with a sword or even a dagger. Now, as his fear mounted, he found nothing on the bed or chair and had to grope around on the floor. In the darkness, he could find only a long wooden object of some kind. He wielded it but did not attack.

'What do you mean, *would have been* destroyed? Your prophecy is the reason why I am in this state! Stopping the Slayer became my obsession, costing me my throne, my powers, everything. Now I'm little more than Jarasandha the Magadhan's pawn!'

You are wrong. Had you not been so fierce in your efforts those many years, the Slayer would have been able to slay you the very day he was born. You have no reckoning of his powers.

Kamsa rubbed his eyes, trying to see in the darkness. All he could make out was a faint vertical shadow against the patch of indigo blue sky visible outside the verandah. 'Really?' he asked.

Have no doubt about it. I am a seer of the future and the past, I can track the movements of the great Samay Chakra itself, the primordial Wheel of Time. Everything you did served a purpose.

'But the Slayer escaped anyway!' Kamsa cried. 'He is out there ... *somewhere*! Waiting to kill me.'

That is why you must act now to stop him.

Kamsa put down the length of wood which appeared to be a broom of some kind, left under his bed by the cleaners. 'How?' he asked miserably, sitting on his bed again. 'I have no powers left. I cannot even expand myself any more. And this wretched loss of time I experience ... even if I plan to do something, I can never be sure of seeing it through to the end. My life is a living hell!' He buried his face in his hands, on the verge of tears.

It is all Jarasandha's doing.

Kamsa jerked his head up. 'What?'

He has a special compound that his henchman Bahuka puts in your food and drink. It causes the effects of which you speak.

Kamsa got to his feet, his hands clenched into fists, fingernails digging into his palms hard enough to draw blood. 'I WILL KILL HIM!'

That is quite impossible. Jarasandha is beyond your ability to kill. Even the Slayer himself could not harm him if he desired. But I can show you how to regain your powers and control of your life once again.

Kamsa thought about this briefly. There was something peculiar about the brahmarishi's offer. 'Why?' he asked at last, tilting his head suspiciously. 'Why do you assist me thus? What possible purpose does it serve you? What do you desire from all this?'

That is not important. All that matters is that I help you. And I do not see anyone else willing or able to do that at the moment. Am I correct?

Kamsa's shoulders slumped. 'No,' he said miserably.

Then sit quietly and listen while I instruct you.

Kamsa sat. And listened.

four

Putana frowned when she received the message brought by an old stable hand who had been in service to the throne since the days of Ugrasena's youth. She nodded brusquely at him, acknowledging the message, but the old Kshatriya still remained standing, ramrod straight despite his frail form and corona of white hair.

'What are you waiting for?' she asked sharply. She knew that the Yadavas, though wise enough not to say so openly, resented her and others who served Jarasandha. She had seen the way some of the men looked at her in passing, and the women too.

The old syce's eyes were dark but clear – a young man's eyes in an old man's face. The man within that grizzled face had no fear of her or of her husband's position. She respected that. She was weary of being kowtowed to and bowed to only because she was the spouse of Pradyota, captain of the famed Mathura Guard. This was the first man she had encountered this closely since arriving in Mathura who looked at her as Putana, a *person*, not someone's wife or daughter or sister.

'I was told to await a reply,' he answered. There was no insolence or affront in his tone; nor any humility or obeisance.

She examined him sceptically. He did not flinch or back down, merely stood and watched her, waiting. She suspected he would wait thus for the rest of the day if required. She grudgingly admitted to herself that this was the kind of Yadavas she had heard of in the old legends and war poems. This man had been a warrior once – the fact was writ large in his every action and word, and also in the silences when he did not act or speak a word. He had stared danger in the face countless times and learnt the essential fact of life: death comes. One can fight it, one may resist it, one could amass skill and art and weaponry and defences, but eventually it comes and takes you. The day you understand and accept that fact, everything becomes clear. The world makes perfect sense. We live, we fight, we die. Everything else we do is just part of passing the time. What was that word the Yadavas liked to use? Leela. Play. Everything else was just leela.

'What is your name?'

The man was silent a moment, gaze locked on her. 'Yadu,' he said.

She raised an eyebrow. 'Like the ancestor?'

He did not reply.

'The great progenitor of the Yadava race? The pitr? Forebear of your entire race?'

He said nothing.

She was about to reprimand him for his insolence, then realized there was no need for him to speak – her question had been rhetorical. There could hardly be any doubt that Yadu was the name of the forebear of the Yadava race. It was no different from saying 'Brahma? Oh, like the four-faced deva?' One did not need to speak to confirm it. She knew his kind. They were accustomed to facing real threat, real danger, the kind that slithered and crawled and flew and ate man-flesh. They were not intimidated by mere mortal threats.

'Did you fight in the Last Asura Wars?' she asked.

He almost smiled. 'I would have to be centuries old if I had.'

She shrugged. She had met men and women who were centuries old, had heard of rishis who were millennia old. 'I asked you a question.'

He smiled openly now, and let the smile stay on his face as his only response – the smile of a boy who was asked whether he was a boy.

She sighed, shook her head and waved a hand dismissively. 'Tell your master I shall attend to his request when I am able.'

He remained standing. 'He desired to know a specific day and time.'

She frowned. In most other men, she would have deemed this insubordination. Pradyota might not be slaughtering Yadavas left, right and centre but he did not run a loose ship either. But she was not Pradyota's wife to this man, or to his master. Merely Putana for both. To call her husband's rank and power down on him would reduce her to the position of Pradyota's wife again. She would deal with this man on her own terms.

'Tell him I shall come to his chambers. Tonight at moonrise.'

He turned and began to walk away without another word, without so much as a by-your-leave-lady. Then again, she had already dismissed him.

She watched him walk across the courtyard, past a group of Mohini warriors, saw the subtle way his walk grew shuffling, his posture bowed and bent. His dishevelled appearance and ragged garb all served to give him the appearance of a servant, in charge of some nameless menial task. None of the Hijras so much as graced him with a first glance, let alone a second look. Yet she suspected that were he to face them in combat, he would do more damage than they would expect, let alone believe. Even at this great age.

She shook her head, grinning to herself. As long as Mathura still had Yadavas like that around, it would remain a formidable force in the Arya world.

The moon was well risen and halfway across the night sky when she made her way to the annexe of the prince's palace. From the lights still glowing in the residential complex of the main place and the fact that Pradyota had not yet returned home, she knew that Jarasandha was still sitting with his flunkeys. There had been a time when Pradyota had been far more than a mere tool of another man; he had desired a command of his own, to be a landowner, and to rule and live free. It was one of the things that had attracted Putana to him at the time. Now he thought the earth and sky and sun and moon of Jarasandha, and all thoughts of his own ambitions had been long forgotten. She had tired of even discussing it with him. There was no point any more.

She paused outside the high wall. No lights gleamed or flickered on the top floor of Kamsa's annexe. The sentries who ought to be on duty were nowhere to be seen; there were no guards patrolling the grounds either. She frowned. She was aware of the change in Kamsa's power and stature since Bahuka and his entourage had arrived – which entourage included Pradyota and herself; she knew that Kamsa was considered an impotent figurehead now, merely the limp hand that held the royal seal that sanctioned Jarasandha's decisions and orders, but she had not thought he was this neglected. To leave a ruler's private quarters thus unguarded – this was beyond negligence. But she knew that Jarasandha did not make mistakes of this nature. If he had left Kamsa unguarded, it was because he genuinely wished him dead. And what better way to have it done than by one of his own disgruntled or disaffected citizens! If Kamsa had not yet faced any assassination attempts – or at least, no successful ones – it was probably only because the very presence of the Magadhan and his legendary and fearful associates was enough to make any Mathuran want to keep his distance from the royal quarter of the city. But it was only a matter of time before Jarasandha left and Kamsa's many enemies realized that he was improperly guarded at night.

She wondered if Kamsa himself realized it. He must.

She was mildly disappointed. She had hoped to meet some resistance on the way in. It had been several weeks since her last active mission and she was itching to engage again. There was also something curiously thrilling about killing her own husband's guards, no doubt handpicked by him to work in this undoubtedly prestigious royal quarter.

But nobody challenged her, called out or barred her way as she scaled the wall easily, dropped over the side and strolled towards the darkened portal. Somewhere in the shadows along the wall, a feline meow rose plaintively and she saw the shadow of a tail flicking back and forth; but apart from that, nothing. And judging from the insolent way the cat called out and roved the grounds freely, there were no guard dogs around either.

She made her way up the stairs and sensed the emptiness of the house. Not a soul stirred, not a sound disturbed the night. This new annexe had been built far, far back from the main palace. It was almost an outhouse in terms of the overall layout. She knew that itself to be a sign of Jarasandha's obvious campaign of Kamsa's humiliation. But its spacious interiors were lavishly decorated and furnished – as befitted a prince regent, if not a king – far more lavishly than the official residence of the captain of the guards.

The bedchamber was larger than her whole house, for one thing. And the verandahs – surrounding the room on two sides in a semi-circular curve that belied the angular corner of the building – were huge. Gossamer drapes rose and fell with every gust of night wind. Moonlight was the only illumination, silvering anything that reflected, shone or glittered. The sleeping area was a dark morass of shadows. She could not tell if anyone sat or lay there, but she could smell him unmistakably. He was here all right.

'You said moonrise,' the voice said out of the darkness.

She shrugged, then realized he may not see the action in this shadowy dimness. 'I am here, am I not? What urgent business do you have that you needed to see me alone in your private chambers at night?' She put a foot out and leaned on one hip to emphasize the undertone of her query.

A shadow stirred among the many shadows around the bed. 'You chose the place and time, remember? I merely wished to speak with you. You could have elected to meet in the middle of the riding grounds at high noon. *You* chose here and now instead. *I* should be the one asking why.'

She smirked. 'So you're not as stupid as they say you are – and as you look.'

'I'm very stupid. But I learn something new every day.'

'What have you learnt about me?' she asked, challenging him.

The shadow moved again, and this time she was certain he was standing beside the bedpost closest to her. It was still several yards away, but she found herself wondering idly if he was clothed or if, in this warm weather, he slept without his garments on. He was an attractive man.

'I have a proposition for you.'

She smiled lazily, and using both hands, swept her hair off her face. 'There is nothing you have to offer that interests me.'

He was silent for a moment. The moonlight streaming through the open verandahs altered slightly. Her eyes had adjusted further to the darkness and she could now make out his silhouette. He was standing by the bed. She could not tell if he was clothed or not, but he was definitely not armed. There was a certain way he would have to stand if he was carrying a weapon, any weapon. She could tell.

'Yet you came,' he said after the pause.

She stroked her hair back, running her fingers through it. She had washed and scented it that afternoon, and it felt sensuous. 'I am bored. There is nothing for me to do here in your great city. I was happy for the diversion.'

'What I have to offer is a great diversion. If you choose to see it that way.'

She walked slowly across the chamber. The floor was cool to her bare feet. She stood in front of the verandah, enjoying the soft breeze that gusted in waves. Moonlight lit the lower half of her body. It made her fair skin seem milky white. She thought she could feel the moonlight and that it felt cool, but of course moonlight had no temperature.

'I think you are mistaking me for my husband,' she said, her back to him, to the whole chamber. '*He* is the captain of your guard. *He* is under your command, not *I*.'

'Your husband cannot accomplish the task I require done. Only you can.'

She glanced back over her shoulder, a smile of contemptuous irony playing on her lips. Who did this fellow think he was? What a fool! 'Flattery will get you nowhere. Certainly not *me* in *your* bed. Not if I do not choose to play along. I am my own woman. Ask anyone; they will tell you. Ask Pradyota.'

'What I seek is far more than the pleasures of your body, woman. Will you not understand that?'

Her smile widened. 'The great prince grows impatient. Will you have me bound in chains and whipped now? Decapitated? Thrown into your dungeon and tortured? What terrible punishment will you inflict on me if I turn down your proposition?'

'None. You are free to leave at any time. I will not ask you to aid me out of compulsion or force. I respect you too greatly for that.'

She turned around, surprised. '*Respect* me? You? The legendary marauder? The tyrant of Mathura? You are a legend, Kamsa! Your atrocities, brutalities, slaughter, massacres, genocides … even for one of Jarasandha's minions, you are quite extraordinary in your reputation for cruelty. What do you know of respecting women!'

'I respect a matrika. Especially a maha-matrika such as yourself.'

She fell silent. Of all the things she might have expected, this was not one of them. She looked around, alert, but there was no danger, no threat. Only Kamsa, alone. And she did not fear him. The only one she feared was Jarasandha and he was not there; she would have smelt him from a mile away – in fact, she *could* smell him, and he was not quite a mile away, but about half a mile away, in the main palace complex. This was not some ploy on his part. Whatever game Kamsa was playing, he was playing it alone.

'I don't know what you mean,' she said stiffly. *He's bluffing. He doesn't know anything, has somehow got hold of some lopsided rumour or idle piece of gossip and is pretending that it means more than it does.*

'I think you do,' said Kamsa.

He stepped away from the bed, emerging from the shadows, coming towards the light very slowly, one step every two or three sentences, like a wolf moving towards its prey.

'You are a maha-matrika,' he said. 'Specifically, you are the one named Chamunda. But you have also been known by other names. Vaimitra. Halebidu. Krittika. Shakti. Brahmi. Maheshwari. Kumari. Vaishnavi. Varah. Indrani. Kaki. Halima. Malini. Brhali. Palala. Vaimitra. Mahalakshmi. These are only some of your names, some of your forms. Some say you have ninety-two in all. Some say there are more. Sometimes you take the form of seven, aligned together: saptamatrika. Sometimes it is eight: ashtamatrika. Sometimes you pose as the wives of six of the saptarishis, the seven great seer-mages of Creation. Whatever your form or your number – you are many who may appear as one if you will it, or one who appears as many – the choice is yours, as are the forms you choose. On occasion you have been the womb-mother to Skanda, bearing him to life on behalf of his spirit-parents, Shiva and Parvati. Sometimes, you have been Skanda's adoptive mothers, hence your given title, matrika. Betimes, you have been cursed for posing as his mother. Betimes, you have begged him to adopt you as his mother. In one instance, you emerged from Skanda himself when he was struck by Indra's thunderbolt weapon, the omnipotent Vajra. You are the embodiment of the feminine force in its purest, most potent form, Shakta Mahadeva's Shakti. You have many gifts, many powers, many accomplishments. But the one thing you can never be is a mother. A maatr. The one thing you can never have is motherhood. The one feat you can never accomplish is birthing a child. That is why you are ironically called matrika or maatr – because it is the one thing you are not, have never been, and can never be. That is your curse, your identity, your destiny, your true nature. Do you deny any or all these things that I say?'

He had reached her now, and stopped a hand's breadth from where she stood. The swathe of moonlight had moved again, rising as the moon dipped towards the horizon as its time ended, and it illuminated him partly, his lower body. His thighs were muscular and powerful as sala tree trunks. Layered with slabs of muscle and taut sinew, his torso was bare and hairless. He was as attractive as she had thought, and then some. He reached out and touched her shoulder. It was a gentle touch. His fingers lingered there as his eyes looked deep into her own, asking for permission.

'What is it you want of me?' she asked, and heard the breathless excitement in her own voice. Gone was her posturing sarcasm, the preening irony, the caustic wit. She was intrigued, aroused, seething with something she had not felt for a very long time – long before Pradyota, long before any man, back when she had shunned the race of men entirely, and had been a creature of the forest and the earth, burning ghats and crossroads, springs and riverbanks, caves and mountain crags. Back when she had been simply maatr. When all women had been maatr and there were no other women but maatr.

He lowered his hand upon her chest. 'To begin with, I wish to see for myself if the legend is true.'

'Which one is that?' she whispered.

A cloud was passing over the moon. She could see the shape and body of the cloud eating away the patch of moonlight that illuminated him and the floor around him. It was moving quickly, consuming him with darkness.

'The legend that you carry a cache of poisoned milk within your body, the milk of the Churning itself. The Halahala.'

She swallowed. There was no way he could know about that. Someone far superior must have told him. But she would play along for now, partly to see what happened next, partly because she found the prince attractive. She had never felt this nervous, this excited, with any mortal man before. 'How will you know that for sure?'

The cloud began to cover him completely but in the last patch of moonlight, she could see the white of his teeth gleaming as he smiled. 'There is only one way for me to be sure.'

The cloud consumed the moon and the darkness consumed them both.

five

Once as a child, Kamsa had tasted a potion being mixed by the royal vaid. He did not know what it was until much later – it was snake venom in the process of being turned into anti-venom. A noxious concoction. He had deliberately consumed it to attract attention to himself. His father had been away at another of his endless campaigns of conquest, and had returned three days ago, only to sequester himself within the queen's private chambers. Kamsa did not know exactly what they were doing in there for so many days and nights, but he had an idea and it infuriated him.

He was even more incensed by the fact that his father had not yet come to him. He felt ignored, unwanted, fatherless. It brought back some ancient memory from his birth when he arrived into the mortal world aware of his true nature and of the true nature of the creature that had sired him upon his mother. Coupled with that awareness had been the knowledge, terrible in its immutability, that his true father would never spend a single moment with him for as long as he lived. He knew this because *that* father, the rakshasa who had actually fathered him, had told him so, taking cruel pleasure in imparting this heart-breaking piece of information to his just-birthed son.

'You will never see me again, mortal-spawn,' he had sneered derisively. 'Live your wretched life in the prison of your mortal flesh!' And he had roared away like the wind, leaving only a dust-whirl that spun in the empty courtyard, frightening horses and passing courtiers.

So when Ugrasena returned yet again from another battle, or war, or campaign of conquest, or whatever the hell he had gone for that time, and ignored his son yet again, Kamsa had decided that if even his mortal father did not acknowledge or care for him, he would show him. He would show him! He had seen the concoction the royal vaid, his father's own physician, had prepared to administer to some unfortunate courtier who had stepped on a cobra, and had picked it up and drunk it whole.

He remembered the unspeakable sensation to this day: the noxious mixture had the consistency of raw egg white and the taste of … a taste like nothing else he had ever tasted before or since to compare it to. And it had scorched his insides like pure rage distilled in liquid form. It had taken him a week to recover from its effects. But to everyone's surprise but his own, it had not killed him. The thrashing he received from his father when he was fully recovered almost did, though, because back then, Ugrasena was a very different man, a hard king for hard times, to quote his own favourite phrase. Kamsa had forgotten the thrashing – one of several he received in his childhood and youth, worsening in intensity and frequency as he grew, until his father's transmogrification into a proponent of ahimsa and non-aggressive governance, his new favourite phrases – but remembered drinking the snake anti-venom till today. And he remembered how it had made him feel after he drank it.

But this, this was far beyond that potency!

This was poison in its highest form possible. The Halahala itself, if the legend was true. And he had no reason to disbelieve the legend. Narada had no reason to lie, and even if he *had* lied, what was the worst that could happen? This fluid that Kamsa was now suckling and swallowing could be mere milk. In which case, he was merely being a good boy and would grow up to be big and strong some day!

He had expected it to be noxious, nauseating, toxic, like the cobra venom.

It was the very opposite – it was the sweetest, most intoxicatingly delectable thing he had ever consumed in liquid form.

And the instant it touched his lips, tongue and palate, its potency was undeniable. This was not mere milk. This was magic, sorcery, asura maya …

It was like drinking liquid power. And as it flowed through his body, he felt himself electrified and seared – as if struck by a bolt of lightning.

He cried out, tearing his mouth away and falling back on the floor. The cloud that had come across the moon, leaving them both in darkness, had passed on, and he could see Putana, still standing with her back to the verandah, silhouetted by moonlight.

He felt his senses warp and burn, his nerve endings flare and fire, his veins and arteries roar as the Halahala coursed through them, entering his heart, his lungs, his brain, his vital organs … He felt the divine poison infiltrate his very bones, his flesh, the cells of his body, felt it wash through him like a flash flood through a long-dried river bed. His consciousness exploded and altered, and the world around him blurred into nothingness as he transcended to a different plane of awareness.

Kamsa returned to his senses to find Putana standing in the verandah, leaning on the balustrade and staring at the horizon. The faint light of a new day was visible in the eastern sky, which told him that he had been lost to the world for the latter half of the night. He lifted himself on his arms and was surprised at the ease with which he was able to get to his feet. Not merely the ease born of well-exercised muscles and a magnificently chiselled body, but something else. He felt himself fuelled by the power of the Halahala as it continued to work its way within his body, catalysing enzymes and engendering new growth. This was not like his earlier power. He felt *more* powerful, yet in a completely different way.

He decided to try and expand himself and strained for several moments, without success. *Damn it!* He tried again. And again.

Putana heard his grunting and straining and turned. She came to the doorway and stood leaning against the jamb, watching him. A faint expression flickered around her mouth. Not quite a smile. Not quite anything.

'The compound Jarasandha has had you consume these past months will have altered your metabolism drastically,' she said. 'I doubt you will ever be able to regain your powers. Apart from everything else, he is a formidable vaid and knows his herbs and mixtures well. He once gave a pregnant woman—'

Kamsa raised a hand. 'Spare me.'

She shrugged. 'Also, the Halahala is a *poison*. You did know that before you chose to consume it, didn't you? And the quantity you consumed ...' She shook her head deprecatingly. 'I have killed entire tribes with less than half as much, simply by mixing it in the well from which they drew their drinking supply. They were wiped out within the day.'

He grunted in response, dropped to the floor and began doing push-ups. He was frustrated by his inability to expand and had energy to burn. Two hands proved too easy, so he switched to one, then to a fist, then to the tips of four fingers, three, two, and finally, he was pushing himself on the tip of a single finger, using the pressure caused by the awkward angle to work his abdominal and back muscles as well. He pushed past a hundred-count and kept going, and felt he could continue doing it all day and still not be tired.

She watched him speculatively. 'On the other hand ...'

He looked up at her from the floor. 'What?' Speaking seemed no harder than it would have had he been seated and talking. He continued pushing. 'Three hundred ...'

'The very fact that you are still alive and clearly not harmed by its effect ...'

'Yes? Three hundred and forty-four ... forty-five ... forty-six ...' He was moving faster now, switching to a different finger with every ten-count, barely an effort.

'Suggests that there is something else going on inside you that even I cannot wholly understand. What exactly was it that you desired when you called me here last night?'

'To consume the Halahala, regain my powers,' he said. Four hundred and two, three, four ... *Faster, now, must go faster ...*

She gestured at him. 'Looking at you, I'd say you've gained *something*.'

He grunted in frustration and pushed himself off the floor, hard. He rose up but instead of being pushed to a standing posture as he had desired, he found himself rising up, up, until his upper back and head struck the ceiling, ten yards overhead, and broke the plaster coating, sending a shower of white powder and chunks raining down. Returning to the ground, he landed on his feet as easily as if he had jumped just an inch. But the marble slab underfoot cracked with a deafening groan and the vibrations seemed to ripple through the entire chamber.

Putana looked around, then at the ceiling which now bore the shape of Kamsa's skull, then down at the cracked marble floor. 'Interesting. There has clearly been some effect.' She walked towards the entrance of the chamber. 'I shall be taking your leave now, Prince Kamsa. It has been an enlightening and interesting experience, which is more than I expected. And in case you fail to comprehend the subtext, that is a compliment I rarely pay men.'

And even though the distance between them was over fifteen yards, he was at her side and grasping her shoulder before one could blink an eye. She raised her eyebrows, reacting to his speed but not commenting on it.

'What does it mean, these changes occurring to me? Where will they end? Will I be restored to my former powers or …? Give me some answers before you go.'

She shrugged his hand off with surprising ease. He was startled by the power in her limbs, which was even greater than his newfound (and growing) strength. 'I don't know how you learnt the truth about me but I suspect you are not intelligent or worldly-wise enough to have gained such knowledge on your own. No man is. Therefore, it must have been imparted to you by someone of a far superior stature. A deva or a devi perhaps, for reasons best known to them. Or a saptarishi, for it is their job to know such things and they do have reasons to resent us.'

She looked at him closely, watching for his reaction. He was careful not to reveal any trace of an expression. Finally, she shrugged.

'It doesn't matter who it was, or what the purpose. I think it has to do with you rather than me. I was merely a tool serving your purpose in this matter. I've served that purpose. Now I shall take your leave.'

She began to move away.

He began to reach for her again but she said sharply, 'Touch me again and I'll break your hand. You may think you're strong but don't forget where that new strength came from!'

'I only wish to know more about my condition,' he said in as non-threatening a tone as he could manage. The old Kamsa would not have been able to carry off that pretence; the new Kamsa achieved it, by a hair. 'What other changes can I expect?'

She looked back at him. 'Ask the person who advised you to call on me. If *you* do not know, *that person* surely does. That's why he or she advised you to do this, isn't it?'

And she left.

six

After Putana had left, Kamsa prowled the corridors of his private quarters, growing steadily more agitated. Like a heavy meal eaten late at night, he could still feel the Halahala being processed inside his body, working its way through a series of transformations. He had no idea what the eventual result would be, and that simultaneously excited and frightened him. His frustration, fear and impatience found expression in sudden bursts of energy. Striding up and down the empty corridors, deserted at the early hour since his personal staff was accustomed to his waking around mid-morning or even after noon, he suddenly found himself leaping several yards at a time, then flying through the air fast enough to land feet-first on the opposing wall, propelling himself back and bouncing off one wall to the other, until he lost his balance and crashed into a pillar, shattering it almost in half and landing in the debris, grinning stupidly at his own newfound strength and vigour.

He was suddenly overcome by a great thirst and felt as if a great fire raged within his veins and he must quench it at once. He sought out the pot of water in his bedchamber and lifted it with one hand, emptying it down his mouth, spilling much of it on himself. When it was drained, he tossed it aside to smash against the far wall, then went in search of more water. He ended up at the drinking trough by the stables, freshly mucked out and filled with clean water. Well, almost clean. Or water as clean as one could expect horses to drink. He emptied most of the contents of the trough, then paused. He looked down at himself. His belly wasn't distended, nor did he feel the normal full feeling that accompanied the consumption of so much fluid. He patted his abdomen; it felt as flat as ever, he could feel the ridged muscles moving beneath his palm. Where had all that water gone?

He sat on the edge of the trough and thought about what to do next. Narada's advice had been more effective than he had expected. Certainly, Putana had provided the much-needed catalyst he had been desperately seeking. Suddenly, he was eager to see if the rest of the sage's advice would prove as fruitful.

He needed a place to try out his new abilities. To learn for himself what they entailed. Could he actually fly? Or merely leap higher and higher, only to land with successively more destructive force? He had to find out! And his strength. How would he measure it, test it to its limit?

He thought of going to the palace akhada, a huge semi-enclosed space where the palace guard and most of the senior military officers exercised between shifts. But he did not wish word of his new powers to spread. He had to keep this a secret from Jarasandha. At any cost. And since Jarasandha had eyes and ears everywhere in Mathura …

He took a horse from the stables. The old syce, Yadu, looked at him with his usual unnerving expression when he asked for a mount, but somehow had the wits to bring him the biggest and strongest in the stable, a massive battle charger accustomed to carrying men with full battle armour, shield and weaponry. It was a choice Kamsa would be glad for by the time he returned, though he did not know it then. He took the horse, mounted it in a single leap, and rode off at an instant canter, breaking into a full-fledged gallop in a few dozen paces. The horse seemed glad for the exercise and did not complain or turn its head when he rode it off the training field and up the hill bordering the palace complex, and onward through the woods.

He took himself a good three yojanas out of Mathura, far from prying eyes or ears, and found a box canyon deep in the woods where he had once been as a boy. It had only one point of ingress and due to the high walls and peculiar acoustics, any rider or pedestrian entering the canyon would be heard easily long before he came into sight. The forest above the canyon was dense and the overhang too sloping and slippery from the recent rains for anyone to watch from above. Here, he could do as he pleased with nobody to witness or report back to Jarasandha. Not without him spying the spasa himself, in which case, he would make sure that the only thing he would find worth reporting was an alarming descent into annihilation.

Kamsa began with some brisk running, warming up to leaping off the walls of the canyon. He bounced from one rocky wall to the other, a distance of a hundred feet or more, dislodging rocks at first, then punching holes as his speed and intensity increased. He experienced a great exhilaration as he flew from wall to wall, bouncing like a wooden stick in the danda game. As his feet hit the canyon walls, he found the impact to be greater with each step, as if he was growing heavier. When he finally stopped, the high sloping walls, rising a hundred and fifty feet above ground, were pockmarked with holes left by his pounding feet, some a yard or two deep. Rocks and rock dust lay everywhere; it looked like the aftermath of a landslide.

He tried punching the wall next, and found that he could punch his way through solid granite rock without harming himself. Again, as his efforts and concentration intensified, he felt the same sensation of growing heavier. But each time he checked himself, he found he was still the same size as before.

It took him the better part of the morning to understand: his ability to expand had not returned. But the corresponding increase in weight as he expanded had come back.

Earlier, if he grew from his normal six feet height to, say, sixty feet, his weight would grow proportionately as well. Now, it seemed, his weight increased if he concentrated hard, and with that, he gained the ability to pack much more power in each punch, kick or blow. But he stayed the same height and size.

He examined his fist after punching a large boulder to smithereens. Apart from the red dust of the boulder, it had no other marks, not even a scratch.

Apparently, he could increase his weight by concentrating, but not his size. He guessed this was a side effect of the compound Jarasandha had had him fed daily for the past several months.

As the day wore on, he felt the Halahala continue working, changing him from within in ways he could not fathom, but he could see no other visible signs of his transformation. He looked the same, remained the same size, and was much the same apart from the considerably increased muscular strength and density.

But it was enough to start. Yes, more than enough.

In the days that followed, he continued to explore the extent and nature of his newfound abilities. He was somewhat disappointed to learn that he could not actually fly, that in fact, one his body grew denser, it grew harder to leap too high or too far. Initially, he had been using more strength without increasing his body's density. Now he realized that his increased density turned his flesh and bone and skin harder, heavier, denser to the point where bone became iron hard and heavy, flesh grew as solid as stone, blood and muscle and tissue and tendon grew as tough as ironwood, and even his skin became impenetrable as oak. He practised turning from normal flesh, blood and bone to this new state until he could achieve full transformation in moments.

Once transformed, he could not only punch a granite boulder to smithereens, he could drill through it with precision if he desired, or pound an entire hill into dust. The proportional increase in weight that came with this gain in density was remarkable. It was difficult to estimate exactly how heavy he turned after these transformations. There were no weighing scales designed to weigh such heavy loads, after all! But after several successively higher leaps, he tried jumping off the top of the canyon's highest ridge and found himself boring several yards into the ground, through solid packed earth and rock!

He had never been very good at numbers, but as he clambered out of the hole, he thought that he must surely weigh as much as several elephants – perhaps even several dozen. He had once seen a dozen-odd war elephants driven off the edge of a cliff and when they landed below, they did not make a crater this deep or large, merely a wide depression in the ground. He suspected that his greater density and smaller size made the impact greater. His ability to focus his power increased and over time he was able to punch neat fist-sized holes in even the hardest boulders, all the way to the end of his shoulder. Then when he slowly pulled his arm out of the hole, the boulder remained intact. One particular rock was left looking like a large fruit into which numerous worms had bored holes.

After each practice session, he was left with the same desperate thirst. Even two or three water-bags, enough to slake a company's thirst for days, was merely a few gulps to him in his new avatar. He went in search of a more plentiful source and on the second day, found it — an old well, its mouth half-covered by overgrown brambles and bushes, probably fallen into disuse when some trade route changed in the past. The bucket was cracked and leaked out half its load before he could winch it up. Frustrated after three or four such half-bucket-loads, he leapt into the well, his thirst making him too desperate to think beyond the immediate need. The water was wonderfully cool and refreshing, if somewhat heavy with minerals. The last suited him perfectly, because mere river water seemed unable to quench his new epic thirst. He drank to his heart's content, then found himself easily able to climb up the moss-lined brick walls by the simple expediency of punching his fingers into the brick and creating handholds and footholds for himself.

This became his routine each day after his training session in the canyon. Each time, no matter how much he drank, his body seemed to miraculously absorb every drop of the water, leaving him as lean and empty-bellied as when he had leapt into the well. He thought it had something to do with the new way his body's muscles and cells had grown denser and heavier. Although not growing larger in size, he was nevertheless growing denser, perhaps even as dense as the giant he used to become earlier, and the water he consumed was absorbed into the denser body mass somehow.

He did not understand the philosophy or science behind such things and did not really care. All that mattered was that he was strong again. Strong enough to fight the Mohini Fauj, or even Jarasandha's champions. And soon, some day, he would be strong enough to face the Slayer without fear and destroy his nemesis. But first, of course, he had to *find* that elusive foe.

Despite his newfound confidence in his abilities and his burning desire to avenge his humiliation, Kamsa was careful to keep his practice secret. What success had been unable to teach him, failure had schooled him in quite diligently. He knew better than to show his hand too soon or at the wrong time and place. Even if he no longer feared confrontations with the Mohini Fauj or the minions of the Magadhan, he still knew better than to think he was strong enough to take on Jarasandha himself. The martial skills of his father-in-law were more greatly feared because they were largely unknown. The effects of his great massacres had been witnessed several times, but nobody had actually seen him in full battle mode during one of those legendary slaughters. The reason was that Jarasandha rarely if ever permitted any survivors to remain to tell the tale.

Because he was so studiously ignored and neglected, it was easy for Kamsa to enter the city and leave as he pleased. Rarely did anyone actually ask after him or bother about his whereabouts. He suspected that Jarasandha's spasas watched him closely enough to know he rode out and back each day, but he was shrewd enough to float a rumour that he was visiting a woman. Another man's wife. From the old syce, Yadu, he learned that they had bought the rumour without question, even laughing at the foolish prince wasting his time on dalliances while Jarasandha ruled Mathura as he pleased. Kamsa gritted his teeth as the old man told him these things in his laconic devil-may-care way, but knew that so long as they laughed at him, they would not suspect him.

The old man knew, though. Kamsa could see it in his eyes.

'Will there be anything further, my lord?' he asked as he took the frothing horse by the bit. Kamsa had practised increasing his weight while riding the horse today, to judge from the horse's reactions how heavy he became. When the beast began to snort and whinny in panic, he had stopped, but the animal had never trusted after that, especially since he tried the same thing several more times. Now, it reared white-eyed as Kamsa walked past, pulling away from him.

Kamsa paused and glanced at the horse which was still bucking in the syce's hands. Yadu seemed unperturbed by the beast. Most men would have been at least a little nervous when a half-ton animal grew thus agitated and began lashing out with those deadly hooves. The syce appeared as calm as ever, and not for the first time, Kamsa wondered just how old the man really was, and what role he had played in his father's coterie before he retired to this menial job.

'A fresh horse tomorrow,' he said and turned away without waiting for a response. There would be none in any case. Yadu only spoke when absolutely necessary. It was one of the reasons Kamsa trusted the old man to keep his part of the secret.

He was startled to see Mohini sentries at the perimeter of his palace. They did not deign to give him even the dignity of a sideward glance and merely continued their inscrutable watchfulness of their area of scrutiny, but he sensed their derision and scorn and felt the urge to lash out and crush them like flies. That would get them to notice him again! But he reminded himself how hard it had been to regain even this measure of strength, and what Narada had said when he told him how to achieve it, and knew he must keep his strength a secret until the right time and day.

There were Hijras lined up along his corridors too, a full force. That could mean only one thing: someone very important had come to see him in his private chambers. Uninvited.

He brushed past the Hijras and strode up to his chambers with deliberate ease. He was pulling off his gloves and whistling when he entered his private bedchamber.

Jarasandha was waiting. And with him were his usual cronies: Hansa and Dimvaka on either side; Bana and Canura off in the corners, skulking and still avoiding Kamsa's gaze; Bahuka, Agha, Baka, Dhenu, Trnavarta, Vatsa, and with them Putana as well. Pralamba and Pradyota were there too, but from their positions relative to Jarasandha, it was evident that they did not enjoy the same favour as the others within the cherished circle of trust. And finally, there were four of the familiar Hijra Fauj, the toughest and most ruthless of the lot. Kamsa knew them from his days with Jarasandha. They had always been the first to go into battle and the last to leave a field; their death count was greater than that of entire regiments. The very fact that they were still alive, despite their many years of service, was testimony to their ability to kill and survive against all odds. They barely glanced at Kamsa; he was nothing to them, not even a hint of a possible future threat. That infuriated him more than anything else, but he kept his self-control. He had gained too much ground with too much effort to lose it only because of his temper.

Leaning back like an emperor upon his throne, legs crossed casually, Jarasandha was seated on Kamsa's bed. Hansa and Dimvaka lounged on either side, as still as bedposts.

'Come, come, Kamsa. We have much to discuss.'

And behind him, Kamsa heard the sound of the chamber doors being shut and bolted.

seven

'Kamsa, dear Kamsa,' said Jarasandha, then clicked his tongue sympathetically several times. 'It seems there is a revolution brewing behind your back that you are blissfully unaware of, my son.'

He paused and glanced at his cronies. 'Although, judging from the way you have been these past months, almost anything could be brewing behind your back and you would hardly know it!'

A round of derisive laughter greeted this quip. Even Putana twitched in a sardonic imitation of a smile.

Kamsa stood impassively, not reacting in any way.

Jarasandha looked at him, chin lowered in his usual way so that his eyes and brow seemed to merge. Like all natural predators, his eyes were close set and intense, and were most accustomed to focussing on the middle distance. His lips were slightly parted and the tips of his split tongue rested on his lower teeth, barely visible. He flicked it out, licked at his left cheek, then withdrew it into his mouth. 'My spasas tell me that your Yadavas are trying to forge an alliance with the Kurus as well as other nations. They will not succeed, of course. The Kurus are far too wise to align themselves with the wrong faction, but the very fact that they make this attempt is an affront to my sovereignty. This kind of rebelliousness cannot be permitted to continue. It undermines the Yadava republic and the power of Mathura.'

Kamsa asked quietly, so quietly that Jarasandha heard only part of what he said, 'What do you propose to do?'

Jarasandha frowned.

Kamsa knew Jarasandha could not have heard him clearly, but he also knew that the 'god emperor' was too proud to ask Kamsa to repeat himself. As he had intended, the Magadhan heard enough to *presume* to have understood him.

Jarasandha shrugged. 'I propose that you quell this rebellion at once, of course! Find the guilty parties, bring them to book, and mete out such punishment as seems—'

Kamsa held up his hand, palm outwards, fingers splayed, interrupting Jarasandha. In a slightly louder but still calm tone, he said, 'I did not ask you what *I* should do. I hardly need advice on how to manage my kingdom. I asked you what *you* propose to do.'

There was a moment of shocked silence. For a brief instant, even Jarasandha seemed at a loss for words. Out of the corner of his eyes, Kamsa saw Putana turn her head a fraction and look directly at him. He did not return her gaze or look at anyone else, but kept his eyes fixed on Jarasandha.

The Magadhan leaned forward on Kamsa's bed, slowly uncrossing his legs. 'I see. So you think you know how to manage your kingdom, do you? Interesting.'

Jarasandha stood up, now facing Kamsa directly. He came forward, one step at a time, pacing his movement with his words as precisely as ever to produce the exact effect he desired. 'In that case, could you explain to me how these rebels have taken matters this far already? Why haven't you done anything about it yet? Instead of standing here and asking me – *me* – what I propose to do to help you! Why must you always look to *me* for help and advice? You are not the young green-eared boy who came to me a decade ago, Kamsa. You are a prince regent now. It's time you started learning to behave like one!'

He stopped less than two yards short of Kamsa.

Kamsa chuckled. He permitted himself merely to make the sound, but not to hold the chuckle more than a second. It was for effect too.

'I do not seem to be able to make you understand me, Jarasandha,' he said. 'I am neither asking for advice nor for help. I need neither from you. I was asking what you intend to do personally! About your own problems! As I said before, I can handle my matters on my own. You're right in saying that I'm not the young boy who came to you a decade ago seeking alliance and military backing to implement the coup which I felt was needed to replace my father's senile administration with a more robust and hard-dealing one of my own. I'm a man now. A king, in fact. I *was* a prince regent, it's true. But I have already made the necessary declarations to proclaim myself king officially at the tribal councils as is the age-old custom. With my father still absent, there will be no opposition. I expect your support, of course, as you have already offered it. And your military resources and aid, which you have officially placed at Mathura's disposal as per the treaties we have signed. But other than those things, I was merely asking about you personally, Jarasandha. Since your presence here is brewing restlessness and rebellion amongst my people, surely you do realize that it's time you moved on from here. After all, it's *you* they want to depose, not me. The Yadavas have never accepted an outsider governing them and never will. So what I was asking, to put it quite clearly this time in order to avoid any further confusion on your part—'

'How dare you!' said Bahuka, stepping forward, whip in hand, ready to lash out, his face red with anger. 'Nobody speaks to our lord in such a manner!'

Jarasandha's hand shot out, surprising Bahuka. Jarasandha waved Bahuka back, without taking his eyes off Kamsa.

'But my lord, he—'

Jarasandha gestured a second time. Everyone who knew him knew there would not be a third time. Bahuka restrained himself with a visible effort and stepped back, lowering his whip but keeping it in hand, ready to use again, and his eyes glowered at Kamsa.

'—to repeat it one final time,' Kamsa went on, as if he had never been interrupted, 'is when do you plan to remove your imperial presence from my capital city and kingdom? That is the question I asked you.'

Jarasandha put his hands behind his back and continued to examine Kamsa. His head tilted slightly, his gaze unwavering, he remained as still as a coiled cobra, but this very absence of motion was fraught with violence. There was powerful threat and aggression in the very lowering of his brows, the narrowing of his eyes, the pursing of his thin lips. Nobody else in the chamber moved either, and the gathering was frozen in time and space, awaiting the next course of action of its leader. The air held the promise of bloodshed and brutality, unmitigated cruelty meted out without hesitation or mercy.

'So,' Jarasandha said at last, 'Kumbhakarna awakes.'

From the frowns on the faces of the others, Kamsa gathered that none of them understood the reference. He might have missed it too, had he not overheard the old stablehand Yadu telling the other stable boys the story of Rama and his epic tragedy just the night before. Kamsa had put his horse into its box as usual and was leaving the stables when he heard the old Yadava's voice, cracked and rough with age and living, speaking over the chirring of crickets and cicadas in the dusk. Kamsa had paused, leaning against the worn wooden boards of the stable wall, sweat drying on his body, and listened with a fascination he could not explain.

'To awaken,' he said slowly, 'one has to first be asleep.'

Eyes narrowing to pinpoints in his straight, perfectly symmetrical face, Jarasandha stared at Kamsa intently. Then he suddenly relaxed his scrutiny. 'Indeed,' he said, then flashed an unexpected smile. 'Indeed!'

He barked orders in a foreign tongue at his men, prompting them into action with startling speed.

The language was Magadhan. Kamsa had learnt enough of it during his time with Jarasandha to know that it was a command to attack and kill him, Kamsa, at once. Or else he, Jarasandha, would kill each one of them and then proceed to kill Kamsa himself.

The last part was totally unnecessary. Bahuka was the first to move. Trnavarta, Baka, Agha, Vatsa and Dhenu spread out to avoid conflict with each other's lines of attack. Even Pralamba and Pradyota moved forward, eyes flicking apologetically at Kamsa. Hansa and Dimvaka stayed back, smiling openly now: they hardly expected their services to be required. Bana and Canura glowered, their faces revealing the long-festering resentment and pent-up hatred they had kept hidden this past year, but waited their turn. Putana hung back to one side, neither committing to action nor avoiding it. She kept her eyes studiously averted from Kamsa, though he knew better than to look at her directly anyway.

But the first to attack were the four Hijras who were closest to Kamsa.

Kamsa had known that would be the case from the very beginning. And every step he had taken while speaking, every gesture he had made, apart from serving its purpose as part of his delivery of speech, also served to position himself most favourably to counter their attack.

He had also been focussing his attention on increasing his body's density as he spoke, extending his words to give himself time.

And now, when the four Hijras moved in to kill him, he was ready to take them on.

Not moving or turning an inch, he remained where he was and was exactly where he wished to be. If they wanted him, they would have to come to him.

He was standing with the closed door to the bedchamber behind him and the verandah to his right. To approach him, they would have to come from his left, his fore, and his right, and that is exactly what they did.

One Mohini slipped out onto the verandah, around a pillar, approaching from the extreme right, his blind spot. Two others came at him from the front and left, with the fourth staying just between and behind them both, but approaching at the same pace.

He had seen quads of Hijras work in the battlefield using similar formations. The first two would attack together, just wide apart enough to make it hard for the target to defend against both attacks simultaneously. Their movements were characterized by perfect coordination and devastating speed of attack. The first duo would strike a blow that would force the target to leap back, or miss a step, bend, twist, turn or otherwise deflect. That was when the Mohini on the extreme right (or, in an open field attack, the one coming from behind the target) would lunge forward, strike a single blow, then fall back instantly, and the first two would move aside unexpectedly, leaving room for the fourth Hijra to come forward and deal the death blow.

The entire manoeuvre barely lasted more than a few moments, and it was rare for the Hijra quad to need more than two strikes to kill the target. Even as the first two Hijras (front and left) finished their action, they would move on to the next target. And so on. Kamsa had witnessed such quads cutting a swathe through entire armies, slaughtering with such precision that the enemy camp often dropped its weapons and ran helter-skelter in panic. Armies or forces that attempted to fight were slaughtered to the last man.

There was a brief pause as the other men watching the Hijras move in glanced at one another knowingly. Kamsa was using his peripheral vision to watch all four Hijras at once, and his frontal vision happened to be looking at the space that Bahuka occupied. In a lupine threat, the grizzled veteran snarled and showed his teeth.

Kamsa offered no response. Later, he was proud of that single action more than anything else he did in that chamber that day. The fact that he had not let Bahuka provoke him at that crucial moment – which, of course, was precisely what the old dog had intended to do.

When he didn't respond, Bahuka instantly lost his snarl and frowned. This was not on his list of possible reactions from Kamsa and it disturbed him. He turned to look in Jarasandha's direction.

Kamsa did not see how Jarasandha responded to Bahuka's look, because Jarasandha was out of his frame of view and he was now focussing his entire body and being on one thing and one thing only: arming himself.

As everyone else in the bedchamber assumed, Kamsa was unarmed.

But there was a bigger truth about which only Kamsa was aware.

He didn't need a weapon.

He *was* the weapon.

The first two Hijras made their move, their short, curved swords blurring through the air with numbing speed as they yelled their high-pitched shrieks, blood-curdling cries that unnerved and startled most opponents when they issued forth from throats that had been deathly silent until that instant.

eight

The most dangerous thing about the Hijras was not their speed, or their unnerving high-pitched shrieks – shrieks which no mature man could duplicate – or even their razor-sharp, short, curved swords. It was their footwork. The reason why most battlefield combat broke up into small units was because warriors attacking together could easily get tangled up with one another. Even a regiment seeking to slaughter a single man would need to come at him one or two at a time, and the moment there were two attacking at the same time, they were more likely to get in each other's way rather than finish off the solitary man. This was the reason why most gurus of combat cautioned their overzealous shishyas: two against one means double the chance of success – *for the solo warrior*! Unless the attackers worked in perfect tandem, like dancers in an elaborately rehearsed performance, pairs, trios and quads against a single man rarely had any significant advantage to offer. As the same wise gurus also cautioned: the only way to best a single champion is to send a superior champion against him.

But the Hijras had turned this basic notion of Arya warcraft upon its head. Bonded together since birth in a way that ordinary Kshatriyas never could be, these wilfully emasculated eunuchs followed only the code of the comrade. When two Hijras were put together, both succeeded or failed. There was no third option; Jarasandha made sure of that. If your partner was cut down, you were cut down as well, end of story. The same applied if you were put in a trimurti: three for one, and one for all. And so on through quads, pentads, sextets, and more. Until finally, the entire Mohini Fauj functioned as one organic unit, an army that breathed and lived and died as a single man.

While the logistics of defeating such an army were mind-boggling, the chances of facing even a pair, trimurti or quad and simply surviving were almost nil.

And in Kamsa's case, with not just the quad of Hijras but so many other champions also poised against him, he had only one chance. He had to take the upper hand from the outset, or the fight would be over in a moment, with him the loser.

Kamsa watched their feet as the first two Hijras came at him, shrieking and whirling like dust-devils. As always, their attack was designed to disorient, confuse, misdirect and maim a standing opponent who was whipping around to try and be able to see both his attackers at once. Their entire strategy was based on that. The shrieks were coordinated in a rising and falling pattern so that the opponent was unconsciously compelled to look at the one on the left, then the one in the centre, then back again, until he was so confused and misdirected that his weapon was poised neither to attack nor defend against either one.

Even if he stayed with one Hijra, the other would be able to slip in past his guard and deal the single maiming blow which the Hijras desired to inflict. Just one blow. Sever the bicep muscle, disabling one arm. Hack at the collarbone, disabling one arm and making it impossible to use the other without excruciating pain. Cut at the upper brow – deep enough to hurt badly as face wounds always did – making blood pour into the eyes of the opponent, blinding him. Pierce the armpit, slice the tricep muscles … there were a dozen other points. None critical or mortal in themselves, but when faced with two men attacking at once and two more following close on their heels, that one disabling cut or piercing was all it took to make a man open to a lethal strike.

But their entire first attack strategy depended on the upper body. On striking at the head, shoulders and upper arms. Hence the leaping and dancing and shrieking to make the opponent look up, swing around, and keep his guard high, enabling them to come in *under* his guard and inflict that one strike. Their chaotic and wild animalistic approach was in fact perfectly rehearsed, choreographed and coordinated. As one Hijra leapt high, his scream rising at that precise moment to force the opponent to raise his weapon and line of sight, the other one slid in to deal the vital blow.

So accustomed were they to this strategy, so habituated to finding success with it that they knew all possible reactions and counter-attacks intimately.

So Kamsa did the one thing they were not prepared for, or expecting.

He ignored them completely.

Even as they came spinning and leaping at him, shrieking like death criers at a king's cremation, he turned around and dropped to the floor in one swift motion, thumping on his buttocks, jarring his spine hard enough to feel the impact all the way up his neck and in his skull. And then he dropped his upper body back, lying flat on the floor as the Mohinis leapt and slashed above him. Several feet above him, in fact. There was a fraction of an instant when the Hijras realized that something extraordinary had occurred. Their opponent had not only failed to react in any of the usual ways adversaries usually reacted, he had done something they had never encountered before in any one of several hundred encounters to date. He had turned his back to them, then fallen down at their feet while they were still leaping in the air, their weapons slashing through empty space where he *had been*, where he *ought* to still be!

By doing so, not only had he removed his entire body from their field of attack in a single instant, he had also effectively put himself below their own high line of defence. He didn't even need to slip in; the Hijras' headlong forward movement brought him within reach of their *defenceless* bodies which were vulnerable even if only for that one fraction of an instant before they adjusted and changed their angle of attack. They were fast. But even the fastest warrior needs a fraction of an instant to adapt to a completely new development.

In the fire of battle, such moment is all the advantage a man needs. It is all he gets, and often he doesn't get even that much. To any warrior, it is a gift. To a champion, it is a gift from the gods themselves.

To Kamsa, operating at the highest level of skill he had ever accomplished in his entire life, it was a great field of opportunity crying out to be ploughed with a blood-axe!

In that fraction of a second, his hands shot out and grasped a single ankle of the Hijra who had been on his left. His new densely packed body strength made the leaping warrior seem no heavier than a straw in his fist. In the same action, Kamsa slammed the Hijra down, onto his fellow Hijra, the one who had been facing Kamsa directly.

The two Mohinis crashed into one another and then onto the marble floor hard enough for the sound of breaking bones and shattering cartilage to be loudly audible, crunching and crackling. Their shrieks ceased abruptly, and where two superb dealers of death had been leaping through the air in a balletic display of warcraft mastery, two crushed and dazed cripples now lay upon the marble floor.

From the position in which he lay, on his back, looking backwards at the chamber, Kamsa could see the twin coals of Jarasandha's eyes glowing from across the room. He took another brief instant to flash a grin and drop a lewd wink at the Magadhan.

Then, without waiting to see the response of the 'god emperor', he regained his feet with a single leap. He had been practising this move as well, and was pleased at his body's response. He landed with a jarring thud and caused the chamber to shake, and due to his body having gained density, left spider webs of cracks beneath each foot. He was growing in density even now, and was yet to reach his full potential; but he had other things to concentrate on for the moment. Such as staying alive a few minutes longer.

The third and fourth Hijras were already moving in for the attack. Stunned though they were by the unexpected manoeuvre and by the downing of their comrades, they were now deadlier than ever. Before, they had been part of a quad that had been emasculated, raised, groomed, trained, punished and rewarded *together* since birth. Now, with two of their comrades crippled, perhaps dying, they were doomed. Even if Kamsa did not kill them now, Jarasandha would. They had nothing to lose or gain, except for one thing.

Jarasandha barked a single word across the room.

Kamsa knew its meaning well, it was so commonly yelled among Magadhans that it might well be considered their battle cry: '*Avenge!*'

The Mohini on the verandah touched one short sword to the marble floor, raking it across sharply enough to cleave the soft decorative stone visibly by a half centimetre. He held out the other sword in an unusual backhand that Kamsa knew would spring back to pierce at the least expected moment. Partly due to the sword held to the floor, he came at Kamsa in a low loping stride. Sparks flew from the point where the deadly sharp blade met the polished stone floor. The other Mohini, the one who had been on Kamsa's right but still inside the chamber proper, somersaulted forward once, twice, then kept coming in that fashion. The bedchamber was palatial, but Kamsa knew that a fighter somersaulting in a closed space always held an advantage over one standing still. For one thing, the somersaulting fighter could change his trajectory at any time and still strike with considerable force – too much force for a standing man to easily fend off without being thrown off balance. The two Hijras were coming at him from the front centre and the extreme right, in two very different yet extremely rapid and forceful attacks that no ordinary mortal soldier would have been able to resist. Coming at him from two different directions, they had turned Kamsa's geographical advantages against him: pinning him against the closed door and wall, and covering both the upper as well as the lower field of attack.

There was no shrieking this time. Just the soft thuds of the somersaulting Hijra making brief contact with the ground each time, and the shirring sound of metal scraping and cutting stone as the other Hijra's sword threw up a shower of golden flaring sparks as he came loping at Kamsa.

Kamsa stood his ground.

Had he been any normal warrior, that would have been a mortal error.

The impact of the somersaulting Mohini striking him with such momentum would have slammed him back against the wall, even as the somersaulting eunuch reversed his movement and bounced off, leaving Kamsa, slumped against the wall and momentarily stunned, an easy target for the second Hijra who would have swung sideways, slicing upwards with the lowered short sword, then stabbed deep and hard with the backheld short sword. Kamsa would have died impaled against the wall.

But he was not the Kamsa of yore. His weight was several times that of a normal mortal warrior. He could not be certain how dense he had been able to make himself right now, but he was certainly at least nine or ten times denser, and weighed proportionately that much more than his usual weight.

For a somersaulting attacker to strike a man weighing a hundred kilos was one thing; but to strike a man weighing a ton or more, with skin like steel, flesh like iron and bones like alloy…

The Hijra somersaulted right at Kamsa, twisting his body with expert grace in mid-air to bring himself into striking position, his feet landing squarely on Kamsa's chest.

There should have been a loud thud, perhaps the cracking of a few ribs, and then the thump of Kamsa's body hitting the wall.

Instead, like dried sticks under a heavily laden wagon's wheels, the Hijra's feet shattered beneath him due to his own momentum and force. It was as if he had crashed into a stone wall, but since he had not been *expecting* a stone wall, the force he used worked against him, breaking his feet. They bent and bent again grotesquely, and the Hijra fell in a broken heap on the floor, silent even in his terrible condition, but only because Jarasandha's ruthless discipline had conditioned him not to express pain through sound. His face screamed his terror and pain instead.

A fraction of a moment later, the second Mohini struck. In a manoeuvre designed to accomplish terrible, irreparable damage, his sword rose up from the marble floor and slashed viciously at Kamsa's upper thigh, groin and lower abdomen at a diagonal. Without waiting to see the effect of this first strike, the warrior swung around, dancing in a diagonal turnaround move that took him from one foot to the other, and stabbed his other short sword directly into Kamsa's solar plexus, aimed at punching through the softest part in the torso to penetrate right through.

Both swords snapped and broke.

The Mohini's action left him at a sideways angle to Kamsa. He turned, expecting to see Kamsa vomiting blood and dying. Instead, he saw the Mathuran standing exactly as he had stood before, and his own short swords broken and useless. He raised them and stared, unable to believe his eyes, then snarled and attacked again, stabbing out with the edges of the broken blades. They were still dangerous enough to cut through normal human flesh.

But when they struck Kamsa's skin, they simply broke again with the impact.

The Hijra stared at Kamsa in disbelief.

Kamsa smiled, reached out, and caught hold of the Hijra's bald pate in his left hand. He took hold of it in a grip so tight, the Hijra was suspended an inch or two in mid-air.

The astounded fighter lashed out with the broken swords, his feet, and every ounce of strength and skill he had left.

Kamsa squeezed, barely exerting more effort than if he had been squeezing a ripe grape.

The effect on the Hijra's skull was much the same. Kamsa tossed him aside, then waggled his eyebrows at the others.

'So let's see if you men fare better than your Hijra comrades,' he said.

Everyone stared at him. There was hatred in their eyes now, not the superior smug contempt that had been there before. Even Jarasandha had lowered his chin further, his eyes barely visible beneath his heavy forehead and brow, and was examining the slaughter with a mind expert in strategy and tactics. His tongue flicked out and back inside.

Nobody said anything.

Kamsa sighed wearily.

'Come on then, get a move on. I've got a kingdom to run and things to do.'

nine

Even through his surprise and rage, Jarasandha could not help but feel a certain astonished pride at his protégé. Some nameless rakshasa might have sired Kamsa, and Ugrasena might have fostered him to adulthood, but it was Jarasandha who had turned Kamsa into a warrior. Until he met the Magadhan, the Yadava had been little more than a rough-houser, winning fights through brute strength, and with a disdain for fighting protocol as well as sheer arrogance. It was Jarasandha's mentorship that had transformed the lad into a carefully honed weapon of war.

But now, it seemed that weapon had grown beyond Jarasandha's own ability to hold or wield.

Initially, he had assumed that Kamsa's cocky arrogance and high-handed attitude was the final stage of the breakdown of the Mathuran's damaged mind. Now he saw that it was in fact the opposite. Somehow, Kamsa had outsmarted him, if only briefly. He did not know how the Yadava had managed to gain such formidable powers or what exactly those powers entailed, nor could he comprehend how the man had managed to overcome the effect of his daily potions. Those potions were enough to drive Kamsa insane by now, or at the very least, make him the same irritable, frustrated but otherwise quite malleable idiot he had been of late. But somehow, Kamsa had dodged the arrow and slipped the noose. Then again, perhaps that was the essence of Kamsa's life story. Jarasandha recalled his spasa's report on how Kamsa had been under the executioner's axe when his rakshasa blood first heralded itself in an astonishing display. Jarasandha had played some part in that as well, secretly feeding Kamsa certain potions which enhanced his rakshasa qualities; it was only a matter of time before nature took its course then. But the fact that it had taken a near-death experience to make Kamsa finally transform suggested that perhaps the Yadava needed that ultimate level of threat to finally effect his change.

And now again, it seemed, he had done the unthinkable, transforming when faced with certain death once more. Except that this time he had accomplished it without Jarasandha's knowledge or understanding, and that intrigued the Magadhan. Like any purveyor of violence and power, he was fascinated by any use of these that he could not comprehend.

'Are we going to stand around all day and stare at each other?' Kamsa asked with just the right touch of irony.

That was another thing that surprised Jarasandha. Until not long ago, Kamsa was little more than a loutish, selfish, pleasure-seeking dolt. This was something new. This was not the result of a potion or even training, it was a change *from within*. How it had been achieved greatly intrigued Jarasandha.

Bahuka and the others looked at him again, waiting eagerly for him to give the command to attack. The fate of the Mohinis had only angered them, not scared them in the least. Superb fighters though the Hijras were, they were still subject to the vagaries and weaknesses of mortal physic. The others, however, had powers which were rarely displayed in public, and about which few even knew. On Jarasandha's instructions, they were to be used only in the battlefield and only on his orders. Unauthorized use would lead to the same penalty as any other form of disobedience to Jarasandha: instant death at the Magadhan's hands. Now, each wanted desperately to be given the opportunity to put his powers to use, to teach the impudent Yadava a lesson. His last lesson.

Jarasandha had no doubt they could do it. Well, perhaps one or three of them might fall too, not quite as quickly as the Hijras had, but fall nevertheless. Whatever transformation Kamsa had wrought upon himself, it was no mere muscle-building or special training. There was real power there. Power that fascinated Jarasandha, made him want to know more, study it further. Whether or not the combined power of his accomplices in the chamber could overcome Kamsa's power could only be determined by an all-out fight to the death. And that would leave either Jarasandha's men or Kamsa dead or damaged beyond use.

He did not want either to happen. Not now at any rate.

For one thing, he wished to examine and understand Kamsa better. To know what had wrought his transformation and whether it could be repeated.

But more importantly, he sensed a greater opportunity. The earlier Kamsa, the giant rakshasa who had all but destroyed his own capital city single-handedly and driven his people to revolt, *that* Kamsa had been useless as an ally. That was why Jarasandha had had to come to Mathura himself, step in and take charge of matters. He had plans for Mathura and the Yadava nation. Long-term plans. And Kamsa the rakshasa was disrupting them with his reckless abuse of power. It had taken Jarasandha the better part of the year past to repair some of the damage, rebuild the city and palace enclave, build ties with the populace, seed future alliances and trade deals, and generally set Mathura back on the path of prosperity and growth that he needed it to stay on. A Mathura at war with itself, destroyed from within by its own mad ruler, was of no use to him in the long run. A strong Mathura with a king who would do his bidding – for a price, of course – and who would rule the powerful and prosperous nation as a proxy for him ... well, such a king would be of great use to him.

This Kamsa just might be capable of being that king. His transformed manner, and mental and physical powers added up to a man who was a far cry from the insane rampaging rakshasa of a year ago, or even the adolescent marauder who enjoyed slaughter too much to even care who he was killing or why. Neither of those were fit to be kings, let alone rule Mathura.

This man, on the other hand, *this* Kamsa, facing a chamber full of some of Jarasandha's most lethal fighters, yes, he could rule as Jarasandha's proxy.

There was a third, crucial reason why Jarasandha did not give the order to attack Kamsa.

All said and done, Kamsa was his son-in-law. And Jarasandha loved his daughters dearly. He wanted them to bear him heirs. And heirs who would inherit the Yadava nation as well would be invaluable in future. Like any truly wise emperor, Jarasandha knew his itihasa. No liege, however strong or empowered with the greatest army, can rule indefinitely by force alone. Statecraft, kingship, diplomacy, or call the blend simply politics, were essential to long-term governance.

Kamsa, as the blood heir to the throne, would ensure that. As would Kamsa's offspring from Jarasandha's daughters.

And if Kamsa had regained his senses indeed, acquired formidable new powers, and even gained a modicum of wisdom and maturity in the process somehow, well, in that case, he had suddenly removed all possible reasons for extermination and made himself an extremely desirable son-in-law and ally once more.

It was with this in mind that Jarasandha shook his head, refusing to give the order that his men craved. They stared at him in disbelief, unable to take in the turn of events.

'No,' he said aloud, ending any doubt they might have.

Bahuka snarled. 'My lord, he has insulted you!'

Jarasandha strode across the chamber to where Bahuka stood, and slapped the man backhanded across the cheek. Though just a casually dealt blow, it was hard enough to split Bahuka's lip and draw blood. 'That is for me to decide. Now, stand down!'

He turned to the others as well, meeting each of their gazes in turn, and said loudly, 'Stand down!'

They lowered their gazes, knowing better than to challenge him.

Beside him, Bahuka glowered at Kamsa even as he wiped the trickle of blood from his lip. 'It is a bad precedent,' he said very softly, just enough for Jarasandha to hear. 'The dog that gets away with a finger may some day bite our hand off.'

Jarasandha looked up at the ceiling. There was an interesting dent there where something had struck the ceiling hard enough to break a piece of the stone overbeam. It would have taken considerable force and velocity to do that. He wondered if it was somehow connected to Kamsa's recent transformation; he thought it did.

'Leave us,' he said quietly for Bahuka's benefit. Firmly but not like a command. The old veteran had been with the Magadhan plunderer too long and fought too many wars and conflicts alongside him to be easily cowed. Beating him down would only end up in another unnecessary death. Some flies were more easily drawn with honey than slapped with sticks.

Bahuka left slowly, reluctantly. The others went too, glowering at Kamsa as they passed him by, but none making a move towards him. Once the doors were opened, other Mohinis came in to drag out their comrades. The faint sounds of necks being cracked outside were audible to Jarasandha's sharp ears; there was no room for the physically challenged in his army. Being a soldier for Magadha was in itself a challenge, physically and in every other way. On the battlefield, he himself went around finishing off damaged soldiers. He called it 'relieving them of their duties'.

When everyone had left and the doors had been shut once more, but not bolted this time, Jarasandha turned to look at Kamsa shrewdly.

'Tell me everything,' he said.

Kamsa looked at him laconically for a moment. 'What does that mean, "everything"?'

'How did this happen? When did it happen?'

Kamsa tore off a silk sheet and used it to wipe himself clean of the Hijras' blood. He also felt the great thirst that overcame him every time he used his powers but he controlled the urge. He wanted nothing more than to pick up the oversized water pot he now kept in his chamber, up-end it and drink until it was completely drained. But he didn't do that. Any need was a potential weakness, and he did not want Jarasandha to know his weakness. Instead, he picked up the pot and merely sipped at it, more as an affectation rather than an expression of need. 'Could you be more specific, Father dear? At least give me some hint as to what you might be referring to?'

Jarasandha smiled wryly. 'You have changed completely. I'm tempted to say "overnight" but of course that can't be true. This has taken time, effort.' Something occurred to him. 'And training! I see now. The question I should be asking is, who has effected this transformation. Who was it, Kamsa?'

Aching to empty the contents of the pot into his belly, let the cold water splash onto his face and shoulders and head, drench him completely, Kamsa took another sip. He could almost feel the water splashing on his sweaty overheated head and torso as he imagined it. But to Jarasandha he showed only indifference. 'What transformation?'

Jarasandha shook his head. 'Come now, Kamsa. You are a different man. A new man. With extraordinary new abilities. That does not come on its own; it is acquired somehow. All I wish to know is, how and when and from whom.'

Kamsa took a third sip, weighed the pot in his hand a moment, thinking. It weighed at least a hundred kilos, he knew, because it contained one hundred litres of water. He knew he could drink five of those right then and still want more. He forced the need to the back of his mind and focussed on the matter at hand. It was important he make Jarasandha understand that the first time, otherwise the process would take weeks or months, instead of days to accomplish. And something told him that he could not afford it to take weeks or months. Each day that he dallied in Mathura with Jarasandha, the Slayer would be out there somewhere, growing up, growing stronger, getting ready to attack him. He had to be ready when the time came. He had to choose the place and manner of the confrontation. It was the only hope he had.

'You are right about the rebellion,' he said quietly, being sure to couch his words in calm indifference. Any sign of urgency would only make Jarasandha suspicious. 'It is led by Akrur, acting on behalf of Vasudeva himself.'

Jarasandha immediately dropped his sardonic smile and came several steps forward. 'I knew it! Did you learn this from your spasas? What else did they tell you?'

Kamsa raised his other hand, waving away the questions. 'It does not matter how I came to know about this. All that matters is that it is true. You can verify it with the help of your spasas in time – but if you do, you will run out of time.'

Jarasandha frowned, lowering his chin again as he was wont to do when he grew suspicious or aggressive. 'Is that some kind of threat?'

Kamsa responded, 'Yes, but not a threat by me. By the Yadavas. If you do not heed them now, your entire empire may be lost to you forever. Already, they have begun to chip away at the edifice; and given time and your continued indifference, they will surely bring you down into the dust sooner than you might think possible.'

Jarasandha stared at him, then seemed to grow aware of the fact that Kamsa still held the pot of water in one hand, with his elbow crooked, as easily as any man might hold a mug of wine. 'You have gained great strength somehow. There are potions that can give you such strength for brief periods, taxing your body to its limits. What they give you in strength, they cost you in years of your life.'

Kamsa chuckled. 'You think my strength is gained from a *potion*?' He raised the pot higher, bringing it to Jarasandha's attention. 'Can a *potion* give any man the ability to absorb a hundred litres of water without it showing anywhere on his body?'

And touching the rim of the pot to his lips, he upended and drained it entirely. It took several moments and he was careful not to spill even a drop. He was trying to make it seem as if he was drinking the water to prove a point – not because of a side-effect that made him inordinately thirsty. When Kamsa had emptied the pot, he tossed it across the room. It flew out of the verandah and landed on the ground below, smashing with a loud crash. A few voices could be heard, Bahuka's unmistakable among them, expressing their disapproval of such careless littering.

Kamsa raised his anga-vastra to reveal his flat, taut belly and ridged abdomen muscles. For Jarasandha's benefit, he thumped his stomach and groin with his fist, revealing it to be hard enough to make it sound like an elephant driving its head against a heavy tree trunk. 'You see now? Is this the work of a potion, you think?'

Jarasandha's eyes glittered. He approached Kamsa slowly, hand outstretched as if longing to touch and see for himself. Kamsa raised a hand in warning, restraining him. Jarasandha's tongues flickered and disappeared again.

'No,' he said finally. 'This is something else entirely. Something I have never heard of or encountered before. It intrigues me.'

Good. For as long as it intrigues you, you will not try to kill me, I trust. Aloud, Kamsa said, 'About the rebellion, then. The rebels have mounted an army and are attacking your outposts. Those nearest to Mathura have already fallen. Now they make their way northwards and westwards.'

Jarasandha frowned. 'North and west? But that would take them beyond the borders of the Yadava nation!'

Kamsa nodded slowly, waiting for Jarasandha to reason it out by himself.

'Exactly. There is an old saying among us Yadavas, when you pour hot daal onto a plate of rice, never try to eat the middle.'

Jarasandha blinked. 'What?'

Kamsa gestured to indicate an imaginary plate of rice onto which he poured steaming hot daal as he repeated himself slowly, 'Never try to eat the hot rice and daal from the middle of the plate. You will burn yourself. Instead, start from the outside and work your way in.'

Jarasandha shook his head, looking irritated now. 'Rustic sayings were never my strong suit, Son-in-law. If there is some wisdom there, it eludes me.'

Kamsa sighed. 'They want you out of Mathura, but rather than defy you here and risk destroying their own capital city and kingdom, they have taken the fight to your territories. That's why they have headed north and west. They have allied with the kingdoms you have taken over and intend to liberate them, one by one.'

Jarasandha now gaped openly at Kamsa, light dawning in his eyes. 'Eating the dish from the outside, working their way inwards. Mathura is the hot centre of the plate. I see it now! How quaint, and quite apt indeed. So they think they can unite my principalities against me, do they? How ridiculous!'

'And yet how dangerous. With a few other allies as strong as Hastinapura …'

'Did you say Hastinapura? The Kurus would never align with these foolish rebel factions!'

'Not officially. But much can be done unofficially. And the Kurus are very powerful indeed. As are the Drupads. And the Bhojas. And the Gandaharis. And who knows who else?'

Lips pursed in the spiteful stubborn way he had when contradicted, Jarasandha shook his head. 'Impossible. Not the Drupads and the Gandaharis! It's true that Pritha, also known as Kunti, is sister to Vasudeva, so the Kurus have some reason to sympathize with the Yadava rebel cause, but these others …' His voice trailed off as he thought for a moment. 'Pritha was adopted by Kuntibhoja, king of the Bhojas, and renamed Kunti by him. Drupad is a close ally of the Kurus. And Shakuni, son of King Subala of the Gandaharis is brother to Gandhari, who is married to Dhritarashtra, the blind king of Hastinapura. They are all connected in some way to the Kurus then.'

'Not *some* way; by blood and by marriage. And by sympathy they are united against your expansionary ambitions. Many more will join them. This is not a rebellion against me or the throne of Mathura. It is a rebellion against you and your empire-building. Everything you have worked for is in danger of being lost, Jarasandha. Heed my advice. Go now. Leave Mathura. Consolidate your empire outside this nation. Leave Mathura and the Yadavas to me to manage, as was our original understanding, and I shall remain allied with you always. I shall also visit your daughters, my wives, and sire children on them. But if you stay, you risk losing everything.'

Jarasandha remained silent for a very long time.

Kamsa waited patiently. From below, he could hear the voices and murmurs of men, the clinking of weapons and snorting of horses. He guessed that riders had arrived, bearing the news he had intercepted the previous day and the information they brought was causing consternation among Jarasandha's advisors.

Finally, Jarasandha nodded once, decisively. 'Everything you have said can be easily proven or disproved. I am expecting riders with news from the outposts even now. If what you say is true, I shall do exactly as you advise and leave Mathura to you.

But if you fail me in any way – whether as an ally, a king, or a son-in-law, I shall return. And the next time I come to Mathura, I shall make her mine forever. Do you understand?'

Kamsa smiled. 'She is already yours. She merely happens to be wedded to me, Father-in-law.'

ten

As he drove the uks cart through the gates of Mathura city, Nanda kept his features composed and his manner as natural as possible. Behind him, in the covered wagon, along with the infantile sounds of Krishna and Balarama babbling excitedly as they spied the high walls and imposing structures of the great city, he could hear the voices of their mothers Yashoda and Rohini admonishing them to be quiet and behave themselves.

He grinned as he clicked his tongue to encourage the uks team to move along faster. Accustomed to the sedate pace of life in Gokul, they too were intimidated by the hustle and bustle of the city and were clip-clopping past at a trot and a canter. Nanda could still remember his siblings and he first coming to Mathura, years ago when he had been a few years older than Krishna–Balarama, and how excited they had all been at the time. Krishna and Balarama were just healthy normal boys, filled with all the excitement and vigour of little children everywhere.

He wished Yashoda would give up her ridiculous theory that their son was possessed of miraculous powers and capable of achieving impossible feats. It was true that Krishna was not ordinary in the common sense of the word; he was their son, and he was extremely special in every way. But he was no superboy or wonderchild as Yashoda made him out to be. That incident with the shattered cart had been so embarrassing. Yashoda had insisted stubbornly – in front of all their relatives and closest friends and neighbours too! – that it had been Krishna who had kicked the cart to pieces! How could such a thing be conceivable? Even if the infant was strong and robust and would grow up some day to be a great warrior, the idea of a babe kicking a heavily laden cart hard enough to smash it to smithereens was too incredible to even consider.

He did not have any alternative explanation for the cart's destruction, or for its remarkable reassembly, almost before their very eyes. But stranger, more miraculous things had happened before, and like all rustic Yadavas, Nanda did not feel a pressing need to question and understand every single thing that occurred beneath the sheltering sky. There were things in this world that could not be easily explained or understood by mortal minds; he knew and accepted this without resistance. So what was the point debating or questioning such events? The only reasonable question might be if the event was of a naturalistic nature or a numinous one. He had already ruled out the event being caused by a sacerdotal act since all the Brahmins present were busy eating at the time and he did not think it was possible that a Brahmin could be feasting and performing wondrous feats using Brahman shakti at the same time!

Personally, he believed, as did all the others present that day, that some calamity beyond their understanding had threatened their infant son on that field, and that the great Protector Lord Vishnu Himself had intervened to preserve his life.

How and by what means these things had been accomplished, he did not know, nor did he think it was comprehensible. But only the devas could do such things as smash a cart and those heavy, laden metal pots to fragments and then reassemble it all in the blink of an eye.

As the cart trundled lazily through the wide avenues of Mathura, Nanda was pleased to see the change in the city since he had visited it last. Just a year before, days prior to Krishna's birth, he had come to pay the taxes to the king, and he recalled how terrified he had been. A pall of fear had hung over the entire city, and the kingdom. That cloud of fear and uncertainty seemed to have lifted at last. He had heard of Jarasandha the Magadhan's departure along with his feared Hijra Fauj. Everyone had been relieved to see them leave. There had been rumours that Jarasandha would use his position as Kamsa's father-in-law to rule the Yadavas with Kamsa as a proxy king. Such an arrangement could be legally justified by Kamsa's own condition, which verged on near-insanity.

But in the past weeks, the political situation had changed dramatically. Kamsa had regained his senses, it was said, and taken charge of his kingdom's affairs once again. And if the word from the palace enclave was accurate, this time he actually seemed to be playing the part of a king in truth, not merely in name.

At around the same time, Jarasandha had received word of trouble at his outposts and an uprising from the kingdoms he had most recently annexed. He had taken his army and left at once, and the rumour was that he would be occupied for a fair while now, struggling to crush the uprising, regain the territory he had fought so hard for, as well as to consolidate the rest of his ill-gotten empire. It was presumed that Jarasandha would not be returning to Mathura for a long time, if ever, and all were glad to have seen the last of him, except perhaps for a few hundred aristocratic families who were said to have formed trade and other alliances with the Magadhan.

Now, as he and his fellow passengers trundled through the city, Nanda could see for himself the air of festivity and gaiety across all Mathura. Buildings and structures and roads and artefacts that had been in near-ruins or disarray the previous year had been rebuilt or demolished and replaced by newer, sturdier structures. Several of these new artefacts, such as the bridges and underpasses, were foreign to Yadava architecture, and were the work of Magadhan engineers and architects. The natural Yadava scepticism of such foreign workmanship had been quickly overcome due to the convenience offered by such devices, and already his kinsfolk from far and wide had begun visiting the capital to study these structures and attempt to imitate them in their own fashion back in their home towns. It was a common misconception that Yadavas resisted progress. The fact was that they welcomed and embraced progress warmly. They merely wanted it to occur at their own pace and in their own style.

All in all, as they leisurely wound their way towards the royal enclave, he thought that the capital had not seemed this inviting in a long time, ever since the day of King Ugrasena and King Vasudeva's peace accord. That had been a fine day, Nanda recalled, smiling and patting his growing paternal belly. Such good feasting, and what excellent conversation and music and dance and company! Ah, truly was it said: Give a Yadava enough wine, music, dance and chatter, and you don't need to use force to take his house – he will invite you to stay permanently!

He prayed that this time, peace was here to stay permanently too. There had been too much killing, too much anger and hatred and reprisals. Violence in any form was reprehensible, a violation of Sanatana Dharma, the unified system of collected beliefs that was shared by the denizens of Aryavarta, the land of the high thinking and right acting. But while all violence was indefensible, Yadavas killing Yadavas was the worst form of violence possible. He still recalled how hopeful and happy the day of the historic peace accord had been, how much it had meant to everyone he knew. When Kamsa and his marauders had begun violating the terms of the treaty even before the wax seal on the parchment was dry, it had come as a shock to Nanda and to all other peace-loving Yadavas. Yet even in the darkest of days, he had never been one of those who exchanged their cowherd's crook for a blade; he had always believed that peace would triumph in the end.

And now, seeing the relaxed, smiling faces of passers-by on the avenue, the uks carts trundling to and fro, horse riders and pedestrians coming and going with a bustling energy that was infectious and reassuring, he felt vindicated. Peace had won out in the end. Fragile though it was, it was the only way to ensure a future for their children and their children to come.

The royal enclave had changed too since he had last been there. Security was stricter than ever, but gone were the loutish oafs who had been too quick with their weapons and too sharp with their tongues. In their place were tough but straightforward men whose queries were terse but to the point and who let them pass without any fuss. Nanda was relieved when he drew the uks cart to a halt in front of Devaki's palace. He had had nightmarish visions of sentries poking spears through the sides and underside of the uks cart, searching for the Slayer. Even now, he had only brought the women and boys there because Yashoda had insisted firmly, and when she set her mind to do something, he had no hope of convincing her to do otherwise. It was odd, though: Yashoda was the one who had wanted to visit Mathura with Rohini and both boys. But she was also the one who seemed most concerned about the risks of taking two infants to a city where infants their age had been indiscriminately slaughtered without mercy not long ago. He sighed as he handed the reins of the uks to one of Vasudeva's men, a distant clansman of Nanda's own brother-in-law, and put the worries out of his mind. He was seeing his old friends after too long to waste precious time with anxieties and fears.

A familiar voice made him break out of his reverie.

'Nanda Maharaja!' Akrur said, greeting him with a roar and hearty back-slapping. 'You look thin, old friend. Has Yashoda-devi not been feeding you well?'

'She has, she has,' Nanda said, patting his belly. 'Here is proof. If I look leaner, it's on account of all the additional running around and work that fatherhood entails!'

Akrur glanced over at the women and boys, then whispered into Nanda's ear, 'Vasudeva and Devaki have been awaiting this day with more excitement than you can imagine. It is a very vital day in the itihasa of the Yadavas, old friend.'

Nanda frowned, wondering what Akrur meant by that. He finally assumed it had something to do with his clansman's other rumoured activities. As they walked up the luxurious but elegantly understated corridors and halls of Devaki's princely residence, he asked Akrur quietly: 'Is it true, then? You lead the Yadu rebellion against Jarasandha?'

Akrur glanced at him, his teeth flashing in a wry grin. 'Don't you know? I am a wanted man. Wanted for questioning at least, if not treason. I am to be apprehended on sight, and killed if I resist. There are soldiers scouring the outposts of the nation in search of me.'

Nanda stopped dead in his tracks. The women and boys, walking ahead, went on without realizing that he had stopped. 'And you are here? In the very heart of Kamsa's garrison? In the royal enclave? There must be an entire akshohini stationed within shouting distance!'

Akrur grinned again, raking a hand through his hair, which he had allowed to grow out, Nanda noted. 'Three akshohinis, actually. Two are stationed in the new military cantonment outside the city. Also, Jarasandha left behind some of his most trusted and feared champions. Officially, they are here to ensure that his trade agreements and other interests are looked after well, but in fact, they are all demons in human form, asuras possessed of terrible powers, each capable of taking on an akshohini himself. I would be more afraid of any one of them finding me here than I would be if all three akshohinis arrived at once!'

Nanda stared at him, nonplussed. 'And yet you are here?'

Akrur clapped a hand on Nanda's shoulder. 'I am here to persuade Vasudeva to leave Mathura. He is in as much danger as I am. I hope your visit will help us convince him of the necessity of going into exile at once. I know he cannot stomach the notion, but it is the only way left. That is why, when I heard you were coming, I made it a point to double back and slip in. If your visit does not convince him, nothing will.'

Nanda frowned, raising his hands in protest. 'But, Bhraatr, I have no great influence over Vasudeva. I can speak to him, of course, and will be happy to do so. But my knowledge of politics is too limited for me to fully understand the complexities involved here, let alone persuade anyone else.'

Akrur laughed, throwing his head back and giving Nanda a fleeting glimpse of his uvula. 'Ah, Nanda Maharaja, ever the simple gopa! My friend, I didn't mean you personally. I meant your son Krishna. He is the one I hope will persuade Vasudeva to leave Mathura and go into exile. Now go meet your old friends. I shall remain at the entrance to this part of the palace and ensure that nobody who wishes any of you harm comes to disturb you.'

And he clapped his hand on Nanda's back once again, turning back to go down the corridor to the last doorway, leaving Nanda wondering what in the world he meant: How could a one-year-old infant who could not yet speak more than a word or three persuade the king of the Vrishnis to go into exile?

eleven

Devaki sensed Krishna's presence long before he entered her chambers.
Maatr, I am coming to see you!
Yes, my son, I am waiting eagerly.
Bhraatr Balarama is coming with me as well. Remember, every kiss and hug you give him, you must give me two in return!
And he had gurgled mischievously.
All the while, as he had approached, she had grown increasingly tense and excited in anticipation. Vasudeva had paced the room endlessly, as anxious as a would-be father awaiting a message from the daimaas tending his wife in delivery. In a sense, she thought, the comparison was apt. Vasudeva would be meeting his sons for the very first time. If not quite a day of birthing, it was a day of rebirth – for the house of Vasudeva, and for all the Yadava people. The day would herald a new beginning. Devaki could not recall being this excited even on the day of her nuptials; but perhaps that was due to that day turning out so badly. She hoped and prayed that this day would not turn out as badly. She could not bear further pain or misery. As it was, the very thought of having her infant son – the very eighth child mentioned in the prophecy – within shouting distance of the very man who sought his destruction was shredding her nerves. What if Kamsa somehow found out about Krishna's visit? What if he suspected that this was in fact Devaki and Vasudeva's son? What if he arrived at any moment?

Do not fret so, Maatr. All will be well. Kamsa-mama knows nothing of our visit here. He will not know a thing until it is time for him to know.

What does that mean, she wondered. *Until it is time. Did Krishna mean ...*

But then the time for anxiety and worries was past. Krishna was here — she sensed his imminent entrance as strongly as she felt the fear and anxiety leave her mind, leaving only an all-pervasive sense of calm and joy.

When Krishna entered the room, still carried tenderly by Yashoda, Devaki gasped and sprang to her feet. Vasudeva stopped pacing and swung around, eyes wide, mouth open. Whatever they had both thought, dreamt of, felt until now, was irrelevant. The past was past, the future was unknown, and there was only the present moment — one in which everything was perfect and their hearts and minds filled with infinite love and understanding and acceptance and patience and tolerance. Nothing was worth worrying about, nothing worth fearing. There was only love, and it was infinite and it filled their consciousness.

A Tulsi plant in the courtyard of Devaki's palace, withered and rotting since the past ten years, unresponsive to every effort to make it grow, turned green and soft and grew prodigiously until its faint but distinct scent filled the courtyard and made everyone in the outer household pause and look up. It would grow evergreen for decades now, even if not watered or cared for.

A female dog who had given a litter of pups in the backyard, and who was in danger of losing half the litter as well as her own life due to complications resulting from the birth, suddenly felt her bleeding cease and her entire being fill with a sense of vigour and good health, as if she herself had just been born anew.

Every last one of her pups survived and lived a long healthy life. She herself lived an incredibly long life, eventually birthing an unheard-of number of litters, every last one of which survived to the last pup, causing the locals to dub her Sarama, after the celestial Maatr of dog-kind.

A large bell – intended for a Brahma temple that was to be built upon a hill, and which rested on the ground and had been kept there only the day before – began pealing steadily upon a hill nearby. The bell-maker's apprentice, frightened out of his wits, went racing downhill to fetch his master, who returned shortly and scratched his head in wonderment as a crowd gathered to view the miracle. What baffled the bell-maker and his apprentice, as well as all the other witnesses, was the fact that the bell was merely a bowl of metal still – the striking rod had not yet been installed inside it, nor had the bell been hung. It was sitting on the ground, with nobody within yards of it. So how did it ring? The preceptor of the gotra sub-caste that was building the temple advised his people to dedicate the temple to Adhoksaja, a form of Vishnu, instead of Brahma. They did so, and for centuries thereafter, the bell would ring every day at that exact time, even without a striker inside it or anyone touching so much as a finger to it.

All those within the household who were ill, ailing, or subjected to any condition, felt themselves glowing from within; as if a beneficial heat blossomed within their bodies, a not unpleasant sensation, and when it passed, leaving a light sheen of perspiration on their skin, they found their coughs and backaches and indigestion and broken legs and irregular heart rhythm and straining kidneys and other ailments healed and their bodies healthier than ever before.

Many similar miracles that have been forgotten by the recorders and editors of itihasa occurred that day.

Within the private chambers of Vasudeva and Devaki, no less a miracle was unfolding.

Yashoda had come in bearing Krishna in her arms. Yet within moments, she felt him grow heavier and heavier, as if some immense weight was dragging him down, until finally she could not possibly bear him aloft any longer. She sought to put him down, but to her surprise he leapt out of her arms. She cried out, fearing that he would fall and come to harm, but instead he remained where he had leapt, in mid-air, floating. He gurgled happily, spreading his arms and legs; a blinding blue glow emanated from him, filling the entire chamber and shutting out all other light, rendering pale even the bright sunlight streaming in through the windows into the background.

It was as if the entire chamber had turned black as night, the walls and furnishings disappearing, to leave only a black void in which floated Krishna, naked as the day he was born, and adorned with the tikka and other accoutrements and jewellery that Yashoda had put upon him as was her wont. He chuckled and turned to look at his brother Balarama, who stood on the floor, legs apart, as if guarding against anything or anyone that might approach. A similar glow emanated from Balarama too, but it was impossible to tell where Balarama's blue corona ended and Krishna's began. They blended one into the other, producing a pervasive light that was one and the same.

Unable to contain herself, Devaki fell to her feet, sobbing with joy and relief.

'Krishna! My son!' she cried.

She wanted to embrace and kiss him, but knew that she would get her chance later. She had waited this long; she could wait a few moments longer. She was just happy to be in the young one's presence.

Vasudeva lowered himself to his knees as well, beside his wife. He joined his hands together in a namaskar. 'Great and blessed child. You do us proud by this visit. It gives us immense joy to behold you with our own eyes at last. You do not know how we have longed for this moment.'

Krishna's baby voice chuckled. Echoing off the very walls of the room, it filled the minds of all four adults present in those chambers.

I do know, Pitr. I have felt every mite of pain you have experienced and I regret you and Maatr having to feel such emotions at all. But being human means feeling pain as well as joy, loss along with love, grief as well as celebration. Even I cannot remove such emotions permanently.

Vasudeva bowed his head in acknowledgement of his son's infinite wisdom. 'What welcome sorrow it was when we parted, that it enabled me to feel this joy of reunion.'

How wise you are. No wonder you fathered me in this avatar. I could not have hoped for a better pitr upon this mortal realm. Only Nanda Maharaja here, who is also my pitr, can compare with you. For what you possess in wisdom and quietude, he possesses in vitality and rustic good sense.

Nanda started at this mention of his name, and dropped to his knees as well, staring at the incredible sight of his son floating in mid-air in a halo of blazing blue light. Beside him, Yashoda exchanged a secret smile with Rohini.

'Let me hold you, my son! I have been waiting to embrace you and your bhraatr for so long!' Devaki said passionately, holding out her arms, tears flowing down her cheeks.

Krishna's voice turned sombre now, and his change of mood was matched by a corresponding shift in the hue of the blue light emanating from him. The light grew darker somehow, a deeper, graver blue.

In a moment, I shall embrace you and you may hug and kiss and bestow as much affection upon me as you wish, Pitr and Maatr. But first, there are things I must say to you and that you must heed well. My visit here is not merely to be reunited with you, my biological parents in this lifetime. I have another purpose. I have come here to warn you that your lives are in grave danger. Kamsa has decided to have you secretly assassinated in a manner that will leave no finger of suspicion pointing at him.

Vasudeva and Devaki looked at one another.

'Akrur has been saying the same thing,' Vasudeva said sombrely. 'Yet what can I do? I will not take up arms and plunge Mathura into civil strife yet again.'

There is only one way. You must leave Mathura.

Vasudeva shook his head firmly. 'I will not go into exile and leave my kinsmen here to suffer the yoke of Kamsa's unjust rule. So long as Kamsa stays in power, I must stay. The people look up to me as a symbol of hope, as someone who would lead the charge in overthrowing the Usurper and restoring King Ugrasena to the throne. If I go, it will break their hearts and crush their hopes. I cannot do such a thing.'

I did not say you should go into exile. I am merely suggesting that you leave Mathura for a while. Travel. Take Maatr and go on a long journey. I sense that both of you have passionately desired to visit several pilgrimage sites, to offer gratitude and appreciation for my bhraatr's birth and mine, and our continued survival despite the Childslayer's cruel campaign. Now is the time to set forth upon that pilgrimage. Visit Badrikashrama, which Maatr has longed to visit for years. Go to every site your heart desires to take you. Offer thanks to your deities. You have accomplished a great task. Now you must take a back seat and preserve yourselves until you are required once again to play your parts upon this great stage of life. When the time comes, I shall summon you back to Mathura. And that is when you shall achieve all your dreams of setting Mathura free of the tyrant's yoke and restoring this great land to her former glory. All your dreams shall come true, my beloved pitr and maatr, but all in their own time. Do as I say and you shall have no cause to regret it. You know I speak the truth as it was spoken in Satya Yuga.

Vasudeva and Devaki were silent. They looked at one another, faces revealing expressions of wonderment and even joy.

'It is true,' Devaki said. 'I do desire greatly to visit Badrikashrama. And many other holy sites.'

Vasudeva nodded gravely. 'A pilgrimage is righteously deserved and called for at this time. We have succeeded in doing the impossible. We have brought the Slayer of Kamsa into this world as well as his brother who will aid him. Krishna is right. Until Kamsa is disposed of, there is nothing much I can do. Akrur is managing the rebellion and the talks with other allies quite well and I can continue to do my part even from abroad. Each day we remain here, we are only an affront to Kamsa and a challenge to his authority. If indeed he has found a way to bring about our deaths without drawing suspicion to himself, we would die without fulfilling our dreams.'

Mathura needs you both alive tomorrow. Not dead today.

Vasudeva sighed and nodded. 'It shall be as you say, Krishna. We shall go this very day. Akrur had suggested that we use your visit as a cover for our own departure. When you leave this palace, Devaki and I shall stow away in the same uks cart. Once outside the city, Akrur and our allies will arrange transport for us for our onward journey. I should have seen the logic of his advice earlier, for he is constantly in touch with the goings-on of the nation and is better informed of the shifting tides of politics, while I have been too long removed from these things. But I was being stubborn and foolish. You have made me see clearly again, my son.'

Krishna chuckled loudly, clapping his hands in joy. His blue aura grew lighter, brightening with his happier mood. It increased in intensity and lightness, warming the spirits of everyone present.

Even Akrur, stationed at the entrance to the private chambers and ever vigilant, felt his heart, burdened with the pressures and stresses of rebellion and politics, lighten.

Now, come embrace and kiss me as much as you please.

After that, there was much hugging and kissing. Perhaps more than was warranted. Then again, how does one decide how much hugging and kissing is too much or just enough? In such matters, it's always advisable to err on the side of generosity rather than on the side of caution. Smack. Kiss. Hug. Repeat as often as needed or until too tired to continue further.

twelve

Kamsa had almost finished his exercises when he saw Putana approaching. She walked in a leisurely way and appeared to have just been strolling by. She paused by the wooden stable wall and pretended to watch him as he worked out, as if interested only casually and in a professional way.

He knew better.

He had been with her just the previous night, and when he had looked out of his verandah and seen her approaching, she had walked quite differently then. There had been an urgency in her step as well as a certain diffidence that he had not known she could possibly feel. Her head had been lowered as if she felt embarrassed at visiting him secretly.

Later, once he had drawn on her store of Halahala, concluding their peculiar transaction, when he was filled with the insight that came of such intimacy, he had known that she was not ashamed or embarrassed because she was a married woman coming to another man's quarters in secret at night. She was ashamed of her own great need to come to him, the hunger that she felt and which he sensed so powerfully within her each time he fed on her poisoned milk.

He had learned her itihasa from Narada – not all of it, but enough to know that after she had been made an outcast from her tribe of Maatrs, she had never found anyone who desired her for her true power and abilities, for the being she truly was inside. Everyone saw only the woman on the outside, a beautiful, desirable, scintillating personality, and only incidentally a great warrior too. Nobody even knew her secret any more, for it had been very long since she had been a Maatr. For Kamsa to know and to desire her for what she truly was, was a great compliment. It had awakened the greatest need of her inner woman, the need to be a Maatr again. Not merely in the simple 'mother' sense of the title, but a Maatr in the most primordial sense. Creator, Protector, Provider ... and Destroyer, if need be.

He finished his routine in moments, crushing the last wooden tree trunks that were set up with the use of elephants for this express purpose each day. He punched the very last one so hard, it was pulverized into a cloud of wood dust, a few chips and pieces falling across the acres-large field. His power had grown steadily with use, and the techniques he had picked up from Yadu were amazingly effective when used with his newfound ability. A normal man, no matter how strong or heavily muscled, would have broken every limb in his body by now, but for Kamsa, it was the perfect technique and exercise. He felt as if he could take on Jarasandha himself. And in a way, he wished that the last encounter, the one in his bedchamber, had gone on a while longer. He would have relished the chance to test his strength and skill on those minions of his. For that matter, he would enjoy testing it on them even today, when he knew for certain that he would win easily.

'So?' he said as he came up to the fence against which Putana leaned with exaggerated casualness. 'How is the wife of the captain of my guard?'

She didn't respond to the jibe. He knew she felt no guilt at being a married woman. What she shared with Kamsa was no mere illicit dalliance. It was a matter of her power being useful. And many people underestimated the simple human need to be of use. Entire continents and cultures had been taken without a single arrow loosed because of it. To be of use, to have one's talents utilized, appreciated, given due credit ... it has been a driving force of human society.

She said nothing so long as Yadu was within earshot. The old man finished rubbing salt into Kamsa's body as he had taken to doing after every practice session. The salt seemed to help him cope with the increasing density of his flesh and bone. Already, he was able to increase his weight by a hundredfold. That entailed other side effects, such as the epic thirst and longing for cold water in great quantities – and a corresponding need for salt. It was the old stablehand and now trainer of Kamsa who had suggested that sometimes salt rubbed into a sweaty body could replenish more effectively than when consumed orally. And like every other bit of advice given by the old stalwart, it proved effective.

'What is it?' he asked, after Yadu had left them alone in the empty stable.

She looked at him in the fading dusk, and he saw something in her eyes that he had not seen until now. A kind of hunger. It was not pleasant to see. It was a glimpse of what she had once been, and might be again. 'I have found the Slayer.'

He sprang to his feet, toppling over a barrel of cold water the size of a man. The water gurgled out, splashed and spread across the entire stable. Horses neighed and whinnied in complaint in their boxes. He grabbed Putana's shoulders, forgetting that he had not yet reduced his density to normal human proportions.

'Where is he? Take me to him at once!' He spoke the words through gritted teeth and as he ground his molars, the sound was loud enough to be heard across the stables. Elephants a hundred yards away trumpeted in protest, disturbed by the unusual yet distinctly animal sound.

Putana put out her hands, grasped his shoulders, and pushed him off her. He was surprised at her strength. It took her some effort, but not much. Yet he knew he had grasped her with enough strength to crush an oak trunk held sideways between his palms. He crushed fifty of those daily, and it was only one of a full regime of exercises. Yet Putana had pushed him off as if he was merely a normal man and she a normal woman.

'He is outside your reach. If you go to him now, it will be too soon. He is already strong and gaining strength each day.'

Kamsa roared with fury, losing his temper for the first time in almost a year.

'I AM STRONG!' he said, and smashed a fist onto the side of the fallen barrel, which splintered into fragments.

'Not strong enough. Not yet.' She was calm, unafraid. She had power of her own. She did not fear his strength or his temper.

That calmed him down. What use was it getting angry with a woman who could destroy you in a moment if she lost *her* temper?

He sat down on the stone bench, basically just a solid iron block. It creaked, and he felt a tiny crack or two appear beneath his thighs. He had unconsciously begun to increase his weight again. 'Tell me everything you know.'

'He is living with a cowherd named Nanda Maharaja and his wife Yashoda-devi in a hamlet called Gokul. It is in—'

'Vrajbhoomi, I know,' he said. 'I know of Nanda Maharaja. He is the chief of Gokul. A popular and powerful local leader. How could his child have escaped my grasp last year? My soldiers slaughtered every last newborn and then so many more as well.' A thought struck him. 'His delegation came to my court this very morning, to pay Gokul's taxes for the past year. He stood there before me; he even spoke to me! How could this have escaped my knowledge?'

She shrugged. 'The Slayer is no fool. He has ways and means to trick you at every turn. Don't forget, he was born to Devaki while she was under your soldiers' watch, and yet your sister was able to give birth to him, and Vasudeva was able to spirit him out of Mathura and carry him all the way to Vraj where he exchanged him for Nanda and Yashoda's actual child, the girl. It was that girl that you then attempted to destroy but who flew out of your grasp, floated in mid-air and then revealed herself to be Yogamaya—'

'Yes, yes,' he said impatiently. 'I know all that, Putana. But if what you say is true, I shall go to Gokul at once. I must destroy the Slayer while he is still an infant, before he grows strong enough to fulfil the prophecy.'

She laughed, throwing her head back and flicking her long hair over her shoulders. He scowled at her, gripping the corners of the iron slab. It yielded beneath his fingers like warm butter. 'He is already strong enough, Kamsa. Why, he was in Devaki and Vasudeva's palace only this morning! He came with Nanda and Yashoda to visit his biological parents. That is how I got to know of his identity. I was watching Devaki's palace, suspecting that he might visit sooner or later. Aren't you glad I was right?'

He pointed a finger at her in warning, and ignored the iron chips that fell to the ground. 'Don't mock me. You may be a Maatr, but I am no mere mortal either.'

She lost her grin and nodded. 'That is so. And in a few more years, you shall be very powerful indeed. Perhaps even more powerful than I am, at least in sheer physical strength. I have never seen nor heard of even a deva who was gifted with the particular power you possess, or the ability to use it in such unusual ways. I suspect that this is all preparation for you to eventually face the Slayer in a manner that would give you the superior advantage.'

Even as Kamsa opened his mouth, Putana held up a hand. 'Do not ask me how or when that confrontation will occur. I am not omniscient, merely prescient. But this much I can assure you: if you go to the Slayer now, you will lose, you will die. In a sense, that is what he wants and that is the reason why he taunted you by coming into your lair today, hoping to tempt you to take this rash step.'

Kamsa thought about this for a long moment, calming himself using the yogic breathing methods that Yadu had taught him. The old stablehand was a storehouse of great Vedic lore and knowledge and it was amazing just how much Kamsa had learnt from him. When Narada had said that he would provide a guru to guide him through the process of rebuilding his powers so he could face the Slayer, Kamsa had been sceptical. Now, he was ready to touch the syce's feet but for the fact that it would appear laughable to the world and also because Yadu himself had warned him that the day he acknowledged him publicly as his guru, Yadu would vanish from his life forever.

Finally, he said, 'Then what do you propose I do? Wait another year for the Slayer to grow even stronger and come back to destroy me?'

She smiled. 'No. You must act. And act now. You are right about doing something while he is still relatively young and somewhat vulnerable. But rather than go yourself, you must send assassins to kill him.'

He nodded slowly. 'Slayers to slay the Slayer. I like it.' He cocked an eyebrow, feeling relaxed enough now to jest about it. 'Did you have someone in mind, or were you going to ask your husband to send his best men?' The last suggestion was a joke, of course. Kamsa himself was capable of taking on an entire army if need be. No matter how many mortal warriors Pradyota might muster, or how skilful they were as Kshatriyas, if Kamsa could not defeat the Slayer, they stood no chance at all.

'I do, actually,' she said. And she explained her plan.

thirteen

It was a peaceful day in Gokul when the assassins arrived.

Gopas and gopis in the pasture fields paused and leaned on their crooks to watch as the entourage of gaily festooned wagon carts trundled by. The construction of the wagons and their decoration, as well as the royal sigil of the House of Yadu and the Andhaka Yadava banner, clearly proclaimed the procession to be an official one from Mathura. Royal processions from Mathura hardly passed by every day, and the life of a cowherd being a quiet, placid one, any news or visitor was akin to a social occasion. Royal visitors meant that a feast would certainly be in the offing, and everyone loved a feast. Word passed from hillside to hillside, racing across the lush pastures and fields of Vrajbhoomi faster than a quad of uks pulling a wagon. Even though the procession seemed to be ceremonial rather than martial, the news still travelled quickly. Just in case.

By the time the convoy came up the hillside atop which Nanda Maharaja's estate was perched, everyone in Gokul already knew of the visitors' arrival.

There were oohs and aahs from the watching crowd as a tall, stately lady of indiscernible age alighted from the largest, most luxurious wagon they had ever set their eyes on. Dressed in rich silks and brocades worn in a manner that most of these simple rustics had never seen before, she was clearly a lady of high birth and great wealth. Those few who had seen such finery and accoutrements passed on the knowledge that this was the current fashion at the court of Kamsa and that only a lady of the king's court could afford such luxury. Gold, diamonds, pearls dripped from her ears and fingers and nestled around her throat, complementing her striking beauty and flawless features. To the older gopas watching, she reminded them of the ancient ideals of Arya beauty: dark dusky skin, sharp, piercing features, frizzy yet flowing hair, and a tall, erect stance that lent an air of nobility regardless of the person's actual stature. She could have been the model for one of the cluster of statues – depicting the eight Maatrs – in the ancient rock temples cut into the side of Mount Govardhana, said to date back to the earliest days of Satya Yuga.

This vision of ancient Arya beauty glanced around at the mooing cows, looing bulls, chattering children and whispering women and men, and smiled an odd sardonic smile that could be interpreted to mean almost anything – and it would be debated and discussed for months and years to come, long after the purpose for which Putana had visited had been fulfilled.

She made her way to the threshold of Nanda Maharaja's dwelling where she was greeted with due pomp and ritual by the chief. When the customary formalities were completed, she disappeared into the residence and remained there for a spell. Thanks to a pair of obliging cousins of Gopanath Mahadeva – as Nanda was also known respectfully – the crowd of curious watchers received a more or less continuous series of updates on the discussion taking place within the walls. Much to their disappointment, it was much less dramatic than anything they had imagined.

The lady was indeed a mistress of the court of Mathura, that much was true enough. She was the wife of Pradyota, captain of the guard, and was independently wealthy in her own right. She was merely passing through Gokul on her way to another unnamed destination, and had heard so much about their festivities on the night of the Ashwin full moon that she had decided to stop by and join them, if they had no objection. Naturally, Nanda Maharaja had no objection at all. That was all there was to it. In fact, Nanda being Nanda was compelled to invite the guests to stay at his own dwelling for the duration of their visit. The visitors accepted happily, praising his generosity and hospitality.

Some of those watching observed the other members of the entourage disembark from the wagons. Even if rich courtiers from Mathura, they were certainly an odd-looking bunch. Apparently, they were all former aides of Jarasandha the Magadhan, stationed in Mathura after their 'god emperor' had departed to ensure that his interests and trade agreements were upheld. One was named Agha, another Baka, a third Trnavarta ... strange names and even stranger men. None of the other courtiers mingled with the locals, preferring to keep to themselves, and they rarely spoke even when they were alone together. If this was how rich Mathurans set out to holiday and attend festivities, what might they be like when they were going through a difficult time or visiting someone for a sad occasion! Even Kshatriyas sent on a mission from which they might not return alive celebrated before they went into battle. These Magadhans, or Mathurans, or whoever they were, seemed not to have learnt how to smile or laugh, let alone feast and celebrate.

After a few rebuffed attempts at friendliness, the outsiders were left alone. The gopas and gopis of Vrajbhoomi did not know how to deal with rude or socially distant people. To them, being alive meant being *alive*. Silence and sobriety were for corpses!

Nobody knew quite what to make of this visit, or of the individuals themselves. But so long as they behaved civilly and had a legitimate reason to visit, Yadava hospitality and Arya culture demanded that they be treated as lavishly as any other guest, invited or uninvited. *Atithi Devo Bhava* as the old Sanskrit saying went: A guest is as a god.

Perhaps some wise ancient ought to have thought of a contrary saying: Sometimes a guest can turn out to be a Demon.

Putana could smell the presence and proximity of any mortal within a reasonable range. It was easier when they were upwind and she downwind, of course. But in an enclosed domicile, where the air was reasonably still, it was simple enough to know who was where at all times. She could sniff out the Slayer by his distinctive odour alone. Not that it was a bad odour. On the contrary. It was like nothing she had ever smelt before, except perhaps ... ah, but that was a long time ago and another realm. Not the mortal one. She might be mistaken.

She had waited for a moment when Krishna would be left alone. Just a moment, she needed no more than that.

It was not long in coming. Due in part to the night festivities, the household had decided to rest for a while during the late afternoon. Not long after their heads touched their cots, every member of the family was fast asleep. This was no coincidence. Putana's accomplices had dropped a little potion into the pot of drinking water before the meal. Not enough to put everyone to sleep for too long, for that would alert the entire neighbourhood's suspicions, but just enough to make sure they did fall asleep.

Now, the house was still and silent at last, which itself was rare for any Yadava house, let alone Nanda's house.

Putana rose from her cot in the section of the house where all the ladies had assembled. Yashoda's sisters, mother, sisters-in-law, cousins, friends and god knew who else, were all asleep, some even snoring. She hoped Baka hadn't put more than a drop in the water. While she didn't care if the whole of Vrajbhoomi rose up in arms once their precious Slayer was dead, the point of her mission was to kill the child without arousing suspicion of a murder. An entire household lying dead asleep and missing an annual festival could hardly be considered not suspicious.

She had kept Yashoda beside her on the pretext of getting some information from her. That was so that the child would be entirely alone when the time came. Yashoda had even admitted that Krishna was a rare child whom she could leave alone without constantly having to worry about; she had smiled shyly when she said this, as if admitting to some great secret. Putana had no idea what she meant, but she assumed it was something to do with the Slayer being who he was.

We'll see just how well you can do on your own when I'm done with you, little tyke, she thought now as she moved through the empty house. She had told the others to stay with Nanda and the men no matter what happened, and to pretend to be asleep as well. The thought of Baka, Trnavarta, Agha and the others pretending to sleep amused her. She suppressed a laugh as she found the door of the room.

The child was a tiny lump on a large cot.

She stood over the cot, looking down at the little bundle of flesh, dark as the darkest shadows in the room, yet still visible since his skin seemed to catch the faintest motes of light in a curious manner, almost seeming as if he was bluish-black in hue.

He was wide awake and looking up at her.

'Slayer,' she said softly.

He gurgled and struck his forehead with a tiny fist. It curiously resembled a military salute.

She smiled. 'I see you know who I am. But I'll introduce myself anyway, just to be polite. My name is Putana.'

Putana-maasi!

The words popped into her head unbidden. She resisted the temptation to look around to see who had spoken. Nobody human had spoken, of course. It was just the Slayer, using an old mind trick, a favourite of the devas and their cronies.

'Why not?' She shrugged, not bothering to keep her tone low. 'Call me Putana-maasi if you like. I would be like an aunt to you, if you were human, and I was too!'

Naughty aunty!

She laughed. 'Yes. Naughty aunty indeed. And I'm about to do something very naughty now. Perhaps the naughtiest thing I've ever done.'

Bad stree. Unfit to be a Maatr. Unable to be mortal. Pity you, Putana-maasi!

She lost her smile. It snapped off like a dry twig. 'What? How dare you, you impudent little brat! You have no right to judge me.'

I don't judge you. I merely assess your past deeds. You have already been judged and found guilty of your crimes. That is why you are here on earth, as punishment for those wrongs. It was thought that once on this mortal realm, you would realize the consequences of your past misdeeds. You would see that here among humans, every action has a consequence and must be weighed carefully. Immortality can go to your head at times, as can great power. The humility of living like a mortal being ought to have taught you to amend yourself. And yet you did not mend your ways. You continued abusing your powers. And once again, here you are, seeking to do the bidding of an adharmic rakshasa and commit the most heinous crime any Maatr can commit.

Through the conversation, he was absolutely still. Putana couldn't even see him breathing. Only once he had finished 'speaking' to her mind did he resume kicking and waving his arms and stuffing his fist in his mouth to suck on it.

'Enough!' she said. 'I have no wish to be reprimanded by one whose only purpose is to take birth on this mortal realm in order to commit murder. Slayer, they call you, and that is all you are, a slayer! But I will stop you before you can commit your crime, you smug superior creature. I shall slay the Slayer before he can slay the one prophesied to be slain!'

Putana had bent over as she said this, to direct the words with greatest intensity at Krishna. Now, he gurgled and spat, spittle dotting her face and causing her to blink. She snarled a deep animal snarl, snatched him up from the cot on which he lay, and sat down on the cot herself. Tearing open her blouse, she put his puckered toothless mouth to her chest, and pressed him so hard, he could be smothered for want of breath. She expected him to struggle or flail pathetically, but he did nothing of the kind. In fact, he raised his little fist and clung enthusiastically to her chest, suckling on her greedily as he did so. She felt the Halahala poison work through her maternal organs and pour into his little mouth, the poison whose single drop could wipe out an entire city. He was drinking it like mother's milk now. She was surprised at how easy this had been, after all.

'Really,' she said, 'I'm very disappointed. I expected much more of a fight from you. If you really are Vishnu's avatar as the prophecy claims, this must surely be your weakest one yet. You didn't even put up a struggle! And now, in moments, you'll be dead and your mission here a complete and utter failure.'

fourteen

Yashoda came awake with a start. Her mouth felt dry, her tongue the consistency of sand, and her throat parched. Her head felt heavy, as if she had overslept and forgotten something vital.

It came to her at once: Krishna!

She bolted upright, looking around at the room full of her sleeping sisters, sisters-in-law and other relatives.

Everyone was still asleep. That was not unusual. The womenfolk had been up late the night before, preparing savouries for the Ashwin festival.

But the way she felt suggested that there was something abnormal about their deep sleep. She felt certain that she had been drugged somehow. She had sensed trouble the instant word of the approaching entourage from Mathura had reached her. She did not trust anyone from Mathura, least of all high-ranking aristocrats from Kamsa's court. They were up to no good; she was certain of it.

Even Nanda did not deny her doubts or try to persuade her otherwise; instead, his brow had puckered in that familiar wrinkling pattern and he had nodded sagely.

'It may be some kind of trick,' he had admitted. 'After Devaki and Vasudeva's departure and their inability to locate them thereafter, I hear they have grown desperate to find some trace of the Slayer.'

He glanced at her with the same expression he had first shown her when speaking about Krishna and Balarama's reunion with Vasudeva and Devaki. That expression that said, *Yes, yes, I do understand that something extraordinary is under way and that we are an integral part of it. But let us not speak of it openly or casually. I am struggling simply to accept what I have seen already, leave alone wrap my mind around what will be in the days to come.*

She had only taken his hand and kissed it gently in response. That was Nanda. A gopa, a king of gopas, and happy to be just that much. He had no desire to get involved with slayers and prophecies and divine interventions. Perhaps that was precisely why he had been chosen to foster the avatar, because he was so unlikely a prospect and so simple and level headed a man.

Now she rushed through the house, towards her bedchamber where she had left Krishna sleeping peacefully before joining the visitor lady named Putana in the other room.

She entered the room, bracing herself for anything …

But there was nobody there.

She touched the cot where Krishna had been lying. It was still warm. And wet. She felt the damp patch with her fingers and lifted the fingertip to her nose, sniffing. She grimaced. It smelt like milk, but not any milk she had ever smelt before. Certainly not her own milk. She knew quite well what that smelt like.

She was about to touch her fingertip to her tongue to taste it when a scream jolted her. She looked around, but there was nobody and nothing to be seen. The house was still asleep, although she thought she heard sounds from the men's section.

The scream rattled her again, louder this time, and more blood-curdling than the first time. She sensed that it was coming from outside the house, not within. She ran out, and a third scream came to her as she ran, and this time, just as she was exiting the threshold, she heard the unmistakable sounds of her family and Nanda's family stirring, rising, awoken by the screams.

'Krishna!' she cried out as she stepped out of the house.

Nanda heard his wife crying out, her voice barely audible through the terrible, heart-rending screams that filled the air. It seemed that everyone in Vrajbhoomi would hear those screams. Perhaps they could be heard as far away as Mathura itself!

His skin crawled and his head ached with each new wave of screaming, and he left his house to see the source that was polluting the pristine calm of Gokul with such ear-bursting violence.

An astonishing sight met his eyes.

It was late afternoon, getting on towards evening. The sun was low on the western side, which was straight ahead, the hill directly opposite his house. Below, in the depression between the hill nearest to him and the one beside it, were green pastures where his cows – the ones that were used for his family's personal consumption – grazed. His other herds were much farther away, of course, spread across Gokul over a yojana or two. These cows in this little valley were barely a few hundred head, just enough to keep his large household fed.

He spied a being in the valley, staggering about drunkenly. It took him a moment to recognize it as Lady Putana, the visitor who had arrived from Mathura with her entourage only hours earlier. At least the being *looked* like her in feature and aspect.

But there was one significant difference between the aristocratic and very beautiful Lady Putana he had met earlier in the afternoon and the being staggering about in the valley.

The being was a giantess.

She was at least twenty yards tall, if not more. The sala trees that grew by the little pond below were about ten to twelve yards tall, and she was at least double that height.

And, if he was indeed seeing right, she was growing taller by the minute. Now she appeared to be another yard or two taller … and she was still growing.

He watched, bemused, as she continued to grow, even as she staggered about like a person who has had too much wine and has grown hysterically drunk.

She bumped against one of the sala trees and it cracked with a loud report, the sound carrying easily to where he stood. The top half of the tree fell into the pond with a loud splash. Startled cows, already nervous from the giantess screaming and staggering about, mooed loudly in protest and began chugging their way uphill, heading homewards to safety. The giant Putana flailed her arms around, beating at her own chest, or at least that was what it seemed like to Nanda from where he stood.

Then she turned around, swinging in a drunken lurch, to face him for the first time.

And he saw that there was something clinging to her chest.

Not something, someone.

Krishna. His Krishna.

Except that his beautiful, dark little infant boy had also grown as Putana had. He was several times larger in size now. Large enough to be at least twice the size of Nanda himself, if he was judging correctly. Certainly larger than the cow jogging nervously past the lurching giantess's feet.

Krishna was clinging to Putana's chest. He appeared to be feeding on her milk.

People had come out of his house and were standing beside Nanda now, some bleary eyed and holding their heads. But they forgot their discomfort the moment they saw what was happening in the valley below. And as they tried to make sense of what they were seeing, their voices rose in a chorus of queries and exclamations.

Nanda saw figures pouring from all directions. The screams were drawing gopas and gopis from all across Gokul. As it is, speculation had been rife about the visitors. Now he was sure that every Yadava in Gokul would be there within the half hour. Armed, possibly.

In the valley below, the giantess continued to grow, as if she was consciously expanding herself. She was now easily thrice the height of the sala trees and still growing at the same prodigious rate.

Nanda could not fathom how such a thing was possible, but one cannot deny such happenings if they take place in front of one's eyes. He shushed the people around him, ignoring their excited questions, and watched the extraordinary show unfold.

Krishna was now thrice the size of a grown man, and due to the increased size of the duo caught in an uneasy duel, uneasy at least for one of the participants, the happenings were clearly visible. Krishna was feeding on Putana's breast, drinking her milk. His cheeks could be seen working greedily, sucking hard. Milk poured into his mouth and spilled down his cheeks, though curiously enough, Nanda noted, not a drop spilled on the ground – neither on the grassy pasture, nor in the pond, on the trees, or even on the cows lumbering past mooing in disapproval at this invasion of their home pastures.

And from the dwindling screams, harried look and staggering drunken lurching of the woman, it was evident that she was suffering terribly.

Somehow, Krishna was sucking the life out of Putana.

How, why, wherefore, Nanda did not know.

All he knew was what he was seeing.

Then he noticed something else, something he had not observed before. So striking was the sight of a giant woman with a giant baby clinging to her chest staggering through his pasture, that Nanda had failed to notice his wife a little way down the hillside. She was watching the giantess and the enormous baby with an expression that Nanda guessed mirrored his own. He presumed she had run out at the sound of the screams, fearing that Krishna was in distress, but had stopped midway when she realized that it was the other way around.

'Stay where you are, all of you!' he shouted to his and his wife's family, then ran down the hillside. He half-slid, half-ran to where Yashoda stood. She started when she heard him coming, then relaxed when she saw who it was. He stood beside her, putting his arm around her shoulder comfortingly.

'What is this?' he asked her. 'What is happening?'

Yashoda answered in a tone so grim, he had to glance at her several times to make sure it really was the same gentle, loving Yashoda he knew. 'That woman ... that creature of the night ... Putana-maasi, he calls her ... came here on Kamsa's behalf to kill our Krishna. Her body contains a deadly poison. She sought to suckle our baby, to poison him to death. Apparently, she has done this before ...' She paused and spat to one side. 'Often before. But she was not counting on our Krishna's divinity being beyond her powers. Now, he is sucking every last drop of poison from her body so that she cannot do it to any other child ever again, whether in this mortal realm or any other plane she goes to hereafter.'

By now, Putana was at least fifty yards tall, and though Yashoda and Nanda were on the side of the hill, they were forced to look upwards. She had stopped trying to run away or was unable to move any further, and simply stood in one place, swaying from side to side. Her face was withering, cheeks sinking like sand into a hole, hair wilting, eyes turning opaque, the entire body losing its lush, womanly contours.

Nanda swallowed nervously.

He is sucking every last drop of poison from her body.

It appeared as if Krishna was sucking more than poison, he was sucking out Putana's life itself. The giantess was dying. He saw now that she had finally stopped growing and was now swaying faster, threatening to topple over. Krishna, about five or six times a man's size now, yet still a baby in every way, kicked his legs and squeezed Putana's body harder with his bunched fists.

Putana let out one final groan. It was more a gasp. A final feeble attempt to breathe. Then she fell heavily to the ground, crashing down on the side of the facing hill and making the ground tremble in the process. Her body covered almost half the width of the pasture field.

Krishna released her body and began to reduce in size. Within moments, he was the size of a normal human baby.

'Come on,' Nanda said, taking Yashoda by the hand. They went down the hill together, and he could hear shouts and cries as others followed suit. He guessed that several hundred residents of Gokul would gather in a few moments.

They reached the body of the fallen giantess and ran around it, seeking their child. The body appeared emaciated, as if all the life-blood had been sucked out of it, and the marrow as well. It was a horrible sight. They came around the head of the creature and Yashoda balked. Nanda resisted the urge to turn his face away. The giantess's face was awful to behold. She looked gaunt and skeletal, unbearable to look at closely. And her sheer size made her disfigurement frightening. Nanda could not imagine a whole army of men facing this giant being and besting it, let alone a single yearling. Yet he himself, along with many other Gokuls, had witnessed it with his own eyes.

He stopped short as they came across another remarkable sight.

Krishna.

He was standing.

Nanda had seen his child creeping about, crawling, and even attempting to stand up by holding onto things or people, mainly his own mother, but he had not actually begun to stand yet.

But here he was now.

Standing. Upon the dead giantess's chest.

Waving his chubby arms up in the air in a gesture that undeniably resembled a victory wave.

And gurgling as usual. Laughing. Chuckling. Giggling. Chortling.

Nanda stood transfixed, watching baby Krishna. He heard and felt people come up behind him and saw them across the field, watching, calling out to one another in amazement and disbelief, some even laughing and crying, for they were simple people and given to expressing their emotions freely.

They watched as Krishna took one step, then another, and then yet another.

'Nanda,' Yashoda said with a mother's tone of unmistakable pride. 'Look! Our son is walking! His first steps!'

Then, as they watched, Krishna clapped his hands in glee, leapt once in the air, landed on both feet, tottered briefly for a moment – the watching crowd went 'Aaah!' in trepidation – and then began to move in a way that could be interpreted as only one action.

He was dancing.

Upon the corpse of the giant demoness who had come to kill him.

As he danced, the Gokuls began to clap, encouraging him. He picked up the rhythm of their clapping and danced to it, delighting them further. They laughed and pointed to one another, the crisis forgotten.

And then, slowly, the chant began to rise. It began with a single voice, then another joined in, then yet another, and so on, until finally everyone present – all the hundreds of Gokuls standing around and watching, including Nanda and Yashoda – was chanting, clapping to keep the beat.

They sang a single word, over and over again. It simply means cowherd, and was a common nickname given to most young gopas in Vraj.

'Govinda!' they sang. 'Govinda! Govinda! GOVINDA!'

And their singing reached a crescendo and filled the entire valley, as the infant Krishna danced and danced merrily, until the entire world seemed to echo with the refrain.

'GOVINDA!'

And above the chanting, the sound of Krishna chortling as he danced on.

Govinda dances on, through many more action-packed adventures, in ...

FLUTE OF VRINDAVAN
Book 3 of The Krishna Coriolis

The mischievous god-child wields the flute to make evil dance to his tune

Infant Krishna and his half-brother Balarama are the most mischievous children in all of Gokuldham, getting up to all sorts of pranks, raiding neighbours' dahi handis and letting the calves run free. But disciplining God Incarnate is no easy task. It slowly dawns on Mother Yashoda that the babe she is trying to protect is in fact the protector of the entire world! As Krishna survives one horrific asura attack after the other, she comes to terms with the true identity of her adopted son.

Meanwhile, Kamsa despatches a team of other-worldly assassins to slay his nemesis. Harried by Kamsa's forces, Krishna's adoptive father, the peace-loving Nanda Maharaja, is forced to lead his people into exile. They find safe haven in idyllic Vrindavan. But even in this paradise, deadly demons lurk ...

acknowledgements

R. Sabarish, my first reader, who read the first drafts of this version back in 2005 when it was still a part of my larger Mba (Mahabharata) retelling, and who shall probably be reading this published version on a different continent now – an achievement that suggests that perhaps I have managed in some way to keep the flame of our epics burning brightly after all. Thank you, Sabs!

Tapas Sadasivan Nair, who read through the final draft of the first two books in the Krishna Coriolis Series years before publication and suggested many valuable corrections and amendments. If not the first, certainly one of my best readers and whose feedback I value greatly. Read on, Kanjisheikh!

For the members of my erstwhile Epic India Group, Forums and the 33,000+ (and counting) readers who have left their wonderful reviews, comments and feedback on my blog at ashokbanker.com over the years. Too many now to name, so I'll settle for ululating without the benefit of a vuvuzela: 'EI! EI! YO!' Proud 2B an Epicindian. Always hamesha forever!

V.K. Karthika, who has turned out to be the editor and publisher who has shown the most faith and support for my work in my entire career, readily buying more books from me, trusting my instincts and giving me whatever was needed to enable the completion of this massively ambitious work. The interesting thing is that Karthika and I first connected not as author and editor, even though we knew each other as acquaintances for years, but as readers sharing a common interest in fantasy, romance and historical sagas. I think that's what makes her such a great editor to work with: she actually reads and enjoys the books she publishes, which is not something I can say for all editors working in publishing today. I am truly grateful for her enduring support and enthusiasm for my work. Karthika, I hope to continue publishing with you for decades to come.

Prema Govindan, whom I didn't even know by name when she turned in the first set of edits on the manuscript of this book, but whose great love for the subject of this book, Krishna, coupled with an intense professional drive to bring out the best book possible and the rare ability to appreciate an author's individual (and very quirky) 'voice' or style – including my penchant for mixing languages, cultures, et al. in an epic khichdi – resulted in the best editing of my career. And since the first book, I have now had the pleasure of working with her on two more books in the series, the experience turning out to be just as rewarding. Prema, it has been a great pleasure and I hope to have your eagle eye and keen mind on every single book in this series and possibly many more as well.

The entire team at HarperCollins India – too many to name, yet each one a star in his or her own right – that is responsible for bringing this book to you, the reader holding this copy in your hands, aided and abetted by the distributors, stockists, retailers and other book trade professionals across the country who are helping the book publishing business defy recessions and break global records. Thank you, all!

As always, my family, starting with my beloved wife Bithika, my daughter Yashka, my son Ayush, and my constant companion

Willow, whose love and support are the fountainhead of my life and work. Our story is the one story that I can never hope to better! Love, always.

And finally, you, dear reader, whether you're new to my work or a long-time familiar. If you've never read anything by me before, then you should know that I approach every book as if it's my first and only book – never expect the same thing twice because I don't write the same book twice. And if you've read every single thing I've written to date, then you probably know that already, in which case, you won't be surprised when you turn the page and find that this book and series is quite unlike everything else I've written before. But what really matters is that you like reading it as much as I loved writing it.

Because I really did. That, and that alone, is the reason why I wrote it. Because I love writing.

And love, like most communicable viruses, is extremely contagious, though thankfully not as harmful to your health.

ASHOK KUMAR BANKER

Andheri, Mumbai
November 2011

Govinda has been weaving his magic since before he was born in …

SLAYER OF KAMSA

Book 1 of The Krishna Coriolis

Cowherd, lover, warrior, god incarnate. The youthful superhero of ancient India is here …

Forewarned by a prophecy, the demonic Prince Kamsa orders every male newborn to be put to the sword. But even in the womb, Krishna uses powerful magic to cast a spell across the entire kingdom on the night of his birth. Now, the stage is set for the epic clash of the child-god and the terrible forces of evil with the birth of Krishna, the slayer of Kamsa …

The fantastic adventures of the Hindu god Krishna have entertained and inspired people for millennia. Playful cowherd, mischievous lover, feared demon-slayer – the legendary exploits of this super-being in human form rival the most rousing fantasy epics. Now, the author of the Ramayana Series®, the hugely successful epic retelling of the ancient Sanskrit poem, works his magic once again with the tales of Krishna. All the pomp, splendour and majesty of ancient India come alive in this extraordinary eight-book series.